Blooming In Death

JASMINE STYLES

Blooming In Death
Copyright © 2024 by Jasmine Styles

Cover art by Danielle Greaves - @designsbydaniellelg
Character Art by Adrienn Zsuzsanna Demeny - @nephelle.art
Chapter Art by -@DigitalCurio
Editing by Callie Rickard - @calliereads18
Formatting by Demi Clorissa - @demiclorissawrites

All rights reserved. No part of this book may be reproduced in any form or by any electronic or mechanical means, including information storage and retrieval systems, without written permission from the author, expect for the use of brief quotations for critical reviews.

This novel is a work of fiction. Any names, events or characters are purely fictional creations from the author's mind. Any resemblance to actual events and actual persons, living or dead, is purely coincidental.

"To those who choose to live in darkness, know your colour is there waiting for you whenever you need it."

Content Warnings

Blooming in Death is a dark paranormal romance and has themes and scenes that may be distressing and triggering to some readers. It is not recommended for those under eighteen years of age. Content warnings within Blooming In Death consist of:

- *Death, murder, attempted murder, graphic violence (including violence against women)*
- *Mentions of blood and gore*
- *Mentions of torture*
- *Childhood trauma and grief (on page & referenced)*
- *Grief / Suicidal Ideation / Anxiety References / Mentions of Mental Health (on page & referenced)*
- *Sexual content and scenes involving breath play, light bondage, primal play.*
- *Swearing*

Please read these trigger warnings and put your mental health first.

Offical Playlist

Blooming In Death

Chapter One

Pale moonlight danced through the thin lace curtains. The gentle sound of rain pattering on the window pane, plinking softly in the otherwise silent evening. The oncoming storm easing our staff into an early night. Grandmother would have been prepared for bed hours ago. A common theme these nights, as if she has grown scared of the night. When you can only admire the world in close to a million shades of grey, you dread a daylight you cannot witness. I had grown to prefer the dark.

Seeing the beauty in life is such a foreign concept. A seemingly delicate concept to those of Florian manor.

People boast of the vibrancy of life, the exuberant colours that shape and brighten the world.

A creation I was still yet to see. The only colours to grace my life were but shades of grey. Bleak slates of nothingness. When asked what colour was my favourite, I would tell them it was pink. A colour supposedly so feminine and soft. Enough to prove to others of my normalcy. I had no idea what shade of grey pink truly was but I really did not care enough to find out.

It was always this way. Long ago the women in my family

were cursed to live in a black and white existence until we met our one true love. A fool's dream. That finding love would enrich a life in colour. A truly ridiculous notion.

I hated the thought. I refused to entertain a world of vibrancy they boasted about. The human race deserved to live a bleak existence. Myself along with it. For all I could see was darkness. In that of both life and death.

People in town often referred to themselves as kind and gentle but to me, they were their own unique form of toxicity. Constantly chasing a life of colour and beauty. But all I witnessed was them chasing a life of greed.

A frown creased my lips as I smoothed my skirts. The rich velvet smooth under my cold palms, the dark grey shimmering under my pale skin. Lighting a candle, I wandered through the halls of our grand manor I called home.

Grandfather was a rich man. A very successful lawyer with a natural wit. Grandmother always boasted of how I reminded her of him. The sentiment was sweet but I secretly longed to know the man he was before he died, to see just how similar we truly were. If any of my so- called 'odd' mannerisms matched his, if he too preferred his own company and if he held a fascination with the darker things that lurked in this world.

My father was always so proud of his father in law. I could not wait for him to return from his travels to greet me in his arms once more. If even just to listen to his boring botany findings at this point. Another fool's dream. He would never draw me into his arms. Not if our lives depended on it it seemed.

I continued through the hall passageway. Drawing short at my reflection in the grand hall's mirrored walls.

Light eyes reflecting back, near black shadows lining my under eye with lack of sleep. Grandmother always said I was the perfect mirror to my mother in all but heart. Same raven black hair, pale skin and hauntingly wide light eyes. Where

Mother was hard and wild, I was soft and tame. Mother had left the manor years ago in the winter of 1845. Just shy of seventeen years ago. Leaving my father to look after me whilst she collected some leaves for him. They found her mutilated corpse floating in a river nearby. A deep x carved into her chest.

Father was distraught for the months following from that haunting image of his wife. Not sparing me a single glance that wasn't filled with hatred before he too abandoned me at age fifteen to be raised by Grandmother. Abandoned like a ghost in these vast halls. Just like his sanity that seemed to falter more often than not.

He had been gone for over five years now. The memory of him fading with each day passing. If I closed my eyes I could still smell his familiar scent, mint and lemongrass. A strange mix that somehow complimented him.

He loved nothing more than studying his herbs. Botany was his one true love. Above us he placed his career. I missed the days spent with him, beside him in the greenhouse. Watching as he crushed each herb. I only wished now that I had paid more attention to his teachings. The information in the books I had read had nothing on his expansive knowledge. My own craving for knowledge and pull to plant life had me growing all kinds of plants through the greenhouse just in the back gardens. Close enough to the manor to feel safe but far enough to feel distant from the endless chill the manor was riddled with.

With a roll of my shoulders, I pressed on to the library. The one place I spent almost each and every day. Losing myself in stories, journals or even studies.

Hundreds of books lined the shelf. Uncle Arthur had filled them for Grandmother when Grandfather died. Each book a different shade than the one before.

Placing the candle down, I ran my fingers over the volumes.

Leather gliding like butter under my fingertips. The covers still vibrant shades of grey despite their age.

Rain fell heavier outside as I lowered myself into my grandmother's reading chair. Her musky violet scent swirling in the dusty room. The maids had always neglected this room claiming there was a dark energy to it. I paid it no mind. It was the only peace I could find these days.

Despite the home being near bare of occupants, the walls screamed their history. An almost eerie feeling as you enter. As if you truly are not alone. I had learnt to block it out. But sometimes, the feeling crept in, the feeling of being watched. I suppose that might be true. Many of our staff over the years had spoken many a time about the spirits that supposedly remained in the home. The book I had been reading earlier in the day sat perched on the small wooden tea table beside me. Placing the candle down, I opened the book to my current page.

'*An Anatomy of the Human Mind.*' the title read.

The volume was fascinating. The book was published under a false name by a female doctor originally in France. Her findings are some of the most extraordinary. She would study each and every one of her patients', in the asylums, minds and report on her varied findings. Reporting on their mania induced hallucinations and actions. The Church of England had banned the book long ago. It was said that those who were found with a copy would be tried for treason.

I didn't mind that though. It wasn't as if the police would so much as dare to search the manor. People had tried in the past to have us searched, labelling us as heretics and vampires as we didn't fit their norm. I laughed quietly to myself each time an officer approached the door, knowing he would leave the moment he stepped into the library.

Thunder cracked overhead, rumbling the ground beneath

me. My heart soared into my throat at the sudden noise. The book I was reading now tossed to the hard wooden floor as I leapt to my feet. The sound of my name being called echoing softly through the halls.

Regaining myself, I headed toward the voice, as if pulled by an unseen force.

Candlelight flickered onto the walls with each step as I passed. Portraits of Florian's past lined the walls. The art was an astounding masterpiece to those who can see colour. To me however, they were an awful mess. I hated their white eyes and bleak smiles. More of a horror story than a legacy told by these horrible portraits.

Each Florian in the portraits had suffered an untimely end. As if the curse also involved a brutal death for each bearer of the family name.a curse of nothing but mostly daughters for the Florian name. As if a higher power had forgone adding them to our line. The only male truly born to the family was Arthur. An anomaly in itself. Each more violent or gruesome than the last. My mother had told me each of their stories just as Grandmother had told her and her siblings. So that we may learn from our ancestors' mistakes.

I always felt a sense of invincibility. I was safe in the manor. The only times I would venture outside of the grounds was to collect seeds for my garden or to visit my only friend Dorian in the town. At this point I was sure I was labelled a spinster but it never really bothered me, not much really did these days.

My name was called louder this time, bouncing off the empty upstairs halls. I shook off the feeling of the eerie portraits watching me and hurried up the stairs to the only person game to call for me.

The weird sense of being watched lingered on my skin with each stride away from the library. My skin prickling under my velvet sleeves. Something felt strange. Well stranger than usual that was. The soft sound of my name being called again swirled around like a leaf on the wind. Gentle and quiet. I turned back to the portraits, straining to hear the strange call again.

"Vespera!" Grandmother barked before letting out a ringing dry cough. My head swivelled back to the stairs. 'You're just being foolish.' I cursed myself, rolling my shoulders back.

"Coming," I called from where I remained frozen on the stairs. I turned to look behind me. Nothing. No one remained. I cursed myself for being so childish before heading into the lady of the manor's room.

"Are you well, Grandmother?"

"You know how I am awfully frightened of the storms," She grumbled, her irritation more at herself than anyone else. She shuffled over in her large bed, her bed covered in blankets and pillows of all kinds. Artwork of all kinds lined the walls. I always believed she kept the art as a way for her to remember she can see colour, that she can see the so-called beauty in life.

Reaching where she lay facing me beneath her multitude of coverings, I extended my hand before sitting in the chair beside her bed. My candle now joining hers on the nightstand, enhancing the glow around her large bed.

Sophia was once said to be the most beautiful woman in all of England. I believe she still is, in both appearance and spirit. She was the kindest soul to those she cherished. Strict, but heartful. Loving beyond reason.

Her long grey hair fanned out across her silken pillows. The strands of white amongst the dark were more evident than last month. Her sweet eyes, once youthful and full of mischief, now drooping with age. She looked exhausted, but the woman was still quick as a whip.

"Why are you still dressed?" Her thin brows creased. Eyes raking over me as I fought the urge to shuffle my feet.

"I was preparing for bed when the rain began and I got

distracted." I had always loved the rain. The beauty of a rainstorm mesmerising as it fell from the heavens to the earth below. Cleansing the world of its filth. The morning after always seeming more lush and vibrant

"You always did like gloomy things." She rolled her eyes but there was no malice behind it. The corner of her thin lips curving up. The howling of wind creaked through the manor. How could anyone be sleeping through this?

"You called me gloomy as a child. Did you not think it would have an effect on me?" I smiled as I took her extended hand. Her wrinkled skin was freezing in mine. I smoothed my thumb in circles over hers in a desperate attempt at keeping warm. The chill had set in. Even the fire at the end of the room blazing away couldn't take away this chill. A chill each Florian knew to be a normality.

Another flash of lightning illuminated the room. The light grey walls near white in the blazing light. A crash of thunder followed not too long after.

She shifted uncomfortably, fear wild in her eyes.

A fearsome storm rolled over many years ago now. My grandfather had left late into the night, where the storm was at its peak, to find his youngest daughter after she had snuck out of the manor. Aunt Magdelena had only been in her early seventeenth year when she fled. No one was ever sure of the reason why. Only that the storm had triggered something within her. Grandfather was the only one game enough to brace the weather to find her. Only to be crushed by a large branch hitting his own carriage as a storm crescendoed with deadly fury. Aunt Magdelena however, was never heard from again.

Mother had told me that Grandmother was never the same after that night. That losing two of her loved ones in the same instance tore her heart apart and was never to be brought together again. To me she was still the sweetest woman I had ever known. I often wondered how my mother had seen her before the accidents. Was she as soft then as she was now? Or was she more of a stern woman. I would never know. Although somehow I suspected the latter.

The townspeople all knew of Sophia. Many intimidated by her, others friendly enough. But Grandmother kept her distance, keeping her list of friends small and only keeping those with a certain type of power and sway close.

People thought we Florian's were cursed and so far they were correct. The outside world knew nothing of our curse. Nor would they ever. If the civilians of the towns found out, we would be tried and most likely be burnt. Knowing my luck, they would bring back the stake specifically for us, after not having done the horrific practice in over a hundred years.

I rolled my shoulders. Trying to shake the feeling of what it must have been like to witness those crimes for myself if I was around back then. I was almost certain I recalled Grandmother speaking of a Florian burnt at the stake for supposedly practising witchcraft. But now was not the time to ask.

"Are you tired, dear?" Grandmother said softly. I shook my head. The lie not needing to be vocalised. I was exhausted. The nights most often had called to me, beckoning me to join the shadows of the night where sleep evaded me. Sometimes amongst the garden, sometimes in the halls like a trapped spirit.

I squeezed her hand, holding her steady as the storm raged on. Her breathing evening out slowly as she fell into an abyss I craved. Lightning flashed brightly through the windows. A roar of thunder following not long after. The silence that followed was deafening.

Chapter Two

"Lady Vespera!"

I woke with a start, my hands wrapping around the maids shoulders in front of me. Sunlight flooded through the windows. My heart galloped. My hands tightened as the woman came into focus with a gasp.

"I apologise," I said softly as I loosened my grip. The young maid stepped back, as if horrified by my touch. Our breathing coming in shallow, on the off beat of the other. My heart racing in my chest, creating a rush of noise and an onslaught of my senses.

"Your grandmother requests you join her for breakfast in the dining hall." The young maid stepped back once more. She must have been new, or more brave than the others. No one young ventured out this far into my rooms, the previous maid claiming spirits lingered here.

Brushing past the light haired maid, I wandered down to the dining hall. Voices chuckled from beyond the large dark doors. I stopped just before the doors, intrigued, smoothing my hair and dress as best as I could before pushing the doors open. Four dining sets lined the table, eggs and toast sat on the centre.

"Were we expecting company, Grandmother?"

"Only the finest." A deep voice said from behind me. I whirled to face the man.

"Uncle Arthur!" I all but squealed before rushing into his arms.

"There is my little bud." Uncle Arthur beamed. He hadn't aged a day since he moved four years ago to London. His light hair longer than usual, curling just below his ear. Bright eyes wide with joy. Even his skin was a slightly deeper shade than usual.

"I am no longer a bud." I laughed lightly. Uncle Arthur shrugged his shoulders half heartedly.

"Yes you are. And I can't wait to see the flower you blossom into." His hands pulled my head to him lightly. His lips touched briefly to my forehead. The sweet gesture warmed my heart. He searched my gaze before stepping back.

"I found this on our travels and thought you may enjoy it." He pulled a small book from his breast pocket. Fingering the pages, he opened the one he required with the utmost delicacy. I wasn't used to gifts. They weren't something our family usually participated in.

Inside lay a perfectly pressed white lily. Such an interesting flower. But I could not for the life of me recall the meaning.

"Thank you Arthur." I smiled, grateful for the gift but unsure of what I was to do with it.

"Your mother and aunt both loved lilies," He said, a note of sadness pulling his features down.

I opened my mouth to thank him again only to close it, offering a smile instead.

"Come now. The meal will get cold." Grandmother's voice

chimed from behind. I shifted away, moving to the table, pressing my lips to the soft hair on the crown of her head.

I took my usual seat to her left. Taking my toast lathered in butter. The lily lay between us. Grandmother snorted at the flower, her lip curled as she looked upon it.

"Hello mother," Arthur said cheerfully, approaching where we sat.

Looking past Arthur, I noticed we were not alone.

A man close to my age lingered by the door. His bright eyes fixed on mine. My eyes raked over him. He was tall, well dressed with soft hued hair. His smile turned up into a slight smirk. Hands firmly clasped before him. Confidence oozed from him, though he didn't look like someone of high society. Which was interesting given he was personally invited to dine with us. Grandmother had a strict no commoners rule that was only broken for the exception of Dorian.

Arthur's gaze followed mine.

"Pardon my manners." He gestured to the stranger. "This is my apprentice, Victor."

Victor bowed small. My focus turned to Grandmother who was looking over him with a fine tooth comb. Her thin lips filled with apparent distaste. I wondered what she saw that she didn't like. He was most definitely handsome, surely he hadn't said or done anything to offend so soon. Surely it was the fact that she had noted he wasn't a man of power. I would be shocked if she could see something I could not. Although, she was rather good at reading people.

Arthur guided him to the table, allowing him to sit and dine with us. Grandmother stiffened but brushed her hand along mine. A rise of her brows the only tell of the disgust morphing into curiosity.

I poured a cup of tea and straightened my posture, my stiff

lace collar digging into my throat uncomfortably. My breathing slowed as if all the air had been sucked from the room.

Grandmother spoke to the men about their various travels. I remained silent, choosing to admire the delicate roses painted onto the china. Broken segments of their conversation made their way into my ears.

"Not married -

"Soon to be a doctor -

"Fine young man for our Vespera."

I choked on my fresh tea at the last words. The liquid scolded into my nose. My gaze flicked to Victor who caught my movement and smirked back. My stomach roiled at the sight.

"Whilst I do appreciate the sentiment, I will have to decline at this current time," I said, my voice rasping from the burn. Smiling as I stood from the table, excusing myself to the back gardens. Grandmother's proud chuckle following me out.

THE GRAND OLD MANOR WAS SEEN AS HAUNTED AND frightening, or so that's what the talk of the neighbouring towns told me. Grandmother had done well to convince everyone it was haunted. No one dared to journey this far into the forest. The rumours were vast and filled with dishonesty. Mother had once believed the manor was not haunted. That no ghosts or entities roaming the halls, just an old grandmother fearful of the outside world and her strange granddaughter.

Living in a wonder of architecture, Florian Manor resembled those of Ancient Rome with long church-like windows, tracery as grand as our line itself. I wasn't sure myself when it was built or why it was built so near to the forest but I did not mind at all.

The days where I journeyed to town were few and far between as of late. Hours spent in the carriage only to enter the colourless city to be gossiped about by townsfolk.

Colour seeing freaks. The lot of them. The young women weaving ribbons through their hair, boasting about the colours of their gowns. My lips curled at the memory of a game young woman rushing over to me to compliment my 'purple' skirts. As if I knew what that colour was. She gushed over the depth of the dye. I tore the fabric from me the moment I stepped inside the manor. Burying it deep in the back of my closet.

I did not care for colour. Nor did I want to know what colour I was wearing at any given time. I didn't want to know beauty. How could I know beauty like this? A cursed existence was enough to taint and sour even the strongest person's mind let alone my own fragile one.

Life for me was simple and uneventful. Unbothered even. I was a recluse, be it against my will, but that was the way it was. I despised those who could go freely and make friends and enjoy others' company without being seen as inferior or weird. That was never my path in life though. My path was a life of darkness and I had succumbed and accepted the fact. Welcoming it home into my heart as an old friend.

The gardens were concealed by a shadow of misty fog. It was unusual for this time of the month. The beginning of winter was nearly upon us but the mist generally came with the harsh season. Grandmother would 'forbid' travel at that time. As if we wanted to leave the place of our own free will in the first place.

Tall trees loomed overhead as I wandered through the garden, my slippers growing damp with muck from the grass below. Clouds loomed overhead, threatening another downpour.

I looked to the forest surrounding the vast gardens of

assorted blooms. My heart thumped in my chest. I was not afraid of the dark but something about the forest set a chill deep in my bones. The feeling of eyes watching my every move pricked my skin with gooseflesh. A cool breeze blew a stray strand of hair into my eyes. I reached up to brush it from my vision, only to catch a flicker of movement amongst the treeline.

"Hello?" I called, my voice hoarse from the sudden fear.

No response came. I took a small step forward. The movement stopped as if expecting me to come closer.

"I know you are no animal. No animal has prowled these lands for a long while now. I suggest you show yourself immediately," I called. The lie coming out easily enough. Taking a deep breath, I gathered my skirts. My voice sounding stronger than I felt.

"I will count to three and if you are not out of there by the end of the countdown, the authorities will be called for trespassing."

No response again. I stepped forward again, closing the distance between the treeline. A rustle of movement broke the silence. As if they lingered close.

"One," I said as I stepped closer.

"Two." Another step. I waited on baited breath, preparing for someone to come and attack me. My hands flexed beside me. As if awaiting the attacker's throat.

"Three," I called, this time strolling to the first tree.

"You have one last chance to make yourself known." I grated, my patience drawing thin. We sometimes had boys from the town come to visit the so-called 'haunted' manor. Though they usually made themselves known by now. The threat of the police enough to scare anyone away these days given how brutal they can be.

Branches rustled in the depth of the forest, the person

fleeing as I drew near. My heart raced. I took another step toward it. A small flicker of movement caught my eye. A single petal fluttered past in the breeze. I tracked the movement briefly before daring to take another step toward the forest and the danger beyond. Only to feel a gentle hand grasp my arm.

My eyes grew wide, heart now pounding in my chest. A scream caught in my throat as I turned to face the person holding me. His hands now gripped both of my upper arms tightly as I stared wildly into his light eyes. Victor's handsome face filled with worry, the cocky smirk now replaced with a concern that felt genuine. I felt myself blanch at the sight of him. The feel of him holding me sending a wave of unknown feeling through my body. Embarrassment gushing through me. He would have seen me talking to the trees and presumed I was mad no doubt. Madder than if he trusted the townspeople's gossiping words that was. The doctor in him would turn me over to an asylum for less than that. I silently begged for him to leave me be, to return back inside where he belongs. Away from me.

"Lady Vespera, are you okay?" He lowered his brow, observing my features for any signs of harm.

"I'm fine." I managed to croak. My eyes still boring into the light of his. Up close I could only just see the small dusting of freckles on his pale cheeks. His lips thinning with concern. The small petal rested on the shoulder of his coat.

"Come, it is freezing out here. You'll get sick." His hands dropped from my arms, instead taking my hand in his as he pulled me back toward the manor. I looked back to the forest. A strand of stray hair covering my face. But there was no mistaking the figure looking back at me through the darkness.

Chapter Three

I retired to the library, still trying to shake off the feeling of the person watching me, the feeling of their gaze burning into my flesh from beyond the trees.

I lowered myself to a cushion before the fire. My skirts fanned out beneath me. The oil lanterns flickering light danced over the walls of books lining the walls. Soft sunlight shimmered over the marble flooring.

Opening my volume in front of me, the knot in my chest loosened. My mind began to wander. Why was Victor in the gardens behind me in the first place? Was he sent to spy on me? Was he the eyes I felt on me? Surely not. They didn't feel the same. His were full of concern, but the eyes I felt were full of loathing. There was another figure amongst the trees. I knew this in my heart to be the truth. My fingers trembled every so slightly as I opened the book before me.

Grandmother had always said it was important for women to read no matter what their class. That a woman should always have knowledge no matter what a man says. My aunt, Magdelena, had supposedly told her on many occasions when she was growing up that Grandmother was delirious for the notion. I did not agree. My grandmother was the smartest woman I knew. Quick witted with a sharp tongue, a great weapon to wield.

My eyes roamed over the book. *A Guide to Human Anatomy.* My lip curled with distaste at the fact that she had changed her name simply for the study to be published. I had read this book weeks ago and found the notion ridiculous. Most of the volumes in the library were filled with medical books. I had read through some of them. Not retaining much of the new information that had been told. The only thing that stood out with each read was just how fragile humans are. If it were acceptable, I would have been a doctor myself. A sudden creak from the halls outside the library tore my focus from a detailed sketch of a skull to Victor walking through the doorway, a silver tray in hand.

"Your grandmother asked me to bring you your morning tea," He said shyly, still seemingly a little tense of my display in the garden. I forced a smile, thanking him as he brought the tea over to where I lounged on the floor. He nodded and sat before me. I took the teacup from him and looked at the dark liquid. Just the way I liked it. No doubt Arthur had made this brew. My lips quirked into a small smile. Victor's face lit up at the expression as if waiting for me to finally acknowledge him.

I bowed my head, looking back toward my book. My stray strands of hair that had fallen from my knot at the back of my head hung like inky black curtains from my face. I looked up at Victor through my lashes as he lowered himself to the floor in front of me. I furrowed my brow, watching as Victor smirked. He reclined back on his elbows, still admiring me as if I was as fascinating as the world's most talked about artworks.

"You shouldn't be reading a book like that." He chuckled.

"And why should I not?" I withheld the urge to roll my eyes.

"It's a bit dark for a woman of your age."

"It is nothing more than medical." I protested. The doctor's study laid open in my hands.

"At the beginning," He shrugged. "The end study was on people who have suffered with near experiences of death."

I huffed out a breathy laugh. "Death does not phase me, Victor. When you have lost as I have, you begin to find death more of a curiosity than a frightful experience."

Victor's eyebrows shot upward startled by my response.

"Then I apologise. I just thought..." He trailed off. A flicker of embarrassment crossing his features. He was truly handsome. At least he would be if I weren't so sworn on not finding true love for myself.

I waved him away. "You do not need to apologise to me, Victor. I am not overly delicate." The smile on my face was genuine. His eyes brightened at the sight.

Victor was the only man to have admired me physically for what felt like years. Most of the town's men already knew who I was and avoided me like I held the plague in my veins. My face warmed at the thought of someone finding me interesting. I didn't need love, but friendship was always a welcome necessity I had never known. My closest friends were the woman who raised me and a woman the town deemed madder than even me.

"I am most glad to hear that." He plucked at a stray thread on the rug beneath him. Gooseflesh pricking his exposed forearm. He was hiding it well. Most people strayed from the manor library. Even Grandmother barely came in here. I noted the kernel for later. Needing to dig a little further into the man before I could know. "I think we will be spending a lot of time together."

My smile faltered. "And why is that?"

"Your uncle has invited me to stay here for the duration of my training."

Well that was news to me. And most certainly odd. Surely Grandmother would say no. She wouldn't stand for this. He was not a Florian. But I suppose if we were to be matched then he would be. He would be forced to take the Florian name. A strange tradition my family held. My stomach roiled at the thought of a husband. The words weighing on my tongue left a sour taste in my mouth.

"How lovely." I managed.

Hopefully the manor would frighten him off soon enough. If it didn't, then the man was made of steel.

Victor left just before lunch with Uncle Arthur, leaving me alone to entertain myself. The maids had taken grandmother to bed for a brief rest. I remained alone well past dinner and into the night. I couldn't believe Grandmother had agreed. She said she felt for the boy. That he had nothing and we could offer him something like a home at the very least.

"You want to offer him to me!"

"I do not!" She had insisted as she stormed through her bed chamber searching for her handkerchief.

"Then why let him stay and disrupt us? I thought you liked the peace!"

"Vespera." She turned to face me. I looked at her from the other side of the bed. My hands on my hips.

"Sophia?"

She stifled a smile at that before clearing her throat and continuing. "I do like peace. But I also like the peace of my mind knowing that my granddaughter will be around people her own age for once."

I snorted.

"Dorian does not count." She wove a finger at me before I could even answer back about my only companion.

"He is staying. He will not be allowed in your rooms nor will he be allowed around you without your permission."

I rolled my eyes before looking down at the floor. A slip of cloth caught my attention. I bent to pick it up. The handkerchief dangling between my fingers.

"Does he know that?" I held it out to her. Grandmother shuffled around the bed.

"Not yet. But Arthur is making it very clear to him as we speak."

"You are unbelievable," I sighed.

"Only when I want to be." She smirked before snatching the cloth from my fingers. "Now go on. Give him a chance. Who knows, maybe love will finally bloom for you, Vespera." She waved the handkerchief near my face. I swatted it out of the way, getting a throaty chuckle in response.

"You..." I started. She barked out a laugh. I turned on my foot and stormed out of her room. Heading toward my own, I could hear Arthur's muffled warnings to Victor from the second room from mine. I didn't bother to eavesdrop. I could care less as long as I was left alone when I needed to be and not be presented as a suitor for Victor to parade around on his arm.

"Like hell would I let love bloom," I murmured as I slammed my door behind me. The pressed lily dangling on my bedside table fell to the floor.

What a joke that was.

BLOOMING IN DEATH

Taking more time to myself, I drew a bath. Hot steam rose from the large chipped porcelain tub, worn from generations of use. Shedding the heavy velvet skirts was a relief but loosening the corset was purely heaven on earth. My chest heaved with a breath of air, relaxation settling deep in my bones. Loosening my hair, I let it trail in waves down my back as I lowered myself into the water. The floral scent of the bath oil coiled over my skin. I was thankful it was not lemongrass. The scent was always like a pang to the heart.

This scent soothed my tired skin. Moonlight poured in from the bedroom window. The night sky on full display before me. Trees swayed gently in the breeze of the forest beyond. The storm from the night before now long forgotten. I lowered myself down further ever so slowly into the water. Allowing the heat to prickle and warm my weary bones. The steam swirled from my fingers as I drifted them across the murky surface before submerging my head under the hot water.

Holding my breath, I opened my eyes under the surface. Distorted visions of the painted ceiling danced before me. I closed my eyes again briefly, only to open them again suddenly, a clatter sounded in the room. My heart leapt to life. A shadow loomed over the surface, their face too dark to make out in the dimming candlelight. Hands plunged through the water, gripping my face and holding it down against the porcelain bottom. One hand holding my forehead, the other tightly wound around my throat.

A scream tore through my throat, bubbling under the water. I thrashed my entire body, fighting the weight of the person holding me down. Their grip softened more with each writhe of my body. My legs kicking up into whatever part of their body I could. The hands withdrew slowly. I pulled myself up from below the surface. Panic running rampant within me. I gulped down air heaving as much as I could down, throat burning from the lack of oxygen. My body trembled despite the heat of the bath. The person was gone no trace of them ever entering here. The door was still closed. Nothing out of order. My eyes darted around the bathing room. Drawing up short. Surely, I didn't imagine it. Maybe I was still haunted by the stranger in the treeline today. That was all it was. Surely I was just in a state of mania. My heart beat pounded in my chest. Blood raged through my ears. I pulled my knees to my chest. The sharp tears lining my eyes now falling down my cheeks. Landing silently into the water below.

That ordeal could not have been all in my head. Pain ricocheted through my body. What was happening to me? Had the looming mania finally taken hold of my mind?

"My lady, are you okay?" A maids soft voice called from beyond the door, left slightly ajar.

"I am fine." I managed to call back.

The door opened slightly, the new maid from this morning poked her head through the gap.

"Lady Vespera! There is water everywhere," She gasped, her eyes darted all over the tiled room now soaked in a layer of water. Her light curls bounced as she shook her head in horror.

My eyes widened as I thought frantically for an excuse. Only to be cut short just as one came to mind by her next piercing sentence.

"Why is there a knife on the floor?"

Chapter Four

"She has told you all she can!" Grandmother's shrill voice echoed through the halls. The staff scurrying about to act as if they were not eavesdropping.

"Now Sophia, we were only asking your granddaughter what we needed to know." The officer tried to soothe.

"And I am reiterating that she was not with a male. She was attacked in her own home. Look at her bruises!" Grandmother's hands waved wildly at where I sat on the chair in the dining hall. My hair was still wet and dripping down onto the dress they rushed to put me in, my foot bouncing on the ground with pent up nerves. Something I had done for years every time I was nervous.

"Vespera, is that the truth?" The officer finally looked at me standing beside the door frame, scepticism in his eyes.

"Yes. I was alone. I intended to remain alone." My voice was soft. The officer shook his head, dark curls swaying with the motion. I trained my gaze on my hands twisting in my lap.

"Thank you. We will move to question the staff." He started before pushing past Grandmother.

She lowered herself before me, kneeling as she took my hands in hers.

"My sweet winter child, I am so sorry," She whispered, her soft eyes searching my near lifeless ones. The attacker drained me of any energy I had to spare so I sat in silence. My eyes prickled as she ran her thumbs over my hands, lip quivering at the tenderness in her touch. A sob heaved in my heavy chest the sound rushed out of me like a broken instrument.

"Oh my sweet girl!" Grandmother's voice rang out as she embraced me, catching me as I fell to meet her open arms.

As curious as I was with death, this was not the end I had thought of for myself. I didn't want to end up slaughtered like my ancestors or stolen in the dead of night. Chills roamed over my body as if cold hands danced over my skin. My head was pounding, the feeling of anxiety rushed through my freezing form. I wasn't fated to go like this. Not yet anyway. How could I die when I hadn't gotten my colour? I was almost sure a Florian had seen their colour throughout our lineage and then died suddenly and often horrifically. I hadn't seen colour. I couldn't go just yet. I was safe. Was it not? I had come to believe my home was the safest in the world. But maybe I was wrong.

The feeling of their hands on me still burned deep into my flesh. Grandmother was alerted the moment the maid left the room. A server being forced to rush into town to get the police and alert Uncle Arthur who was yet to appear.

Grandmother apologised over and over as I sobbed into her embrace. Who would do this? What had I done to make someone attack me?

The sound of the front door opening caused my blood to run cold every fibre of my being freezing at the interruption. Have they come back to finish me off?

Two sets of heavy footfalls hurried toward the dining hall.

Grandmother turned quickly standing before me as if to protect me from another attack. I stood behind her, a good head taller than the frail woman.

"We came as soon as we heard." Arthur grunted as he entered the hall. Grandmother stepped aside allowing him to come closer to me.

I shied away from his touch. I couldn't bear the thought of another person's hands on me so soon.

My attention caught behind where he stood frozen to the spot. Unsure of why I had shied away from him. Victor looked at me with wild eyes.

"Why are you both here?" Grandmother demanded.

"We came to see if Vespera was safe." Victor spoke first.

"We came to stay. You will need protection and I presumed it would be better to have two men than just one," Arthur pressed.

I could feel the concern roll off the woman before me. I didn't say a word, choosing to push past them as they bickered about having too many people surrounding me. The new maid lingered beyond the doorway. Her terrified eyes met mine a million apologies falling from her plump lips. Her smooth pale hair a mess around her shoulders. As if pulled amongst her realisation of the situation she had just gotten herself into. I could only imagine the plethora of emotions she must be feeling. What a lovely welcome for her to Florain Manor.

"What is your name?" I managed to ask keeping my voice as level as I could.

"Rosemary. But my family calls me Mary," She said softly, fearful of my reaction. I nodded, holding the name to memory.

"May I call you Mary also?" I crossed my hands in front of me.

"Of course, my lady. You can call me whatever you please."

She smiled. The anxiety leaving her quickly. I nodded once it was too hard to smile at that moment.

"Will you escort me up to my rooms to prepare for bed?"

She accepted eagerly, a warm smile still spread on her face. Leading me up the stairs. Her hands clasped in front of her.

I sat in silence as she dressed me in my sleep gown and brushed my damp hair, weaving it into a tight braid.

Mary didn't say a word, content in her own silence.

She couldn't have been no older than I was. Her skin still tinged with that youthful glow. Whereas mine grew lifeless in the reflection of the dressing table looking glass. My appearance now dull with exhaustion. A ring of bruises lined my neck and forehead. The police believe it was a man who attacked me due to the strength of the attack but I wasn't so sure. The thing that attacked me was no short of the devil himself in clothing. A man of nothing but darkness.

"I'll fetch you a cup of tea to aid your sleep, Lady Florian," Mary said gently as she left the room.

The fear of being alone crept over me. What if the attacker came back? What if they never left? Maybe the police had missed a room when they searched. My heart began to race once more, my breathing coming in short. I tightened my gown around me. Throwing the door open I hurried into the hall, my mouth opened to call for Mary when I collided with a hard chest. A scream lodged itself in my throat, the scent of oakmoss tingling my nose.

"It's only me." Victor's voice rang out. My chest heaved up and down as I drew breath. Swallowing my scream. I wrapped my arms around him. Not knowing what I was doing or why I was seeking this stranger's comfort. His warmth poured into me, sinking deep into my skin. The feeling making me want to curl tighter into his embrace.

"Shh." He soothed. "It's only me. I'm here." I held him tighter, as if he could scare the monster away.

His delicate hand moved from my spine to my hair. Smoothing it as he held me close.

"I'm here. No one will hurt you now." And somehow despite myself, I chose to believe him.

My eyes stung the moment I opened them as the morning light poured in from the windows. Whatever herb Mary had slipped into my tea had put me to sleep in minutes. I pulled myself out of bed, my mind a whirlwind of thoughts. Was it all a nightmare? Did I imagine the whole thing? Did I imagine the strange man holding me until he disappeared like smoke?

I moved to the dresser. The looking glass reflected back my broken appearance. The bruises standing out against my stark pale skin. My light eyes haunted, dark circles lining the sunken skin underneath. Slowly, I raised a hand to feel my throat. My fingers glided over the skin. Whoever it was wanted to watch as the light left my eyes. I didn't even want to acknowledge the fact that they saw me free of clothing. I shuddered at the thought, disgust coiled in the pit of my stomach.

A brief knock hit the door three times, softly as if not wanting to wake me. I ripped my hand away from my throat, embarrassed at being caught in a moment of weakness.

"Come in," I called. Trying to mask my inner fear as best as I could. My voice still sounding strained.

Victor stood in the doorway, his hair dishevelled an aura of sleep still hanging over him.

"I'm glad to see you're awake," He said softly, a smile on his lips.

"As opposed to dead in my bed?" My attempt at humour fell flat. Victor's features dropped brow furrowing.

"Why would I wish you to be dead in your bed?"

"Never mind." I waved a hand, shaking his concern off. Victor frowned deeper but stepped forward.

"Lady Sophia thought it may be a good idea for you to distract yourself. She suggested you garden this afternoon."

I slumped my shoulders. I hadn't tended to my private garden outside in a long while.

"The flowers would be dried out or overgrown with weeds."

"We can venture into town. I'll buy you more."

"Victor, that is too much-"

"Nothing is ever too much. Not for you, Vespera." He cut me off with his sweet words. My heart warmed at the sound of them as did my cheeks. Despite all I was feeling, the thought of his kindness gave me the briefest sense of hope. Hope that not all was lost on humanity.

"Grandmother wouldn't allow me to leave the manor after last night." I smiled before reaching up to undo my tangled braid. The hair still damp from how tight Mary had wove it.

"I think that would be a rather fine idea! It would be safer than being here." The lady of the house called from somewhere down the hall.

"Get dressed. I'll meet you downstairs." Victor's grin widened. I returned the bright smile before looking in the mirror, hoping my expression was believable.

Was he the one who attacked me last night? The thought hit me like a lead brick. Surely not. He was sweet. I cocked a brow as I took in my reflection. I would find out more about

Victor. I had to. Curling my hair into a knot, I selected the sharpest hairpin I could and poked it through.

One thing was for certain though. No one would touch me again. I wasn't sure I would survive another attack. But I wouldn't go without a fight.

My dark skirts swayed as I hurried down the hall and passed the spare bathing room. A shudder ran through my spine at the memory.

Victor stood waiting at the bottom of the grand staircase. The dark stone almost the same shade of grey as my dress.

Victor took my arm and led me through the front doors.

We journeyed into town in comfortable silence. The only breaker being the sound of stones crunching under the carriage's wheels.

I gazed out the window as we passed, watching with curiosity. The Florian Manor's black carriage was a rare sight as it was, let alone with myself and a male my age inside.

I could only imagine the gossip the town would spread. No doubt it would be heard even to the palace in London. Queen Victoria herself would most likely hear of it too.

Victor's gaze however was solely focused on me. A smile playing on his lips. I quirked a brow and his smile broadened into a full grin.

"What are you looking at?" I narrowed my gaze. Hoping my hair hadn't fallen from the braided knot on my neck.

I didn't like bonnets. Useless things. Thank the lord Grandmother agrees too and refused to put me one. I didn't care for hats either. Although maybe I should have invested in one to hide the bruise on my forehead. I noted the idea for a later trip.

"You just have the most beautiful blue eyes."

I withheld the urge to roll the "beautiful" eyes. I noted the colour he mentioned despite myself. Wondering what that colour would be. Was it beautiful? Or was it as plain as the rest of me? I wondered what other things were blue. Were Grandmother's eyes blue? I was told they were the same as mine but I could never remember the colour they say.

"Thank you," I said small, my hands twisting in my skirts. "I like yours too."

Victor smiled, accepting my bluff. I turned back to the glass window.

I truly hoped this man wasn't going to try to woo me. I was content in my colourless world. But I had an inkling that even if I married him, my world would still be lifeless.

THE CARRIAGE CAME TO A HALT OUTSIDE OF AN OLD building now covered in dirt and grime. Where was the owner? He would have never allowed his garden store to fall to pieces.

The dark facade of the building now splattered with dirt and dust. I held my nose as I exited the carriage. The overpowering stench of the town further reminded me why I hated this place.

Victor's arm snaked through mine. A warm expression on his face. I inhaled as sharply as my corset would allow. Willing the air to calm me at his touch. Grandmother said the first time Grandfather has touched her, the gift of colour arrived. Whilst Victor's hand was bare against my long sleeves, I fretted my lip in nerves. Making a mental note to not allow him to touch my skin. The door swung open with the ring of a bell.

"Ahh, Vespera! It has been such a long time." Donovan's deep voice called from the doorway.

"Good day Donovan!" I called as I approached.

"I thought you had forgone your garden with how long it's been." He teased, his wide eyes sparkling, Irish accent as thick as ever.

"I would never forgive myself if I did." I managed to force out. It wasn't a lie. I did feel bad for not resuming gardening as passionately since father had left but the words felt like ash on my tongue.

"Then you must come." He ushered us in. Victor said nothing but remained silent as I led him down into the small store.

The scent of blossoms and dirt swirled into my nose. The smell feeling like a home I could only dream of, pure unfiltered bliss. Although I couldn't see the colour, I was still able to create a work of wonder within the blooms.

Donovan was the only person outside of the family who didn't shy away when I approached. He was always the one to support my craft. Never once judging my use of unusual colours of blooms. Always just watching with an approving smile.

"I assume you need a restock?" He called from behind his large wooden counter. The walls around him were full of every seed variant possible and bloom of every plant kind there was. I preferred flowers. I loved the texture of petals against my skin when I wandered the garden.

"Yes please. All my usual seeds." I smiled, watching as the large Irishman moved around the store selecting my seeds for after winter. There was no use planting them now. But I could still plant some in the greenhouse.

"Do you like to garden?" Victor said.

"I have since I was a child." I smiled, the memory of my mothers hands guiding mine as she helped me plant my first gardenia. The briefest memory of her scent came over me. Paint and indigo.

Victor said something but I paid him no mind. Moving to look at more bushes in terracotta pots. Donovan eyed Victor as he admired the store. An expression of wariness crossing his face. I said nothing, taking note of the strange interaction.

Donovan continues to talk about the new exhibition in a garden he had seen in London and even offered to take me when he goes. It was a dream to visit the Queen's garden one day. But that was all it could be. A sweet dream. Victor stiffened by my side.

"I would love to accompany you and your wife on your next trip. If Dorian was there as well of course." The words left my mouth quickly. As if trying to show Victor that Donovan had no romantic interest in me. A warmth flooded my cheeks. What was I saying? Why would Victor care about that?

I didn't really like light haired men. It was always the dark featured men that caught my attention.

"But of course." Donovan beamed, endless pride bloomed from him when his daughter was mentioned.

For years, she has been my only comfort outside of the manor. Years spent growing in the store together and making an absolute riot of the town. We were the same age when we met. Two outcast children. The townspeople gossiped about her just as much as they did about me and our antics. Dorian was not entirely sane by their standards. Always talking to herself and rushing around, seeing things no one else could and glimpses of what she called the future.

Paying for the seeds, I left the small shop. Eager to visit my friend to discuss the trip.

Chapter Five

I led Victor up the town centre only six streets from the store. Dorian had moved out of her parents' house to reside in her grandmother's run down old cottage. The weeds in the garden climbed toward the roof along the walls of the brick house. Dead blooms lined the chipped stone walkway. Victor mumbled something about the state of the cottage but I paid him no mind. My thoughts solely focused on how Dorian would feel about a stranger in her home. She screeched so loudly the last time, her distant cousin ran far and never returned. I knocked once, my fist rapping lightly on the wood before it creaked open.

"Dori? It's Vessie. I'm coming in." I called before stepping over the threshold.

Victor's hand fell on my back, the somewhat soothing movement left my body feeling tingly, and not in a good way.

I stepped forward once more through the main entrance. Weeds crept through the broken floorboards. Dust lining every surface, each window coated in a thick layer of grime. Dorian had tried to clean the home on multiple occasions but it never lasted long. The weeds would always grow back within no time through the floorboards.

"Are you sure it is safe in here?" Victor whispered cautiously.

"Safer than the manor." I released a breath. Victor snorted behind me.

The floor creaked as I took another step. The sitting room was bare, the only furniture not covered in bundles of fabric was an old armchair in the centre of the room. A teacup perched on the seat.

I called out for Dorian one last time.

"Maybe she isn't in." Victor stepped beside me, his hand not having moved from my lower back.

The sound of shuffling sounded down the short hall.

The slight woman poked her head through the doorway. Her smile widening as I walked toward her. She sprinted toward me, throwing her thin arms around my neck. I shifted at the feeling, remembering the strangers' hands around mine. The pain of that night fleeting like a ghost over me. A shudder followed in its wake.

"Oh Vespera! I was so worried about you!" She cried, her grip tightening a fraction.

How she knew I was attacked was beyond me. No one outside of the manor and the police knew. Grandmother herself made certain. Sometimes Dorian knew things no other soul could know. That's why the townspeople talked, labelling her a witch.

The visions would sometimes render her near useless, she could become a recluse for days, studying as much as she can, or a manic episode follows. She shies away from any form of physical contact, but will lean in to her wit to compensate

Dorian pulled back. Her dark eyes staring at me through strands of frazzled hair. Her hands cupping my face. She tore her gaze from me, moving to Victor. Her limbs moving ungracefully from my neck as she took a step back. As if she had forgotten to use them her searching gaze narrowed.

"Not him," She mumbled. Her hand slowly reaching up to touch his jaw. Victor's hand left my back but I caught his wrist before he could brush her away. It was best to let Dorian come to her senses. Her eyes glazed over. Victor's uncomfortable gaze slid to mine, his expression pleading for help. Her mumbled words soothed the anxiety in my chest though. I didn't know how she meant them but I took them the way I needed them.

"Dori." I urged softly trying to get her attention. Her hand finally made contact with Victor's clean shaven cheek. He stiffened at the touch of her fingertips brushing over his skin.

"Calathea," She whispered before stepping back as if his skin burnt her. She cradled her hand in the other. A frown lining her thin lips.

"Vespera," She said suddenly her eyes clearing.

"Yes, Dorian?" I loosened a pent up breath.

"You shouldn't be out." She snapped. "Someone tried to kill you. Yet you come see me, you silly little fool."

"Yes. I did." She rolled her eyes at my response. Her dirt covered sleeve hung off her arm as she gestured toward the kitchen. I walked first, guiding Victor down the hall. I really should have forewarned him about her. She wasn't this bad the last time I had seen her. She looked like she hadn't slept in weeks.

I sat at the small table, Victor moved to stand behind me, seemingly my new protector.

Dorian mumbled to herself as she brewed a pot of tea. Measuring assorted herbs and placing them in the pot. Once the water was over the flame, Dorian turned her attention back to Victor.

"I apologise for my actions earlier. I have not been myself as of late." She tried to smile. The expression still seemingly forced and unnatural.

"I understand. None of us have been ourselves as of late," Victor said as he laid a hand on my shoulder. Dorian hummed, raising her eyebrows at the sight. A twinkle of mischief in her gaze.

"Dorian. This is Victor. Arthur's new apprentice." I pressed. Knowing she would pester me for answers the next time we were alone.

"Charmed to meet you. I am Dorian. Vespera's only friend." Possession ebbing through her tone. She looked over Victor once more. Nodding as she moved from the stove to the table. Pouring a splash of her strange brew in a single cup.

"To help your mind," She whispered. Knowing my whirlwind of thoughts never ceasing as usual. I thanked her before blowing on the boiled murky liquid.

"Do you see colour, Victor?" she bubbled.

"Ah, yes. I do…" He trailed off, noticing Dorian's wicked grin.

"How curious," She practically sang. Humour and amusement brightening her face.

I shifted my leg under the table, kicking her shin. Anger flashed in her eyes at the impact before clearing back her strange mischief. I frowned before sipping the bitter tea. The horrible taste filling my mouth. My nose scrunching at the distaste.

"Victor, would you be a dear and fetch me some daisies from my garden." Dorian waved toward the door. Victor hurried off as if grateful for the excuse to leave. The front door clicked shut and Dorian leant forward. Her foot colliding with my leg. I winced in pain.

"You bring a man here without consulting me first?" She hissed. Keeping her voice low. Her gaze glowering at me.

"I couldn't leave without him. It's not as if you would visit me at the manor." I matched her tone.

"Too much death. You know that." She waved me away, straightening in her chair. I shook my head with a frown. Her face a mask of arrogance

"Speaking of which, I have a salve for the bruises on your neck." Her eyes darted toward the door before continuing. "Be careful around him."

"Why? What do you see?"

"Nothing. That's the problem. I just can't seem to see a thing about him." She exhaled with frustration, nodding her head in the direction Victor disappeared.

I slumped back in my chair. Another person to fear. Just what I needed. The anxiety came running back.

"He does see colour though." Dorian teased as she took the cup from my hands.

"What does that mean?"

"Your soulmate is supposed to be just like you, are they not?" She winked before downing the cup of tea. Her face screwing up with blatant disgust.

"No wonder you didn't drink it," She muttered. Throwing the liquid over her shoulder to land on the tiles behind her.

"What do you mean Dori?" I pressed.

"That drink was putrid. Did you not taste it?" Her eyes grew wide. Irritation rose to the surface of my skin. I was eager to press on and get exactly the answer I wanted.

"Dorian, I swear to God-"

"Found some!" Victor's cheerful voice cut me off.

"Perfect." Dorian bubbled. Her knowing smirk plastered on her face. "I'll make the salve."

We left the cottage to return to a bustling town centre. The townspeople all going about their daily life. My mind swirled with thoughts. What did Dorian mean by just like me? Were they almost killed? Could they see no colour also?

People drifted past as we walked in content silence to our carriage just up ahead. Some stared, others ignoring me as usual. I glanced across the bustling street. One person caught my attention.

"Can I interest you in a luncheon, Miss Florian?" Victor's voice tore me from the strange man across the street. Although I could not see his face beneath his hat, shivers still ghosted over my skin. My body froze at the sight of him staring at me. My fingers clenched my bag of seeds and salve tighter.

"Victor." My voice cracked. The stranger across the cobblestone road took a step toward me.

"Yes?"

"We need to leave," I whispered, keeping my gaze on the strange man in the dark coat.

Victor looked from me to the man. His hand wound its way through my shaking free hand. The bruises on my neck hidden from sight now tingling with a sudden pain.

"Come." Victor urged, pulling me softly toward him. The man stepped forward once more, my heart leaping into my throat.

I squeezed my fingers against Victor's before hurrying into the awaiting carriage.

My breathing came in hard and fast and as I slumped back in my chair, I could finally focus on getting my breathing back to normal. Not caring about being proper in my posture as I reclined. My heart thumped in my chest.

Victor sat in front of me, cautious eyes alight with worry. I clenched mine closed not wanting to look into his any further. I could still feel his hand on my bare skin.

He was touching me. His hand was on mine yet no colour came to fruition. Despite the strange man lingering outside, a weight in my chest lifted.

Victor was not the man I was set to love.

But that only poses another question.

Who was?

Chapter Six

Victor left past noon to gather some things before coming to stay at the manor. The interaction with Dorian throwing his perception of me off for the moment. He eyed me with caution the entire carriage ride home. I couldn't hide my smile. The man probably thought I was as manic as Dorian. Having been attacked one night and smiling the next day. I was content to be left alone though. Now that I knew he was not the one I was fated to be with. Maybe I could grow to love him.

Even then the thought repulsed me. I didn't want love.

The house was freezing when I entered. As if a harsh frost tore through the walls. It wasn't uncommon in the manor. Most rooms had a chill to them but no maintenance was required. The manor was as well looked after as the palace itself.

Grandmother prided herself on the state of her home. Just as her mother did before her.

We ate in silence through lunch back at the manor. Both not wanting to discuss the strange man watching us. Even though I could still feel his eyes on me.

I retired to the greenhouse until sundown. The steamed glass walls bore the outside forest to me, I watched as the sun became one with the ground. Deep inside me harboured a young girl who longed to see the colours of a sunset. Grandmother had told me about them years ago. I had never forgotten how sad she looked when she described it. As if she despised her ancestor for the curse that had taken away our beauty in life. No matter how many times I told her that just because colour was non existent to me, I could still find the beauty in everyday life and appreciate it more. She always told me to not argue and that I would understand when I found my colour.

What she didn't realise though, is how I would grow up to despise colour and how happy it seemed to make people. I didn't understand how people couldn't find contentment in darkness.

The earthy scent of damp soil and plant-life swam around my senses, radiating a wave of calmness through me. I strolled through the rows of pots I had accumulated. Bunches of leaves poking out everywhere amongst the array of flowers I had brought to life. Extending my fingers, I ran them over the leaves. Some soft, others sharp. Some like a kiss of smooth silk to the skin. A smile tugged at my lips. The greenhouse was one place I always felt at peace. Closing my eyes, I ran my fingers over a petal of a peony. A distant memory resurfacing.

Father's voice echoing around me. "Not pony, Vespera, peo-knee." The sound of his once bright joy hit like a blade to the chest. I had longed for him to return for years. To come see how I had grown. But it has been years since I last heard from him. Sometimes I wondered whether I truly liked gardening or whether I was simply keeping it up to standard for when father arrived back home. If he ever did. Grief tugged at my shoulders, pulling them down.

I was never enough for anyone.

Grandmother had called me gloomy for many a year. I would seek comfort in books of anatomy or medical research. Something no young woman should supposedly be interested in. I never gravitated toward light colours or small animals. I would always reach for dark shades and fearsome animals. Although I could not stand ravens. Noisy little beasts, I much preferred the silence to their chatter.

Pulling myself from my thoughts I began to prune the bush before me.

"Lady Vespera?" Mary's voice tore through my concentration on the petunias.

I hummed as she approached, waiting for whatever it was she wanted. The oil lantern flickering in her hold.

"This was delivered for you. Victor said he quite enjoyed the study and thought you might too," She said softly as she entered my safe space, her hands in her apron pocket, hiding whatever was concealed.

"Is he here?" I whispered, looking briefly behind her for him. She shook her head before producing the gift. A small leather bound book lay between her hands. I reached for it warily. What kind of study was it? Opening the first page, I almost giggled at the title. *A Study of Madness.*

Mary quirked a brow at my reaction but said nothing. I thanked her before turning back to the petunias, putting the book beside the pot.

Mary lingered in the pathway, watching intently as I snipped the dried leaves. She cleared her throat loudly. I slid my eyes to where she stood watching me.

"What exactly are you doing?" She tilted her head, eyes filled with curiosity . Her voice as sweet as honey.

"Tending to the dead leaves. If I don't remove these ones, the rest of the plant will die."

"Fascinating," She breathed, stepping forward. I mumbled a brief yes before turning back to the pot. Mary remained exactly where she was, watching with awe as my hand wove through the plants.

Whilst I didn't usually like company, something told me Mary needed the companionship more than I ever did.

"Would you mind finding me a trowel please? I think I may begin planting some seeds."

Mary's eyes glazed over with a sudden mystification. As if the mere thought of planting a seed was the most fascinating thing for her. My lip quirked up at her quick nod before scurrying around the benches. The sound of her footsteps falling in line with my pruning shears. She hurried back holding the trowel like a beautiful treasure.

I thanked her warmly before pushing past her gently to get a pot.

Mary watched as I filled the heavy pot with damp soil. Poking holes into the surface with my finger every inch. I placed each rose seed in with delicate care before smoothing the soil over each small hole, remaining silent as I worked.

"That will do for tonight." I wiped a filthy hand over my brow, leaving a trail of mess lining my skin.

"Will you come back and complete the others tomorrow?" Mary asked softly.

"Yes. I think I will do the ones I can."

Mary brightened in the light from the oil lantern beside her. I withheld my own smile, knowing she would be back by my side tomorrow.

The moon hung high above us as we walked through the narrow path back to the manor. Content silence filling the vast night.

Uncle Arthur sitting watch outside my door writing notes by candlelight. He smiled as I approached my room but said nothing. I washed the muck from me quickly before collapsing into bed, staring at my reflection in the mirror. Nothing had changed. I still looked as cold and plain as usual.

I shook the memory of my shallow reflection from my head. Turning my focus back to the strange medical study book from Victor in my grasp.

The pages opened easily, the old book clearly had been read multiple times over. How many people had touched this book and studied the contents? Understood the supposed truth in the words? Excitement jittered through me as I read the first page.

"*Madness has been found in many places around the world but seemingly more evident than ever before in the heart of London,*" it read. I grinned despite myself. Of course London housed a multitude of madness and hysteria. It was too large not too. Too many tales told. Too many horrors held in the streets.

I read deep into the night. Desperate to reach the end of the study. It was in the middle that froze me to my core.

"*Under stress, the mind can conjure images of things that are not there and can cause them harm. Many cases of near death have resulted in the patient declaring that a man of shadows came to take them away.*"

I hadn't seen a shadowy man. Just a strange blurry attacker that no one else had seen.

Was I the one who was mad? I couldn't be. My mouth opened and closed. Silently protesting the teaching of the book. I scolded myself. How could I have imagined it if there were bruises on my skin. Scowling, I closed the book and rolled over, forcing myself into a fitful sleep.

"If the soil is too dry, the seed won't grow. Same as if it were to be too wet"

Mary nodded as I spoke, drinking in each fact that I provided. Her sweet face was lined with dirt and sweat.

It was exceptionally warm in the greenhouse, the sun now high in the sky.

It had taken all morning for me to convince Mary that she was allowed to help me plant the seedlings into the pots. The poor soul was terrified to mess anything up and be the cause of their deaths. It was sweet in a way. I didn't mind if she misplanted them. It was all part of learning. Only God knows how many seeds I had planted only to have them wither and die or not even blossom at all.

Mary's tongue poked out from the side of her mouth. Her focus solely on covering the seeds, patting the soil ever so gently so that they were sealed in.

I praised her for her work, feeling pride for the young maid. A small giggle left me as she cheered for herself. Her pleasure filling the empty space. The sound of her delicate claps bringing a small smile to my lips.

"When did you start here?" I asked suddenly, the mood deepening.

"Only a month ago. Your grandmother put out an advertisement for someone to come tend to the house."

"And you came despite the rumours?" I cocked my head. Listening intently for her response.

"Every house is haunted. There is not a single inch of this earth where something hasn't died on some stage." She shrugged, as if truly unphased by the entities in this manor.

I straightened, taken aback by her words.

A brief flicker of movement flashed behind her. I glanced over her shoulder looking out beyond the glass walls into the forest.

I froze.

"Vespera, what is it?" Mary's tone softened, like a mother soothing a babe.

"I think there is someone in the forest." I kept my voice low. Fear ribboning through it.

Mary turned to face the forest. Her eyes darted over every tree. I stepped beside her slowly, searching again. Mary gasped but stepped back. Her hand flew to her mouth. My stare catching on what she had seen.

A figure covered by a dark hood loomed on the outskirts of the trees. Facing where we stood in the greenhouse.

My heart pounded in my chest. The sound echoing in my ears.

Mary gripped my arm. Her stare still locked on the stranger.

The door to the greenhouse suddenly creaked open. Mary's hands darted for the trowel. The handle in her shaky grasp as she stood before me. Trowel ready to attack if she needed to. It was admirable really.

"Jesus Christ, Mary. It's just me." Victor materialised, his hands raised in a sign of surrender.

Mary exhaled heavily.

"What are you staring at?" Victor breathed. Too afraid to make mention of our terrified appearance.

I swallowed thickly. Unable to form a word. My fingers raised to point at the treeline.

The figure stood as still as stone watching the interaction.

"Mary, take Vespera inside." Victor ordered. His arm extended for her to take the trowel and move out.

"She is not going out there with that mad man!" She exclaimed, her voice shrill.

Victor held a finger to his lips. His expression lethal. "Get her inside now." He hissed.

Mary puffed before thrusting her hand back for me. I took it easily, noting that she still held the trowel in a white knuckle grip rather than giving it to Victor. She pulled me toward the door.

Victor dashed out before she made it, moving toward the strange hooded man.

"You are trespassing on private property. I demand you state your name and reason for entering the manor yards." His voice demanding. A tone I never thought I would hear from him. He was always so gentle and kind. Mary tugged me down the path, urging me to continue as I stopped to catch a glimpse of the man.

The figure remained silent but lifted an arm. A gloved finger pointed at me. Mary tugged once more before I moved. Looking over my shoulder as the figure stepped back, melding into the tree line once more.

Chapter Seven

The moon was hanging high in the sky by the time I retired the next night. Arthur had already checked on me, as had Victor.

Grandmother had been asleep most of the day. I didn't blame her though. She had been up most of the night by my bedside. Or so Arthur had told me. She hadn't wanted to leave my side after the stranger was found in the trees. The men of the manor all searched the surrounding forest but to no avail. It was like no one had been there at all. Not a single footprint where he stood against the brush. Only a single rose lay amongst the grass. I hadn't been left alone since. If it wasn't Grandmother, it was Mary or Victor.

I didn't need to be watched. I needed to be left alone. To stare into the night and think of how many critters were in the woods. Not how many mad people were lurking around for me.

I wandered through the cold manor, a candle in hand as I made my way to bed.

I passed the large dining room. The only light flooding in from the large windows lining the entrance way. The candlelight flickered in my hand as I looked around. My heart raced. A small but distinct creak sounding toward my left, beyond the door into the dining room. Another creak sounded. Closer this time.

I hurried forward. Rushing to the stairs as I made my way to my room.

My foot fumbled in my skirt. Blasted things. My head pounded with each step.

Another creak behind me sent my heart galloping. Dropping the candle, I abandoned the light. Moving straight into the darkness beside the stairs. I lowered myself to the ground. I find the darkness more comforting, it lets me forget that the light brings distorted faces.

Footsteps closed in behind me. Making their way up the stairs.

I shifted ever so slightly. Looking up at where the figure would be walking. The only thing visible was the soles of their shoes.

The man walked slowly. As if hunting its prey.

I clenched a hand over my mouth. Wishing to god my breathing would be silent.

The man's breath echoed in the silent manor. Heavy and thick. His footsteps drifted higher as he walked up to the second floor.

I took my chance. I crawled away from the staircase. Hurrying as quiet as I could to the library. I looked back just in time for the man to spot me.

A scream lodged itself in the back of my throat as he leapt down the staircase.

I turned back and ran. My legs moving as fast as they could in my dress. My own breathing coming out shallow. I couldn't turn back. My hand reaching for the doorknob of the library.

The sound of the man drew closer.

The doorknob was cold in my grasp. As if all of the heat had been sucked out of the room. The knob refused to turn. The scream in my throat finally breaking free. The shrill screech blasting through the still air.

The man was close. I pushed back. Dashing toward the kitchen. A broken sob falling from my lips. The kitchen doors loomed in sight. I threw myself through them.

The names of servers called from my lips. My voice now hoarse. Where was everyone?

I opened my mouth to scream again. Not caring that the man could find me at any second. I couldn't run any further. My legs and chest were on fire, my throat burned with the force of the scream that busted from my lips

Only to be cut off by the man's hand on my mouth. He pulled me against him. Hot tears lined my eyes, spilling over onto my cheeks. The gloved hand, almost familiar, grew my terror beyond reason. Flashes of the other night in between this nightmare had my head growing lighter with fear.

No, no, no! I thought as I thrashed in his hold. The stranger's hot breath curled over my ear.

The hand he rested on my belly now clenched. As if he held something. I didn't dare think what was there.

The man pulled me back into the shadows of the hall.

No one had heard my scream.

I tried again and again as the man held my mouth, the leather of his glove muting my scream. I bit into the fabric. Hoping he would release me. If anything it only made him stronger.

His grip tightened.

As if on instinct, I stamped my foot. The sole of my shoe landing directly on his toes. He grunted but regained himself.

The words "little bitch." rung in my ear. The voice unfamiliar but haunting all the same. The smell of dirt and leather filled my nose as I sobbed. Weak pleas fell from my lips behind his hand.

The hand holding something flicked.

Pain like no other tore through my abdomen. The sharp slice sending another muffled screech through the air.

"Please for the love of all things holy let me go," I screamed, my words falling behind the glove doing little to no good.

No one was coming. My stomach burned as the stranger removed their blade. I could feel my own blood leaking from the wound. Dropping down onto the marble floor.

My fingers tore at the hand holding my throat. The scream trapped within stifled with the lack of oxygen. The man's hot breath met my shoulder. Puffing with exertion as I fought his hold despite my ceaseless pain. His strong arm pulled me back, throwing me to the cold tile floor beneath me. He was on me in seconds. The mask covering his face as menacing as his form. The stranger straddled me, his hand back on my throat stifled the air once more. The weight crushed my ribs. The pain of his hands on the still prominent bruises, twisting with the pain of my stomach... With his free hand, I watched in mute horror as he pulled a long knife from his boot. I thrashed wildly beneath him. My hands reaching up to claw at whatever part of the masked man I could. Panic overtaking me. My blood pooling beneath me.

This was it. He had finally gotten what he wanted. The man who haunted my every nightmare was now here to drag me to hell. The blade slashed straight across my exposed chest, searing with agony. Tears fell from my eyes as the knife moved again. This time marking the opposite way. I could feel my blood pouring from me. Running down my sides only to pool beneath me. Pain ricocheted through my body.

The man moved quickly. My screams concealed under his hand now firmly holding my mouth. He held the bloody blade before my eyes. I clenched them closed, terrified of what he could do next. My torn flesh burned upon my chest. As if laced with some type of acid. The sound of the masked man's breathing echoed through my ears. My hands reached up to claw at whatever I could.

The attacker moved from me. My arms dropped to my sides, exhaustion eating into me. My life drained with each drop of blood from the wound. My eyes closed once more. The sound of his retreating footfalls echoed through the halls.

My head lulled to the side, metallic blood leaking from my lips.

"Sweet girl, it's time to come home." A deep velvety voice echoed through the room. I couldn't move. Frozen in agony on the floor. My eyes fluttered open once more. Moonlight pouring in from the vast kitchen windows. The cool air of the manor brushed against my skin. The pain dulled as my breathing drew light.

A dark hooded figure stepped forward as if out of the shadows of the room. I couldn't contain the whimper in my throat. My hand reached for him. As if my subconscious knew he was safe. He had to be, or at the very least he would end this misery. He stalked forward. Slow and gently as if used to looking upon Death. I couldn't see beneath his hood. I didn't need to. The darkness he produced was darker than any I had seen. His gloved hand moved toward mine. Calm radiated from the stranger.

"Time to come home, Vespera." His voice was soft. Like the stars at midnight. My fingers inched toward his hand. Now suddenly free of the glove.

His hand met mine. A sharp pain burst through my mind. The man stumbled back with a hiss holding his hand. I couldn't see anything but black. My hand brushed my open wound on my chest. I blinked once more. Willing my vision to come back. Slowly, the shadows began to dissipate. Amongst the grey scale was something I never expected to see.

A shade of colour lined my hand. My blood. The colour is so vibrant against the grey of my skin.

Footfalls came closer from beyond the door. A shrill scream sounded beside me. I paid it no mind. The only thing I could focus on was the one strange colour I could now see. Before everything went back to black.

Chapter Eight

I woke to my name being whispered to me. Light pouring in behind my eyelids. The soft fabric of the sheets warm against my skin exposed from the thin sleeveless nightgown.

What a horrible nightmare that was. I tore open my eyes. My body heavy with exhaustion.

Grandmother's gasp rang through me, echoing off my skull. I cringed at the sound.

"You came back to us," She cried, her hand reaching for mine.

"Of course I did?"

"You've been asleep for three days Vespera, dear." Her tone grew worried. Her hand moving to stroke my ruffled hair from my face.

"How could I have slept that long?" I didn't believe her. I wasn't out that long. It was only a dream.

"You really don't remember do you?" Her voice softened.

"Remember what?" I croaked, my throat suddenly dry. No. This couldn't be happening. This wasn't right. It was wrong. Everything was still grey.

I sat up too quickly. My body screamed with agony. My right side of my abdomen feeling as if it was tearing apart.

I almost howled in pain. What was this?

Grandmother's voice rang out for Arthur. Two pairs of footfalls raced up the hall.

The two men burst in, Arthur with a bandage in hand and Victor with a pair of scissors. The sight of a blade causing vomit to rise in my throat. It wasn't a dream. It was real.

"No." The word fell from my lips.

"I am so sorry, Vespera." Arthur's voice sounded sincere. As if he felt responsible for my attack.

My head spun. Confusion setting in.

How was I alive? I was carved like a beast. My hand trembled as I lifted my hands to my chest just above my breasts.

"I'm sorry. The scars will remain." Victor's voice was thick.

I clenched my eyes closed, fisting my hand in my sheets.

"Who?" I said softly.

"Who what, dear?" Grandmother said gently.

"Who attacked me!" My words rang loud, bounding through the silence.

"We aren't sure."

"Then become sure. I want them hanging from the gallows!" I cried, laying back in bed.

Arthur gripped my arm. A small prick in its place.

The world faded to black once more.

THE WORLD SPUN BENEATH ME. STICKS AND STONES littering the forest floor, sharp against my bare feet. Rain pattered around me, landing softly on the branches of the trees above. The scent of the earth filling my nose with the calming scent of the downpour.

My hair stuck to my face with each gust of harsh wind. A tremor ran through my spine. I turned through the forest. No one lingered.

My voice was hoarse as I called for anyone at all to hear me. Slight crunching caught my attention from the left. Branches crushing under weight. I stilled bracing for the person.

Long dark hair flicked behind a tree before a tall woman in white stepped out. Her long damp hair loose around her waist. Her feet bare and covered in muck. Her beautifully cheerful smile on full display, brightening the dark woods. Her eyes alight with the purest of joy.

"Do come on, my love," She called. Her arms stretched out to me. I moved forward. The sting of tears lining my eyes. My heart leaping to life as I took a step toward the woman whose soul I ached to see again. Movement sounded behind me. Quick footsteps hurrying forward, heavy and purposeful. A deep chuckle sounded close to my back, another tremor running through me. The chill of a hand pushing into me radiated from my chest. I glanced down, watching in horror as the man walked through me. As if I wasn't there.

My mother beamed at my father, watching as he approached her. The moment he was in arms reach she leapt upon him. The two locked in a passionate embrace. My heart creaked inside me. I had always remembered them like this. Never the arguing or the fighting. Just the love that filled their hearts day in and day out. A love I had once longed for but grew to despise.

Love weakens you to your surroundings. Love can twist a person apart and put them back together but it can just as easily leave them broken and in pieces on the floor. The tears on my face began to fall harder. The rain still falling over them. It was my mother who pulled away first.

"We must protect, Vespera," My mother said softly, a sense of urgency in her voice.

"Nothing will happen to her." Father insisted, his voice smooth and loving. The familiarity crushing my heart. Another thing I desperately ached to hear.

"He will come for her, John. As he always has and will do." She urged as he lowered her to the ground. Father towered over her as he brushed a kiss to her damp forehead.

"Adele, nothing will happen to her. I swear on my life that no one will take our daughter away." His gentle stroke of his thumbs against her cheeks brushing calmness over her skin. Mother's eyes flickered closed, leaning into the touch.

"Our child will be safe." Father insisted once more.

The lie settled deep in my bones as I watched. An internalised anger now threatening to break free.

I wasn't safe. He left me. Alone. He left me to be attacked. He failed her.

"He failed you!" I screamed at her. "He failed you!"

My words falling on dead air. I stood forward, my anger running through me. He was meant to protect me but he failed.

"He failed you," I screeched. Willing for her to hear me. To see me. To see the strange and horrific wound on my chest. My anger simmering to despair as the rain fell heavier. As if it too felt the weight of my emotions.

"He failed us." My voice shook as a sob wracked through my body. "He failed us both."

WHEN I AWOKE, I WAS ALONE IN MY BED. THE FOREST now but a distant memory to be lost. The warmth of the room filled my bones. My mania from earlier still simmering beneath the surface. I needed to act as if all was well. Or they would send me to the asylum three towns over. I shuddered at the thought. I wasn't hysterical. I was in pain. I was confused.

What in God's name had happened to me? Why had I seen my parents? What did they mean he was coming for me? Had they known my attacker all along? And surely the brief single colour I saw was not real. It can't have been. For it was only Death's hand that touched me. I looked at my hand. Now clean from any blood. Still the same pale hand. I moved up the bed. Preparing for the pain. Only there was none.

"Curious." I noted to myself. The drug that Arthur injected me with was truly working wonders.

I managed to shift from the bed with no further pain. Rolling all of my limbs and joints. None stiff.

"Lady Vespera!" Mary's voice called from behind the door.

I responded before thinking. "Come in."

Mary opened the door slowly, cautious for what she might see.

"You should not be out of bed, my lady!" Her eyes widened like saucers at the sight of me.

Panic ran through me. I needed an excuse. My eyes ran over the room before me. The empty crystal glass on my bedside table throwing light in the afternoon sun.

"I was desperate for a drink, you see. So I thought I would fetch myself a glass of water." the lie fumbled from my lips. *Nice one, Vespera. Really believable.*

"You should have called for me." Mary lightly scalded before collecting the glass. Offering a silent warning to get back on the bed with a nod of her head. I withheld my sigh of relief as I lowered myself.

Mary came back with the glass in hand, her eyes lined with concern. I made an effort to smile despite how mixed I had felt. The smile fell flat as Mary eyed me, her gaze falling on my partially exposed chest.

My smile dropped. No doubt this would look vile when I took the bandages off.

Mary shook her head as if shaking whatever thought she had before picking up a hair dress from my dresser.

"Seeing as you are up and walking, we should prepare you for dinner. You have not eaten in three days." I nodded weakly. Not willing to fight her. I needed to find out who knew what about my attack.

Mary dressed me in a low cut gown. "So the pressure doesn't touch the wounds," She had said as she loosely tied the laces on the light grey gown.

THE DINING HALL WAS EMPTY WHEN I ARRIVED. THE pain in my abdomen slowly ebbing back in. I lowered myself to my usual seat and waited for the rest of the house to arrive. A waiter came and poured a glass of deep wine to which I swallowed quickly. Requesting another. He didn't say a word as he poured another. Voices echoed in the hall beyond. I strained to listen.

"You will find, sir Maaier, that the house may look imposing but it is simply just a facade. Keeps the gossips at bay." Grandmother joked. I snorted into my glass. Of course she makes light of this horrid situation.

"This is the dining hall." She continued. I expected her to stop and open the doors but her voice drifted away. Who could she possibly be giving a tour to in a time like this? I stood slowly. Following the sound of voices into the kitchen. The pain in my belly throbbed. My chest however not radiating a single discomfort.

My hand found the spot on my stomach. Holding it against it as if that would do anything to help the pain. I pushed forward.

"This is where she was found." Grandmother's voice carried from the kitchen. "We are ever so glad that Victor had found her when he did. The poor soul was torn to pieces right here on the floor."

I neared the door, keeping my footsteps quiet. Why was Victor the first to find me? He was the first to retire to bed and the furthest away. Surely he would have slept through my scream?

"Your granddaughter was stabbed here, you say?" A deep velvety voice spoke. Warmth tingled within me. Who was this strange man? I leaned against the doorway. Stabilising myself as another wave of dizzying pain overtook me.

"Yes. I was terrified of losing her. Vespera is my humanity, you see. She is my one light in this gloomy existence." Her tone thickened with emotion.

"Then I will do my very best to keep her safe. We will find who did this, Lady Florian," The deep voice said.

The pain in my abdomen throbbed once more. I stumbled forward. My feet falling out from under me, knees hitting the cold marble flooring. My name fell from Grandmother's lips as she hurried toward me, thick skirts swishing around her. I clenched my teeth. I was a fool for leaving my bed. I was too stubborn for my own good.

Grandmother's thin hands looped around my shoulder pulling me upright.

A second set taking my waist, pulling me up gently to face them. The sight before making my mouth run dry.

The man was easily the tallest I had seen. Strength exuding from his form. Eyes so dark I could see myself reflecting in them. His long hair tied back in a knot behind his head. His skin a middle shade of grey, not too deep, not too light. An interesting mix.

The man's thumbs smoothed circles over my waist whilst grandmother rubbed my shoulders.

My hands gripped the man's arms for support, hard flesh pressed against my fingers. A warmth pooling deep inside me that I had never felt before.

"Maaier. This is Vespera." Grandmother's voice drifted from behind me. I couldn't focus on anything but the smirk that filled Maaier's plump lips. My own tongue running along the seam of mine. By God. What was wrong with me? I shoved him away quickly, as if burnt by his lingering touch.

"Please excuse me." I faked a smile. Maaier bowed low before me.

"Of course. We can introduce ourselves formally later." His velvet voice soothing against my frayed nerves.

Like hell we would.

I turned on my heel, shaking off Grandmother.

Now where was Arthur and that magical tonic?

Chapter Nine

"Vespera, I don't know what you are talking about." Arthur grunted. We had been arguing for nearly an hour.

"The tonic you administered me when I was in bed. It was sheer relief."

"It is the same as the one I just administered you."

"No. It is not," I snarled through clenched teeth. "The one I had earlier gave me no pain!" Falling back into the abundance of pillows on my bed.

"It is!" He exclaimed. His arms thrown wide with exasperation before storming out of the room.

I withheld my scream. This was torture. I was like a prisoner in my own bed. After my fall earlier, Arthur had taken it upon himself to lock me in here until I was healed enough. I had been in here for three hours already and I was already prepared to be taken to the asylum. This was madness.

Mary spoonfed me soup and even she was told to leave me be. They believed it was safer to have me alone in my room whilst someone guarded my door. I rolled my eyes. The attacker would get past them easily. He was not human. He was a beast. The sound of the door creaking open caught my attention from my self loathing. I sat slowly, my eyes meeting Maaier's as he entered the room.

What was this stranger doing here? Was this even safe?

"I thought it best to introduce myself. I am Lord Maaier of Contsa Manor up North," He announced, standing beside the bed. Peering down at me with his hands clasped in front of him, eyes lingering on my bandaged chest.

He couldn't have waited until I was dressed could he. And not in this ridiculously thin nightgown.

"Pleased to meet you, Lord Maaier." I managed, not wanting to come off as impolite.

"Pleasure is all mine." He smiled, the expression causing my heart to race.

I watched with curiosity as he lowered himself to the chair. Now dwarfed by his large frame. Why was this stranger in our house?

"Your grandmother hired me to watch over you," He said as if reading my thoughts.

"And you are what exactly? My protector?" I wanted to snort. The only way to keep me safe is getting me far away from this manor.

"I suppose you can call me that." Maaier smirked, his tone grew teasing.

"What else would I call you?" I cocked my eyebrow. What was I even saying? Why did my mind wander when this man was near? Maaier's smile widened into a grin.

"You can call me what you like, little bird."

"Why am I a bird?" I narrowed my gaze. I hated the birds. Such noisy creatures.

"Would you prefer bloom?"

"I would prefer if you addressed me as my name." I snorted. What was this stranger playing at?

"As you wish, Vespera Florian." He smirked before leaving the room.

My hand collided with a pillow. Why could I not be left alone to heal? And where was Arthur with my tonic?

***

I SAT AT THE BREAKFAST TABLE ALONE.

I had hardly slept. The thought of the attacker coming back plaguing me like a hound. Even with Arthur and Victor protecting me, I now had Maaier to contend with. As I watched the sunset rise over the treeline beyond the large window, I allowed my mind to wander.

Images of a hooded man flashed through my mind. Reaching his hand out to me. Gentle words reminding me it was safe to come home. Wherever that was. A loathsome part of me wishes I did join him. Maybe it was my time to leave this life. Who knows, it may have just been divine timing.

The steam of the teacup tickled my nose as I held it to my face. My legs propped up on the dining table as I leant back on my seat. The only sounds were my breathing and the birds awakening outside. My eyes fluttered closed, relaxation willing its way in despite the past week's events.

"Is this seat taken?" A low drawl sounded behind me. I stiffened slightly before gesturing to the chairs opposite me, keeping my legs on the table. My skirt full enough to still cover them.

Maaier slid into the chair directly across from me, pouring himself a tea before mirroring my posture. He placed his own booted feet on the edge of the table. Leaning back as the sun shone over his skin, he inhaled deeply. The portrait of utter bliss in the morning. His thin white shirt tight on his frame. The man was strong that much was certain.

"It's rude to stare." He raised a brow but kept his eyes closed. I rolled my own and faced the window, sipping on my tea.

"You're up early." I noted, wiping away the excess tea from my lips with my finger. Maaier lolled his head to the side, watching the movement.

"Couldn't sleep," He muttered before looking out the window once more. I don't know whether it was the lack of sleep or the relaxation of the sunrise but something drew me to speak to him.

"Do you go to London often?"

"No." He smiled.

I nodded, accepting his simple answer. A beat passed before he spoke again.

"I'm a friend of the family. I used to come down often throughout my youth to visit the manor.'

"You knew my mother then?" I felt the corners of my mouth lift ever so slightly at the memory of her.

"Yes." Maaier smiled but it didn't reach his eyes. "She was a beautiful woman from what I can recall."

I smiled into my teacup. She truly was. My heart ached for her.

"I'm sorry for that loss. It was a deep one indeed," He said, his voice low.

"Thank you." I managed, turning my attention back to the sun. The silence filled the air as we sipped our teas. Content in the company of another. I should have been terrified. I should have called for someone else to join. But a small part of myself won over, telling me to trust him just this once.

"Do you..." we spoke at the same time. A warm blush coated my skin as Maaier chuckled.

"You go." I nodded, facing the window once more. Silently hoping he couldn't see the flush of colour that warmed me. What was happening to me?

"I was going to ask if you made plans for today."

I slid my legs off the table, twisting to face him fully as he did the same thing.

"No." I admitted as I placed my teacup down. Running my finger over the edge of the rim.

"Good. I think it is a good day to stay inside," he nodded "your body will still be trying to recover."

I snorted. "Are you a doctor too?"

"No." He smiled. The expression lighting up his entire face. "But I do care deeply for the Florian's."

I sucked a tooth. Noting the strange sentence but saying nothing. Instead choosing to nod and pour another tea.

Maaier stood slowly, walking over to the window. His expression wistful. As if remembering a simpler time. A happy time judging by the smile gracing his lips. A time I secretly longed to know more about.

The dining hall was freezing as I entered later that evening. Maaier was right, it had rained all day. The once beautiful sunrise, now tarnished by endless dark clouds. The tall vast windows covered in a thin layer of condensation. My steps boomed like a drum with each step of the bare room.

When my mother was young, Grandfather had made it mandatory for her to learn the piano. A skill she thrust upon me.

I was not overly creative but I did love to press the keys and produce a sweet melody. I glanced at the piano in the corner. The dark wood dull with age.

My fingers ran gently across the dust ridden surface. The smile tugging at my lips more genuine than I had felt as of late.

Lowering myself to the padded bench, I traced the last keys mother ever played. My eyes fluttered closed as I was thrown into another world.

THE DINING HALL WAS FULL OF PEOPLE OF ALL SORTS. Mixed dresses and fabrics swaying to the melody playing. I wove through the crowd like a wraith. Drifting through each couple to where the masses gathered, pure joy decorated their faces.

I turned to where the musician sat on the bench. My mother's smile beaming back as her long fingers pressed into the ivory. Notes swirled through the air. Beautiful and full of life. Just like her. She was young, only a few years shy of myself. She grinned once more, looking at the congregation before her. Each reflecting the expression. My gaze drifted over them. Hoping to see my father amongst them. Maybe this was the night they fell in love. That blessed night they would tell me about often.

My mother's gaze finally stopped on one single person. Her spine stiffening the only tell of her hesitation. Who was she looking at? I moved forward as the song ended. Each person clapping and cheering a near deafening applause from every corner of the room.

The crowd shifted slightly, preparing for the next song. Bodies moved as I made my way to mother, careful not to touch as I traced her line of sight. I looked up to find an oddly familiar face. Dark hair and intoxicatingly dark eyes. His hands slowly clapping. His stare fixed on mother. I gasped quietly, taken aback by his hungry expression. The man's eyes drifted at the sound of my gasp. His stare meeting mine. I opened my mouth to call his name. To ask how he was here too. Only to be cut short by the feeling of being yanked back to reality.

"Do you play?" Maaier's velvet voice crooned from behind me. I spun to face him. My hair swiping wildly over my face at the force of the turn. The breath caught in my chest as my heart thundered within.

"How did you get here?" I said. My voice tight with emotion. "I just saw you..." my hands trembled by my side.

"I walked through the door," Maaier said after a moment of silence. Amusement in his features.

I exhaled finally. Shaking my head.

"I apologise, Lord Maaier. I think I haven't been myself as of late." I turned back to the piano. Looking down at the keys.

"That is more than understandable. You've been attacked twice."

I huffed, stifling a dark laugh. That was one way to phrase it. Maaier's gloved hand brushed against the nape of my neck. His touch ever so gentle, like a ghost kissing my flesh. I shuddered under his touch. My body coming to life. What was happening to me? A man had never caused me to feel like this. The fingers brushing now gripped my neck, pulling me back to look at him.

His deep stare boring into mine, searching for something. Did he see that strange vision of the past as well?

His gaze finally fell lower to where my chest was now heaving with restraint. A quirk of his lips the only readable part of his expression. My tongue darted out despite myself, licking my lips almost on reflex, as I watched him do the same. His hand snaked from the back of my neck to my throat. His grip tightening. My heart began to pound, nerves subsiding to excitement. Maaier's thumb reached up. The pad of flesh pulling at my lip.

"Soon," He muttered to himself.

I furrowed my brow. He lowered himself. His breath warm against my ear.

"Soon, you will find yourself enough to know."

I stiffened, disgust and confusion roiled through me. Before I could retort, he was gone. Leaving me more confused than I was before.

THE NEXT TWO WEEKS PASSED QUICKLY. I WAS ABLE to walk again with little to no pain. The wounds on my lower abdomen and chest both healed. Nothing but a scar lining the flesh. A scar so close to resembling my mother's. I had told the police that. Their only input being that the attacker could be simply copying past methods. My mother had been dead too long for the attacker to be the same. Or so they thought. I wasn't disregarding anything.

The police hadn't found any trace of the attacker and no threat had come to pass again.

Maaier had become a walking pain in my behind. His eyes never straying too far. He would watch in silence as I would read in the library or sketch at my desk. The worst always being when I was in the garden.

"You should have gloves on." He huffed as if the dirt under my nails offended him.

"Why? So can I be just like you?" I cocked a brow staring at Maaier's gloved hands. The man never went without them. A strange part of me longed to know what lied beneath them.

"Ha." He jeered. "You will be like me soon enough Vespera."

I chuckled at his words. This man was a damned fool if I would become as arrogant as he. Maaier's smile broadened. As if my small laugh was the greatest sound in the world. I shifted on my feet. A rose between my fingers as I looked at him. His gaze was solely fixed on me. Something about him simultaneously thrilled and terrified me. Like there was more to his story.

THAT WAS A WEEK AGO. THE SUN HAD FINALLY COME through the clouds after days of being lost to the clouds. Nothing but roses dared to blossom in the harsh cold. I knelt in the dirt. My hands packing soil around the trunks of the rose bushes. The small warmth from the sun bringing a genuine smile to my face.

I stood quickly, ready to face the heat on my face. My hand caught on a stray branch. Thorns pricked into my flesh. Small beads of blood pooling from the wound. Hurried footsteps moved toward me. Maaier's gloved hands holding mine.

"Are you alright?" He said. His worried gaze falling to my eyes.

"I'm fine." I tried to assure him. I was used to it. Gardening was my favourite hobby. Maybe someday I will be able to see the colour they brought to the earth.

"But you could have hurt yourself worse." His concern wafting from him like waves in the ocean.

"Maaier. I am fine." I laughed. The strange man's eyes widened at the sight. Horrified by my tiny cut. I was only glad it wasn't as red as I had seen it that fateful night, only a slight hint of the colour amongst my grey skin.

Part of me wanted to know who the strange man was who brought the slightest hint of colour to my world. The other however was terrified of seeing a world in colour. I was content in my shades of grey.

The moment registered slowly. This was the only time Maaier had dared to touch me. His gloved hand covered mine. My mind wandered to what his bare hand looked like. If he hid them due to an affliction or something worse. What would they feel like against my skin? Warmth flooded my cheeks. A shiver ran down my spine. My tongue ran over my lips. By God. What was happening to me? This man was a stranger and here I was in turmoil of whether I distrusted him or not. This man could very well have killed me but here I was alone with him, fawning over his touch.

I shrugged Maaier off, withdrawing my hand. Maaier straightened, clearing his throat.

"I apologise, Lady Vespera. It was a misjudgment on my part to touch you without consent." His voice was thick. As if now embarrassed by showing his more tender emotions.

The man was hard in all aspects. Mind and body. He truly was a wonder to study.

Chapter Ten

The days were blending into one. I didn't usually mind being kept in the manor, but lately I was going mad. I wasn't allowed to see Dorian let alone even contact her, the staff were scared the attacker would intercept the note. Going as far as forcing a fetched lie when I demanded to know why. My every waking moment spent under watch and my every sleep monitored.

I needed to get out of here. If not for a day then at least for an hour. Anything would do at this point, a minute alone would be a well craved blessing.

Winter was on its way and the roads would soon be too slick to travel on. One wrong move and death was certain. The idea blossomed to life in my mind. That's it!

"Victor!" I called through the halls. Maaier had taken leave for the day leaving me feeling at peace.

Victor's head popped out excitedly from his doorway.

"You called?" The young medic having a day spare from his apprenticeship.

"Come." I held out my hand. "I want to go for a walk." The weather outside clear and seemingly dry.

Victor smiled, happy for my interest in him as a protector. My own joy still shimmering through me.

Victor took my hand in his the moment we stepped off the front entrance stairs. We walked in content silence down the outskirts of the forest in the driveway. Tall trees reaching up for the last embrace of the autumn's sun. A cool shift near. Birds sang as the wove through the branches, chirping merrily to each other.

"To what do I owe this pleasure?" He asked softly.

"I needed a break from the manor. It's starting to become suffocating."

Victor huffed. "I'm surprised it's taken you this long to admit that. I was growing worried about you."

I furrowed my brow.

He continued "You never seem overly happy there in the manor. Like you are content but not overly satisfied with your life."

I stilled beside him. I had never considered it that way.

Maybe I was content, but maybe there was a part of me that wanted to know more than basic anatomy. Maybe I could be the first female doctor for our town. A laughable thought. The towns folk would burn me for simply trying. My gaze flicked to Victor.

Maybe he could teach me some things. He was training to become a doctor himself after all.

"Maybe you have a valid point," I mumbled, kicking my skirt as we headed further up the garden path.

"We could always run away together." He teased, knocking

his hip into mine as we continued down the path. I chuckled lightly.

"And where would we go on our secret runaway?"

He remained silent for a while, considering his options. His brow furrowed in thought.

"Rome." He smiled, "I think that would suit you well."

"Doubt the attacker would find me there." I joked with a light hearted shrug.

Victor's smile turned to a frown, dropping instantly. "Vespera," He said my name ever so softly.

I turned to face him. The breeze blowing my hair over my face.

"Do you trust this Maaier fellow?" His voice low despite the solitary surroundings, his eyes focused on mine.

"I honestly don't know." I admitted. The memory of seeing him at my mothers piano like ash on my tongue clashing with how peaceful he looked in the sunrise.

"Me either. Something seems off about him. Like a darkness lingering around him."

"The entire manor is filled with darkness." I shrugged again. Victor squirmed on the spot. As if he too felt it.

"Almost makes me regret moving in," He mumbled under his breath. I stilled, pulling Victor back to me.

"You moved into the manor as well? I thought they were kidding." I all but gasped. Victor's warm gaze searched mine. He nodded slowly. I could feel a sudden hesitation closing in. A familiar need to pull away. No one who stayed in the manor was ever normal again. Dorian stayed once but even that was enough to twist her already twisted mind further. People seemed to be plagued by something lurking in the dark. Unwilling to stay but unable to leave.

"Your uncle thought it would be a good idea considering how much time was intended for Maaier to be around you.

Arthur thought it would be easier to keep an eye on you if I remained there," He explained. His hand grazing my shoulder, a warm touch intended to sooth.

"Victor, you have to leave," I whispered. My shaking hands rose to grasp his shoulders. The slight muscle tensing beneath his shirt.

"I'll be fine-"

"No you won't." I cut him off. My eyes pleading with him. My hand squeezed tighter as I continued. "The darkness in the manor will consume you. Haven't you noticed that all the maids bar Mary are old and withered? It's because they can't leave. They're trapped. Once you enter the manor Victor, you can't ever leave. You can run from its halls but it will always lure you back. Always."

Victor stilled as if made of stone as he listened to my words. The rising and falling of his chest the only movement.

"Your father left and is yet to return." He countered after a moment of heavy silence

"My father was already driven mad by the manor. Please Victor, please believe me. You need to leave."

"I won't leave you, Vespera," He said softly.

"You must. I can hold my own. And if I can't then I will meet my mother at the gates of heaven once more." I admitted, a weight lifting from my chest.

Victor released a sigh, "It's not that easy."

"How? You can just run!" I raised my voice, the tone now shrill with desperation. It was as if he was lost, trying to find where he fit in. An insecurity I hadn't felt in a long time. My heart ached for him to leave to be safe. Something was lurking in the walls and I didn't need Victor falling prey to the darkness of the manor as so many before him had.

"I have nowhere to go." He hissed, his shoulders drawing

tight. Apprehension sparking in his eyes. "I have no family back home. No house. No one. Nothing."

A hard lump rose in my throat. I swallowed thickly, dislodging my sudden emotions. This wasn't how this was supposed to go. I needed him to trust me and leave.

"I'm not just staying for you. As selfish as that sounds. I am staying for myself as well. You are not the only one who has felt death Vespera." Victor's voice grew daringly low.

It was never even a thought that crossed my mind. I was a selfish fool. Thinking I was helping him when all I was doing was turning him away to a life of nothing. A place he seemed so familiar with already.

"Victor, I am so sorry." I managed.

He shrugged, turning his attention back to the road.

Chapter Eleven

I moved through the day like a ghost trapped in the halls. Not speaking, not seen. Victor's words sounding like a chant over and over in my head. *"You are not the only one who has felt death, Vespera."*

Had he felt the cold embrace of death's hand too? Or had he experienced loss as I had? I couldn't press him to talk more about it. I didn't know him well enough. I was still slightly wary of him as well.

My mind was a mess as I made my way back to my room. Concentrating on the floor beneath me as I stepped. I didn't even notice that a door had opened and someone had stepped out in front of me. My forehead hit them first, followed by the rest of my body as I fell into them. A spicy scent warmed my nose as my face had unwillingly buried itself inside the man's chest. Their chest rising and falling with a silent chuckle whilst I pulled my face away.

"Something on your mind, Vespera?" Maaier's voice teased.

I narrowed my gaze, staring up into his dark eyes. God, I just wanted to be alone. But every single area of the home had been taken up by someone. I hated it. The silence now constantly filled.

"Yes, actually." I threw a false smile, more of a sneer than anything.

"And what was that?" He mirrored my sickly sweet tone.

"I was thinking that I wanted to be alone," I said as I pushed past him. Maaier's hands shot up quickly, gripping me by my upper arm. I froze in his touch, tiny currents of heat flickered over my body. What was happening to me? I had never felt this before Maaier. Who was this man?

"You aren't alone, Vespera. Not anymore."

I was tired and still on edge from my altercation with Victor earlier. All I wanted was to retire to my bed and read until nightfall.

"Why? Because you are here?" I huffed.

"Yes, actually. And if you don't believe me. You will with time."

I studied him then. His dark eyes flicked over my face. Dark hair falling loose from the tie holding the long strands back. My fingers twitched, as if desperate to run through the thick black locks. His throat bobbed as he swallowed. My tongue almost escaped my lips to feel the movement. Jesus above, what was wrong with me.

I pulled back from him. His hands loosened slightly as he watched me in silence.

"You don't understand." I said with a sigh, turning back to the stairs. Maybe the old library would be peaceful for a moment.

Maaier's gloved hand darted out, grabbing my wrist before I took a step. He pulled me to face him once more, our eyes locking as he said, "I know what it is like to truly be alone, Vespera. And it is something I do not wish upon anyone. If you wish to be alone for a moment, so be it. But it is not forever."

I searched Maaier's gaze, warmth and concern lingered behind his eyes. I had only just met this man. Why did he feel the need to tend to me?

"Come." He ordered, pulling my arm through his whilst I was still distracted by his words.

I trailed along beside him, curious and demanding to know where he was taking me. Only to be met with no reply. He opened the library door and led me through.

The fireplace was already lit, casting a glow over the shelves of books, the scent of the woods smoke like a warm embrace.

"If you wish to be left alone, I will allow that. But if you need me, all you must do is call. I will be right outside the door." He bowed his head before walking backward through the door frame, shutting it behind him.

My heart thumped in my chest. His actions brought a heat to my cheeks. Was he the one who had prepared this for me? Every detail oozed comfort, the warmth of the hearth with the blanket perched and folded on the lounge. Along with the pot of tea on the table beside it, a lemon tart poking out on a plate. My mouth watered. This was perfection. But how did he already know so much about me?

Surely he got the information from my grandmother or the staff.

That had to be it. Didn't it?

My mind wandered to the attack once more. The fear in my heart rising to my throat. The man was tall but not too tall that he towered over me. I remember that much. He didn't have a scent. No cologne or aftershave to recall. How I wished I had tried to pull his hooded cloak off to look at the face of the man who tore my body open. If I had, maybe he would be rotting in a cell or even hanging from the gallows. I shuddered at the thought of how long he must have been watching me. Stalking me like a predator to his prey.

The thought ran through me as I sunk into the lounge. What if this was not the first time I had seen the man? What if it was the strange figure in the forest from that morning Victor arrived? My fingers massaged into my temples, circling the tension from my pounding skull.

This was too much. I had nothing to go on. Nothing but the fact that this man was either close to the family to know his way in or he was simply copying that of the murder of my mother. Unless it was the same person who had attacked my mother.

A pent up sigh escaped me. It was fruitless to consider the possibility of who it was, I truly had no idea. Only one fact rang clear. They knew their way around the manor. The thought chilled me to the bone. My fingers drifted from my temples to my hair twisted atop my head. I plucked the pins free, letting the waves of hair fall over me.

Maybe him coming back wouldn't be such a bad thing. Maybe the next time he would be successful and I will have the pleasure of seeing the man who brightened my world again. If only for a second.

The fire crackled beside me. The wind outside only growing stronger. Shuffling sounded beyond the door. An ever so slight smile covered my face.

"Has being alone this long been sufficient?" Maaier called through the closed door.

"Not quite." I called back.

Maaier didn't respond. Instead choosing to let me be for a brief moment longer.

With a bite of the lemon tart, I started to read. Only I couldn't focus on the book. Only the strange man beyond the door occupied my mind.

Chapter Twelve

Stifling was the only way to describe the manor. Being held like a freak at a circus with five different sets of eyes on you at all times. The air became harder to breathe with each day.

As much as I loved my solitude, I needed an escape. I needed to remind myself that there was light outside of the darkness that plagued me. I had returned inside from the morning walk only to be ambushed by Grandmother in a strangling embrace. Her words spilling from her lips about losing me again and how worried she was. I gazed over her shoulder. Maaier leant against the wall, his shoulder just shy of the frame of my portrait on the wall. His face level with where my chest was immortalised in oil paint. A glimmer of amusement flickered through the dark abyss of his eyes. Mischief pulling at his smile. I furrowed my brow. His lips lifted at my obvious annoyance. This strange man would be the death of me. A mystery I couldn't solve.

After being released from Grandmother's scolding hold, I stormed past Maaier, heading down to the kitchens.

Mary stood chattering in the doorway. Her voice was more alive than I had ever heard as she conversed with the cooks. Her attention focused on one dark haired boy at the stove.

I drew up next to her, she stiffened at my touch.

"Only me," I whispered. She softened instantly, the tension deflating immediately.

"You really have to try it, Mary," The young man bubbled. He would have been close to her age in his early twenties. Average build and height, rather plain looking if I was honest. But it was the way he looked at Mary as if she was the most important thing in the world to him. A ripple of jealousy ran through me but I was quick to shake it away. I was content not to fall in love. And I was hell bent on keeping it that way. That didn't mean I never craved the feeling that someone saw me as they saw the sun. A bright and mysterious thing they couldn't live without.

Stepping past Mary, I stepped off the stairs and further into the kitchen. My gaze focused on the floor. Not a single splattering of blood remained. Nothing to remind anyone of the horrors of that night. I tore myself from the spot and moved to the pastries on a plate in the centre of the bench. My mouth watered at the sight of a lemon tart as it teetered on the edge.

I took it before anyone could argue and moved out to the back lawn beyond the manor. A groundskeeper looked up from his post.

"Hello, young Lady Vespera!" He called. I smiled at him and waved back

"Good morning Gregory!"

"What brings you out back?"

"Would you aid me in something?" I smirked.

Gregory's smile quirked at the side. His usual mischievous self shining through.

Gregory was an old friend of the family. His wife and daughters still lived in town but he journeyed out here day in and day out for thirty years to help out where he could.

"You busting out of here?" He whispered as I drew closer.

"You know me too well."

Whilst Gregory saddled a horse, I stood watch, waiting to see if we would get caught. Many times, I had snuck out of the manor with Gregory using an excuse of me picking flowers in the forest. Once the horse was ready, I climbed upon its back and began my small journey into the forest.

THE TOWN WAS BUSTLING AS I TROTTED THROUGH the streets. People fluttered about like birds in the wild. Weaving in and out of shops in their ridiculous bonnets and dresses. Although some of them I did quite admire, I was never quite game to ask where they had purchased it.

I came to a halt outside a strange bookstore. The old storefront illuminated in the afternoon sun. Paint peeling off the owner's hand painted sign. The store beyond beckoned me like an old friend. The door creaked as I entered, a loud bell sounding shortly after. Not a soul wandered through the aisles, bookstores were rare as it was. When did this one arrive here? Surely I would have noticed that before.

"Hello?" I called out, my voice echoed through the halls. Frowning, I moved forward, my hands ran over the various stationary lining shelves in the centre table. The room was only small but the multitude of titles filled the space just enough to feel cosy and not too cramped.

I looked along the volumes, stories ranging from romance

to medical and encyclopaedias facing me. I wanted them all. To know all of the knowledge they held on their pages. To feel the facts and emotions in my soul. I looked toward the end shelf. A single book caught my attention. I drew near slowly, my heart beating in my chest. The cover was worn and torn in places. Black with a lighter pattern on the front. A flower of some sort. I narrowed my eyes. Looking closer at what it was but the leather was too badly damaged. The title was faint but still readable. *The Cursed Life of Death.*

My fingers shook ever so slightly as I opened the cover. The words handwritten on the page in an elegant scrawl.

"*For my sweet lost soul,*" The dedication read. I turned the page, masses of the same elegant scroll filled each page as well as small detailed sketches ranging from dancing to something more intimate, the words blurring together as I flicked through.

Warmth filled my cheeks. Was this a diary? I knew deep inside me that it would be wrong to read the diary of another person. But somehow the book pulled me in. As if it had tethered itself to me. I couldn't put it down. I needed it. I needed to know what it was about and why it was all handwritten.

I called out again for the keeper of the shop. Again no one returned. I walked to the counter, placing an assortment of money on the counter. Hoping it would be enough to cover the cost.

The town had quieted down beyond the window. I stepped outside. The crisp autumn air tingling against my exposed neck. I stepped forward. The world teetered as a body slammed into me. Their hands wiping around my body, catching me before I hit the pavement. The scent of cedar and saffron filling my nose. I cringed at the scent. The smell warmed my entire body, awakening a deep need I kept buried far inside.

"I apologise, I didn't see you there." Maaier's voice was full of concern until I faced him. Pulling myself from him. I slid the book into my satchel and stepped toward the horse.

"Vespera, what are you doing?" He hissed as he reached for me. His hands wrapped around me, pulling me close. My body met his and a rush of heat, his front warmed through my back into my entire being. I wrenched myself away despite the underlying draw to be close to him.

"Do not touch me, Maaier." I warned over my shoulder. "The townsfolk already gossip about me enough. If you are seen with me that is deathwish enough on your social standing."

"To hell with that," He swore before coming close. I reached for the saddle, lifting myself to sit. Maaier's strong hands gripped my waist. I revelled in the touch. Why did this do things to me?

I thanked him briefly before shifting slightly. In the blink of an eye, Maaier was seated behind me. My shaking body pressed against his. His arms wrapped around me, taking the reins from my grasp.

"Come, you little escaper. Back to your cell." He teased.

I snorted, not knowing how to react. Not to the situation nor to the feel of his chest pressing against me.

"What were you doing in town anyway?" I asked. Swallowing thickly as I tried to avoid the intrusion prodding my behind.

"Am I not allowed to take a day off from being your keeper?" He pressed his chest to my back.

His breath fanned my ear. "Obviously not. You clearly love looking for trouble."

Rolling my shoulders back, I taunted him over my shoulder. "Trouble has a way of finding me. Not the other way around."

Maaier smirked in return. "Whatever you believe. But you and I both know you tempt trouble each and every day."

I rolled my eyes and faced the road once more, pulling the reins, I moved down the road back home.

Chapter Thirteen

Maaier escorted me in through the back door. The excuse of escorting me through the forest enough to starve off any concerns as to where I was.

The secret book still in my satchel, I headed to my room. It was late in the afternoon and the staff were all preparing for dinner. My eyes darted around the room. Where could I hide this book? I didn't know why but I felt compelled to keep it away from prying eyes. This was just for me. If Grandmother caught me looking for death again she would either pass or send me to a colony.

The room was cold already, but with each step I took, the air became colder. I shuffled to the window. The cold was the worst here, biting into my flesh despite the roaring fire in the fireplace. My fingers ran along the underside of the cushion. Feeling for a tiny sliver in the wood. My fingers found a small imperfection. I lifted the seat to show the hole below.

A tiny compartment I used to hide some of my most prized treasures. A copy of my father's journal of herbs, my mother's composition book. The first drawing Dorian ever sketched me and letters my mother used to send me from her room down the hall.

The game would start out with a request. Only turning into a hunt and game of chase as I ran after through the manor. The sound of her girlish laughter echoing in my memory. I looked at her beautiful handwriting. The ink slightly faded from time. I closed my eyes, imagining I was back in her embrace, my head pushed against her chest. The feeling was almost real on my cold skin. Her chin resting upon it as she smoothed circles into my spine. What I would give to feel that again.

I looked amongst my treasures once more. Brushes from Mother's art room scattered through the bottom as well as Father's small knife he used to take trimmings of plants and propagate them. If there was one single thing I would trade all of these memories for besides their touch, it would be my other necklace. The small silver heart shaped locket with a rose etched into the centre.

'*When you are old enough, my heart, I will show you what is inside but for now, it will be my little secret okay?*' She had said every time I had asked what was inside. The sound of her voice playing as if were echoing around me. All I had ever wanted to know was whether it was me or my father whose picture graced the inside of the heart around her neck.

I hadn't watched as they pulled her body from the lake. My father's howl scaring the birds in the trees. The necklace was gone from her throat. The police had said that her killer had most likely taken the necklace as a sort of trophy. My father had not believed them. He had searched diligently through the water and the depth of the river to find it only to come up short each time.

The cold air became frigid once more. I shivered as I pulled out one of her paint brushes before putting them back. The memories had always hurt. I had hoped they would have faded over time. But that was a lie. The pain never goes away. You only need to manage it to have it go numb for a short while but it is in the core of your soul. You will always carry that pain with you. To live is to carry the burden of grief and sorrow with you. To die is to be buried with them. So that slowly, over time the memory of it all will fade with you.

I placed the strange book into the compartment and closed the lid. It would pain me to open that door each day but something in me told me I needed to. That my answers were in the books.

I stood slowly, bracing my hands on the velvet seat by the window. A silent tear rolling down my cheek as I reopened the wound my parents had left.

A shuffling sounded behind me but I paid it no mind. Another fat tear rolled down the other cheek, one after another. My chest heaved, my fingers curled into the soft cushion. I would find who did this if it was the last thing I do. And if I don't, their afterlife will be nothing but a hell in the shape of me.

"Oh my winter child. I knew you would break soon." Grandmother's own watery voice sounded as she placed a warm hand on my back. I choked out a sob. She said nothing but continued to soothe me in the only way she knew how.

"I want him dead." I snarled through my teeth, the rage quickly taking over my moment of sorrow. I wanted him dead and rotting in a shallow grave. I wanted to carve his skin as he had ours. I wanted him bleeding out on the floor like I had. I wanted him to drown in the lake like my mother with my hands around his throat. I. Wanted. Him. Gone.

"Then so shall it be. Vespera. So shall it be."

My fingers brushed against the ivory keys. Dust from years of neglect collecting on the surface. The strange vision resurfacing. What was Maaier doing here that night? How has he not aged? The thoughts swirled around my head, mixing like the dust in the afternoon sun.

My eyes still burned from my onslaught of tears earlier. The emotions weighing me down.

I stood before the window behind the piano, raising my gaze to the horizon.

Maybe Dorian could shed some light on the vision situation. Surely she could aid me. Hell, I might even give her the book. I made a mental note to bribe Victor into escorting me back to Dorian's cottage. A cringe ran over me at the thought of asking him to be around her again. He was scared enough the first and last visit we had.

She was the only one who could help. I couldn't dare ask Grandmother why this was happening. She would commit me to the sanitarium in a heartbeat just like that maid from years ago who swore on her own eternal soul she saw a ghost talking to death themselves. Grandmother wasn't superstitious. She just trusted in fact. As far as age was concerned. The curse was an anomaly. Albeit strange, but explainable. But only if she decided to explain it. Only she never would. Just that it was a strange generational curse.

The sound of light footfalls sounded behind me. A smile formed despite my sombre mood. I turned to face the old woman.

"I thought you hated this old room." I teased. My smile fading as I faced the person.

"I do. But not for the reasons you expect." Maaier's voice was light, gentle almost.

"What do you want?" I sneered, turning back to the window.

"To apologise," He said, walking toward where I stood with my back to him. He drew close. Not enough to touch but enough for a cool sensation to run down my flesh at his proximity.

I snorted. Maaier swallowed before meeting my gaze in the reflection.

"I didn't intend to pull you close to me."

I frowned. The needy feeling that blossomed from the feeling of his hold now faded like the sun at dusk. Much like my patience for him.

"Sure," I muttered.

Maaier returned my frown, his scent washing over me as he stood beside me. Cedar and a brief hit of saffron warmed me despite myself.

"Anyway," He pressed on, "I brought you this."

He faced me with a small package in his hands. I eyed the parchment wrapped gift before I dared to reach out for it.

Maaier waited on bated breath as I gently tore the wrapping.

A light leather bound book sat before me.

"An English Guide to Flowers," I read aloud, cocking a brow at Maaier.

He brightened as I opened the cover.

> *For Vespera, sorry I am an ass. Love always, Maaier.*

I managed a small laugh at the inscription. There was no love between us.

"I found it in town and thought it might be good for you to rediscover your love of gardening. Your grandmother assured me it was your favourite besides the piano."

"I haven't done much of either lately." I exhaled, turning the pages of information about roses over.

"You'll get there. Besides, I think you'll be seeing the greenhouse a lot more often."

I scrunched my nose, "You truly are the strangest man I have ever met."

Maaier chuckled darkly. I stared into his dark eyes, now alight with a twisted amusement.

"Sweet girl, you haven't even met the real me." He smirked, "Yet."

I opened my mouth to protest but Maaier was gone in the blink of an eye. The only reassurance that he was here was the book in my hands. What a strangely thoughtful gift.

There was more to it. There had to be.

Chapter Fourteen

"No way."

"Victor please!" I pleaded, pulling on his tailored jacket.

His groan vibrated through his chest before he cringed.

"Why do we need to see her? She gives me the chills. And not in a good way." He all but shuddered at the thought of her.

"Dorian is harmless. I assure you." My pleading gaze met his. I needed to turn up the charm. I battered my eyelids, a slight pout to my mouth. I probably looked ridiculous but it was what the girls in my novels did to sway their match in their favour.

Victor eyed me before gritting his teeth., the word fine grating through them.

"Oh Victor!" I gripped his shoulders. "Thank you!"

"Yeah. Yeah. Get in the carriage." He waved me away. The hint of a smile playing across his face. I tugged at my lace cuff on my sleeve excitedly. Dorian would have the answers I just knew she would.

I tucked the book in my satchel before racing out the front door. An icy feeling ran through me. I turned to see Maaier standing in the hall, silently watching as I turned to leave. Irritation radiating from him even from this distance. I stood frozen to the spot, caught in his gaze. Victor brushed by him. Unphased by Maaier's stature before taking my arm.

"Come along then. Let's go visit this extremely odd friend of yours." He bubbled.

"Sure," I mumbled, my body feeling like lead as Victor gently pulled me toward the carriage outside. Looking back over my shoulder, Maaier met my gaze once more.

Dorian was outside in the garden as we approached. Tending to her final clippings of the season. Victor had distracted himself with a new study on life he found in Arthur's personal library for the majority of our journey. I listened as he babbled on but continued to look out the window. What colour were trees? Were they red too? I imagined them as that shade. Almost laughing at how ridiculous it was.

Dorian greeted us warmly, her smile as bright as the sun now high in the sky.

"I had a feeling you would come see me today." She held my cheeks in her dirt covered hands. Leaves and petals littered her knotted light hair. Light glistened in her eyes, pure joy she rarely sported. Just like the Dorian of old that I loved so dearly.

"I see you brought little old Daisy boy." She teased a no doubt uncomfortable Victor who shifted behind me. The scent of soil and honey swirled from Dorian, her smile infectious.

"Come. I have a surprise for you."

Dorian tugged me inside her house. Victor followed closely

behind. The smell of dirt eased away, leaving room for something more sweet. More warm and comforting.

"Happy almost birthday!" She sang as she spun us toward her table. In the centre of the old wooden surface sat her gift. A homemade orange cake. The scent alone caused saliva to pool in my mouth, the thin pale icing dripped onto the plate.

"Dori! You shouldn't have." My cheeks warmed as Dorian pulled me close.

"I knew you would like it." She winked, pulling me into her embrace. My chin resting on her bony shoulder.

"Almost birthday?" Victor questioned. I looked at him over Dorian's shoulder. His perplexed expression sealed with a quirked brow.

"One month and fourteen days until she's officially a spinster." Dorian chirped before spinning to face him. "Daisy, be a dear and fetch me some marigolds from my garden."

"I don't know what they are, but sure," He mumbled, shaking his head as he left us be.

Dorian's expression darkened, her hand outstretched. "Give me the book." Her fingers curled

"You amaze me." I retrieved the book.

Dorian stormed toward the door, shouting "Not daffodils, Daisy boy. Marigolds." To wherever Victor was beyond the entrance.

"Right." She huffed as she sat down, urging me to do the same.

"You want me to study the book to find out why you are seeing things?"

"Yes." I pleaded with my eyes.

Dorian cut the cake, nodding as she passed me the plate of delicious dessert. "Fine. But on one condition."

"And that is?" I said through a mouthful of heavenly cake. The sweetness was like an explosion in my mouth.

"You keep him around. There is something about him I can't quite figure out."

I rolled my eyes. Of all the things for her not to know, of course it was Victor. But Dorian would figure that out surely.

My best friend's eyes glazed over. A sure sign she was seeing something beyond. I watched intently as her eyes flickered beneath her now closed eyelids. Her lashes fluttered. Her hands trembled on the table before her. Dorian's breathing turned sharp and shallow. I watched as she experienced the vision. Just like I always had, with rapt fascination.

She scared the life out of me the first time. I had never forgotten how she looked that day. Haunted and hollow. The face of a girl who seen such a horror she couldn't shake.

Her eyes snapped open. An annoyed yet infuriated expression marring her face. She mumbled a brief pardon before she stormed from the room.

"They are peonies. You silly fool." Her tone shrill as she descended the hall.

I frowned at the thought of poor Victor copping the after effects of the vision. Dorian was often terrible to be around after a vision. The scenes often rendered her angry and sometimes violent, though she would never harm anyone. She just throws something in frustration and refuses to speak for days at a time. Whatever she had seen always troubled her deeply. I knew better than to question her. The last memory of the time I had pressed her caused a shudder to run through me.

The book lay on the table between where we had sat. I picked it up cautiously. As if the book were to come to life at any time and devour my hand. I opened to the middle page, the scent of old pages wafted to my nose. A scent I had so long desired and often craved. It was like no other comfort I had experienced. My eyes lingered on the top of the page. The chapter heading branded into my memory.

"The Mark of Death." sat in curled text. As if someone had written the book themselves like a journal. I read on.

'Whilst Death doesn't usually make himself known to his victims until he comes to escort us away to the heavens we desire, there have been noted occasions where a man dressed in all black robes has been sighted watching his souls. As if fascinated by the way a human moves or lives their short life. But Death has oftentimes been said through legend that he is searching through these people for his soul. For the soul who always seems to evade him. The only thing the reaper craves more than death is life.'

The sound of footsteps pounding on the floor sent my frozen heart racing. Why was learning of this death persona having this effect on me? I was frozen to the bone.

"Vespera." My name called through the hall. In a rush, I threw the book down on my lap.

I looked up to find Victor with petals riddled through his hair, now a matted mess on his head.

I smiled, biting back a laugh.

"You owe me big time for this." He pointed a finger at me before moving to stand behind me.

Dorian entered not long after Victor's hands met my shoulders. Her enraged expression fell the anger now replaced by what seemed like grief and hopelessness. The marigold's dangling from her fingers.

I asked her what was wrong, rising from my chair. She swallowed thickly and pushed me back down.

Dorian's voice shook as she apologised, sitting back in her chair. Her eyes flicked between me and the man behind me.

"We should go," Victor said softly, his palm rotating on my shoulder like a caress.

Standing, I swept over to Dorain who was slicing the cake. My lips brushed against her forehead. I slipped the book on her lap.

"Read it when you feel able."

Dorian's large eyes met mine, shining with an onslaught of tears that I was certain she would shed when I left. It happened more frequently. Normally she would beg me to stay. To be with her. But today, she was different.

She remained silent as she passed me a plate full of cake slices. Her face now dim as her expression sombered.

"I'll be back soon okay?" I whispered into her hair, running my hands through the locks of light silk. She nodded as her bottom lip trembled.

Victor watched the interaction, his head tilted to the side. Watching as Dorian took my hands, her eyes pleaded with mine. I wrapped my arms around her thin shoulders. Holding her tightly, I pressed a brief kiss to her petal covered hair.

Whatever it was that she had seen had deeply rattled her. The only question was, what had she seen that had affected her so?

Chapter Fifteen

The carriage ride home was sombre. If dark clouds could form from the mood inside of the carriage, everything would be drenched in heavy mist. Victor sat beside me, his fingers drawing lazy circles on the back of my hand. No warmth bloomed from the spot. No sparks ignited my body. I let him continue, as he seemed to need the comfort it provided.

'You knew it wasn't him' I cursed myself. I glanced back at Victor. His gaze far off out the opposite window. The touch merely a soothing gesture. For him or myself, I could not tell.

How a day so beautiful turned out so horribly dreary I will never know but it was always like that with Dorian, however, it was never something I would hold against her. We all had our inner battles and demons and it was no one person's right to judge how we fought them. Some people threw themselves into the bodies of others or a drink of any and all kinds. Some hid, some screamed for attention. Some gentler souls became recluse. It was never my place to hold it against them. For I too knew how deep those emotions could run.

My heart ached for my sweet friend. Knowing she was

alone again, crying, in the house. It hurt to leave her behind. But I knew better than to stay. To stay would only cause her more harm. She needed to release her woes. To release the pain she felt. I had a sick feeling coiling in my stomach. The way she looked at me was enough of a clue as to my thoughts being the truth. The vision was of me. But what could have hurt her so badly she took it out on Victor. Was he involved in whatever happened to me? Was he the one who would attack me this time?

I shifted in my seat, unease running rampant. Victor tore his gaze from the passing trees and looked over me. His eyes assessed as I watched him from the corner of mine.

"Does she do that often?" He spoke timidly.

"More now than she used to. She used to only have outbursts once every while but as she grew so did they."

"Has she seen a doctor?"

I shook my head, teeth fretting my bottom lip. "No. They would take her away to a sanitarium for hysteria if they found out."

Victor nodded silently. His eyes falling to where his fingers laid on the back of my hand.

"You are good to her."

"She's too good to me." I exhaled. And she was. It was the truth. No one soul knew me quite like Dorian.

Victor smiled small, taking my hands in his. The warmth almost burned my cold skin.

Tiny pings hit the top of the wooden carriage. Dark rain clouds settling over, their heavy wrath not far behind.

Rain was falling heavily as we approached the manor. The road now covered in a slick downpour. Victor exited first, holding the door open for me. I stood to exit only to spot Maaier leaning against the main entrance. My eyes rolled at the sight of his smug expression. Taking a deep breath, I gripped Victor's outstretched hand. He balanced me as I stepped out of the dry carriage and onto the muddy dirt beneath me. My skirts grew heavy as they brushed along the ground, the rain drenching them further.

"Welcome back," Maaier called over the heavy rain.

"Fetch Mary to run Vespera a warm bath." Victor ordered back. Maaier stood rolling his shoulders as his expression fell dark.

"As you command, *doctor*." He condescended before disappearing inside. Victor's hands gripped my waist as he pulled me back against him.

"I got you," He whispered in my ear, rain falling between us. His arm wrapped around mine as he bent down.

"Victor, what are you doing?" I squeaked as his other arm met the back of my thighs and I was hoisted up in a flash, my body bouncing in his hold.

"Victor, this is highly unnecessary," I said, wrapping my arms around his neck to hold myself up. The heavy rain pounding over us. Victor exhaled deeply before taking the stairs with me useless in his grasp.

"I can walk." I assured him, to no avail.

"Shh," He hushed, sighing, I let it go. If he wanted to be a hero, then I would allow it. I knew in myself it wasn't winning him any favour. I was already very fond of him. Just not in the way he wanted. Nor I for that matter. If I were normal I would have fallen for his charm in a heartbeat but I didn't. Or couldn't. I wasn't sure which.

Victor stepped forward. My fists tightening around the

collar in his shirt. The scent of honey and tincture wafting into my nose as I drew in closer, praying to high heavens he didn't drop me.

I remained silent as Victor pressed up the stairs, wobbling in his grasp.

The rain pounded on the concrete stairs. I pulled my face from Victor's neck, meeting Maaier's stare through my drenched hair stuck to my face. His anger was palpable.

"I presume she persuaded you to take her out?" He called out over the downpour hitting the roof like hail.

"What do you think?" Victor chuckled back.the sound vibrating against me. The ice cold water seeped through the fabric of my gown sending a shiver down my spine. God I wished he would let me go. I'll catch my death in this dress. I stifled a smile. Catching Death wouldn't be too bad I supposed.

Once on solid dry ground, Victor finally lowered me to the floor. Allowing me to stand on my own two feet.

"You silly fool!" Grandmother's shrill voice tore from down the hall. "You could catch a chill!"

A sigh fell from my lips. I was already trembling in place as Mary rushed forward with a towel. Her voice was soft as she led me down the hall. My dress weighed a tonne more than when I had first put it on.

"I needed to see Dorian and besides, it's not like the weather was bad this morning," I said through chattering teeth.

Grandmother huffed as she moved beside me, taking the lead into my room. The men both made themselves scarce.

"Sometimes I think the soul of your aunt came back to haunt me in the form of you." Grandmother clucked her tongue. The frown etched into her face as I unlaced my corset. Mary helped to peel the layers from my wet skin.

I rolled my eyes before leaving her in the bedroom. The sound of the bed creaking sounded softly behind me.

I stepped into the hot water, my skin burning on contact with the surface. I hissed through gritted teeth as I lowered myself further. The dark scar illuminated against my pale chest. A disgusting sight to behold.

The water lapped around the edges of the tub. The soothing sound overpowered by grandmother's shout from beyond the partially closed door.

"I suppose it's good to see you bonding with Victor."

"Oh no. Don't say anything further!" I called back. Lolling my head back to the edge of the tub.

Her chuckle brought a blush to my cheeks.

"As wild as your mother you are."

My lips quirked despite myself.

"But in all seriousness, Vespera. I think it's time for you to find your colour."

My groan echoed off the walls. Mary snickered from the side of the bathroom where she laid out a fresh change of clothing. As if she knew about the curse. Surely she couldn't know yet. It was too soon. If she knew about that then surely she would see the spirits in the halls.

"I've spoken to you about this," I sighed. Dragging my fingers over the steaming surface.

"And I still think you're being childish!"

I couldn't handle it anymore. I lowered my head beneath the surface. The sounds of the outside world now warped and distorted beneath the sound of my pulse in my ears. I kept my eyes closed. The sensation of hands ghosted over my neck. The memory of his pressure on my face resurfacing.

I burst from the surface gasping for air. My hands raked over my skin, making sure there were no fingers still pressing into me. My name was spoken beside me as I heaved in a breath.

Mary called out to Grandmother beyond the door, letting her know I was okay.

"See Vespera. A husband could keep you safe."

I glowered at the water. Maybe they could. But there was only one person I could think of protecting me. But that person was the one I was certain got me into this mess in the first place.

Chapter Sixteen

I woke close past midnight to a shadow over my face. The moonlight cascaded into the room through the thin curtains. My eyes adjusted to find a man over me. Maaier's hand pressed over my mouth. My heart thundered in my chest as the panic set in. He pressed a gloved finger to his lips. A brief shush filling the silence. My body obeyed the demand despite myself. His dark eyes searching my wild ones. Lungs catching with the lack of air.

"Come." He ordered, slowly removing the gloved hand from my mouth.

"Where are we going?" I said warily. My voice cracked from the almost scream that had built in my throat.

Maaier just smiled darkly. The gleam in his eyes brighter than the stars in the sky above. If time stood still, I would happily gaze into their abyss for eternity. Despite the man they belong to.

He held out his hand for me to take. I took it slowly, hesitation stalling my movements.

I pulled my cloak on before following him out into the hall.

Maaier's hand held mine tightly. Holding me tight as he led me down the stairs.

"Where are we going?" I whispered. Maaier remained silent, gently tugging me down the hall. The halls feeling like winter roamed the narrow passage. The air like a fogged haze hanging over the portraits, made worse by their disapproving gaze bearing into me.

I whispered Maaier's name only to be tugged into the east rooms of the manor.

Soft light reflected under the doorway of the ballroom.

"Why are we here, Maaier? It's the middle of the night and I can't play. It'll wake everyone up." I hissed as we entered, keeping my voice as low as possible.

A single candle sat on top of the piano. Why was I here? This man exhausts me. What was his game? The only way I could find out more was to be around him. The thought of that made me nauseous. I stifled a shudder.

Maaier led me to the piano, stopping just before the bench. His hand still held mine.

He dropped it slowly. His hands found my waist. My body met the piano as he sat me on top of the bench. Right next to the candle flickering with the disruption.

"You really are a curious little one," He purred.

"How so?" I quirked a brow.

"You stare at me like the most fascinating thing in the world but you run off with strange men into town."

"Victor is not a strange man." I snorted. "He's my friend."

"Are you sure about that?" He smirked. His gaze dark in the brief candle light. I opened my mouth only to close it shortly after. Victor hadn't hurt me. In fact he had been the kindest soul to me, seemingly always interested in anything I did or said. That could be a facade but I highly doubted it. He didn't strike me as an overly skilled actor. The man could barely stand Dorian. How would he bear to be around the crazy beings of the theatre. The stories people shared about the acquired tastes of the local theatre group both terrified and intrigued me.

Maaier chuckled and the candle flickered as he reached behind me. .

Maaier's breath fanned across my face as he leaned in close. His fingers closed over my neck. A thrill ran through me, sparks awakening in my veins. I clenched my fists closed, desperate to hide my desire to run them through his hair. Why did this man have this effect on me?

"Do you remember what I told you the other day?" He said softly, an undertone of menace lining his words. I shook my head, too breathless to speak.

"Look at you, pretty little bloom, too stunned to speak." He tightened his grip but it didn't scare me. Only sending another thrill through my body. "I warned you not to go out without me again."

An apology whispered from my lips. Maaier's eyes flashed before he released his hold. His free hand slowly pulled the gloves off his fingers. One by one, achingly slow.

"I don't appreciate you disobeying me," He said, his voice low with warning.

"I'm sorry." I managed.

He released a pent up breath. "It's fine. But really do try to keep yourself out of trouble."

"Why should I?"

"Because you have people who care for you. People who want you to see the next dawn."

"Right and as my bodyguard you believe you have a say in my life?" I raised my brows, daring him to fight me on the matter.

"Yes. As your personal guard, it is my job to make sure you survive." He narrowed his gaze, staring me down as I stood from the piano. There was truth in his words.

"I shouldn't have been so daft. I shouldn't have ran into the town but I felt safe. It was silly and immature, I know. But I couldn't be trapped here any longer." I stared up at him, meeting his eyes. "It's one thing when you have the freedom to leave but chose to stay but when that choice is taken from you, it is another."

"I understand," Maaier said after a beat "Truly I do."

"Now why did you bring me down here?" I asked, trying desperately to change the subject.

"Well I was trying to think of a punishment for you. And the only thing I could think of was the most horrific thing you can imagine."

A lump rose in my throat, fear cooling my warm skin.

"You will teach me how to dance."

"What?" I burst out laughing, surely he was not serious.

But he was. Maaier stood with an unimpressed look on his face.

"Wait, you are serious?" I sobered.

"I was never taught."

"You're a lord. Surely someone would have-"

"There was no time." Maaier cut me off. A twinge of sadness crossed his features before he schooled them back to his usual cocky smirk.

"Alright," I said slowly, "where would you like to begin?"

"From the beginning?"

He was not wrong. Maaier's dancing level was below that of even my father's. Someone who could not dance to save his life. Maaier held my hand in his with one on the small of my back as I guided him through a simple step. No music playing in the background only by brief instructions. I praised him gently after each correct step he did.

After what felt like an eternity of silence on his part he looked at me and said "Have you often danced with men, Vespera?"

I shook my head, pulling my gaze from the flush lining his cheeks.

"No," I said as I stepped back, "No one really comes out here unless it is for a big party. And even then it's just to see if the rumours are true."

"What rumours?" Maaier said as he stepped back into me.

I smiled before offering a small laugh. "Rumours of ghosts and madness."

Maaier chuckled, the sound like a summer breeze. "But of course they would think that. How could they not?"

"Exactly. They are all as daft as the next, I say."

Maaier grinned as he spun me around. The movement caught me off guard, causing my breath to hitch in my throat.

He spun me around and tilted my body back in his strong grasp. A small gasp escaping my lips.

Maaier's eyes shone with mischief as he looked down upon me. His hand was still cupping my back as the other reached up to smooth my hair from my forehead.

"All ever so daft," He smiled before lowering his face to mine. My breath caught once more. His spiced cologne tingled my nose.

His lips brushed my forehead ever so softly.

"Please do take care, Vespera," He said gently as he pulled back, pulling us both upright.

Without a word, he dropped my hand and walked out the door. My forehead warmed where his lips had graced my skin.

My gaze fell to my heaving chest. Why had that small

moment affected me so my whole body was alight with warmth. As if a fire had been lit from within. My stare caught on the scar crossing my chest. The cross now redder than I had ever seen amongst the grey.

Chapter Seventeen

My mind was a whirlwind. Why was I seeing only that single bright colour? If Maaier were my soul mate then I would have seen full colour. Or would I? The details of the curse were hazy to even the most well versed Florian.

I rushed into the halls chasing uselessly after Maaier. A wave of frustration crashed through me. How dare he abandon me like that in the dark hall at night with only a single candle to light my way. Useless bodyguard he was. My skin warmed where his hands had been, as if craving more of his gentle touch. My footsteps echoed through the corridor, clapping lightly on the floorboards. Moonlight cascaded down the misted windows through open rooms.

God damn that wretched man! My hands twisted into fists. How dare he call upon me and simply dance with me. What was he waiting for? It's not like I'm overly delicate. I want someone to set my body on fire but not bring anything more.

Candles flickered as I walked. The cold chill in the air settled deep in my bones. I wrapped my arms around myself for warmth. My breath fogged in the air. The eyes of the portraits on the walls following my every move. Their details were hazy in the condensation of the night air.

As I made my way toward the one person I missed most, my heart raced in my chest. Coming back to life.

"Hi Mother," I whispered as I approached. Her features so like mine. The only portrait not covered in a haze.

Her loving stare forever captured in the painting. Grandmother always told me she held me behind the artist and that's why her smile was so adoring. I liked to believe Father was the one holding me and she was looking upon both of us but according to Arthur he had disappeared for almost a year. Mother took him back with open arms much to the family's dismay.

Slowly, I stepped toward her, admiring the detail in her eyes. My gaze landed on the heart shaped locket around her neck. My mood deflated further. I lifted a palm. My hand making gentle contact with the canvas, the rough texture of the old cold and harsh under my touch.

A sudden pain erupted in my arm. I withdrew my arm with a hiss and stumbled back. A harsh white light took over my senses until all I saw was the shade.

THE HALL WAS THE SAME, ONLY ALIVE WITH PIANO notes and singing drifting through the halls. People wove through the rooms. Chattering and giggling.

"Vespera?" Mother's voice called. She swayed into the hall. Her smile was luminous as she looked at me. Her long light skirts swaying around her. She opened her arms. I stepped toward her.

"Mummy!" Called a small voice back to her. Without

another word, small hurried footsteps moved toward me. I watched as my own child form ran through me, leaping into my mother's arms. She pulled me into a tight embrace, kissing my hair over and over again. Her smile blazed brighter as I smiled back at her with a wide grin. Nothing but adoration in my eyes.

A smile lifted on my own face. Mother ushered me out to the back garden. I followed behind her, wishing my hand was still in hers. Mother led me to a patch of petunias. The flowers swayed gently in the warm midsummer breeze.

"See how beautiful they are?" Mother knelt before me. Not phased by the soil beneath her mating her beautiful skirts.

"So beautiful." My voice so innocent as a child. So untouched by the cruelty of the world.

"What about those ones?" Mother pointed at a small bunch wilting in the back. I moved around behind her. Watching as child me observed the blooms peeking through the brush.

"They're dying." I noted. My small voice sad.

"Yes they are. Death comes for us all, sweet girl. But soon enough he will come for you."

"I know," I sighed.

"You need to find your colour before he finds you." Her hand grabbed her child before her. Her eyes staring into mine. As if baring her message into me.

"But mummy. I don't want colour." A pout forming on my lips.

"You do baby. Trust me you do. But Death will take that from you. He will take you far away from me." She urged.

Tears pricked my eyes. If only she knew that he took her first.

I looked at her necklace. The same locket glinted in the sun. I reached forward over my head. Tears stinging my eyes. I remembered this day. It was Mother's twenty-seventh birthday. She petted my child hair. The tears fell down my ghostly cheeks. This was a week before she died. She warned me of Death coming for me when in reality he came for her.

"Baby. Look at me. Promise me you won't trust anyone who says you belong to them," She said looking so panicked. I had never seen her like this. She was genuinely terrified.

Movement caught my gaze from behind her. I looked past the sweet moment. Only to find a familiar stable hand. Only now he wasn't a stable hand. He was my protector. I looked back at him. His gaze fell from my mother to me as a child until it lifted. His gaze darkened as he saw me lingering behind them. The first person to notice me in this strange ghostly form. His eyes locked on mine. Wild and confused. He stepped forward. I stepped back.

Mother turned to face him. As if sensing his presence too. Her gaze narrowed, assessing the strange man. She said nothing as she rose. Facing him head on. As if she truly had no fear. Her warm hands reached back for me. Despite myself, I leant forward. My hands reached for hers. My heart dropped as my ghostly corporeal hands fell through them. Younger me clutched hers tightly.

"Come now, gloomy. Let's have some cake."

WITHIN SECONDS I WAS HURLED BACK TO THE present. My back collided with something hard as I stumbled back. A warm body stood firm behind me. Victor's cologne hit my nose. I sighed heavily in relief, the feeling of Maaier's eyes still clinging to me. My hands trembled. Once warm, now frigid and cold.

"What were you doing down here?" He said. But his tone wasn't angry or upset but rather curious.

"I came to find a book. I couldn't sleep." I lied. Mother's warning lingering in my head. Her smile still warming me slightly. I turned to face him. He looked like he hadn't slept in a week. The manor would do that to you.

"Can I make you a cup of tea?" He offered. His hand outstretched.

I nodded. My mind whirling as he took my hand, leading me down to the kitchen. Why was I seeing these weird visions? Why was Maaier there? And what on earth was Victor doing up this late?

I LEANT AGAINST THE COLD BENCH. THE SMALL teacup pressed against my lips. Inhaling the leafy scents did nothing to calm the throbbing in my temples. Victor remained silent as he stared at me.

I lowered my gaze to the murky brown water. At least this was better than Dorian's brew.

Seeing Maaier in that memory was much like seeing him now. He hadn't aged a single day. Not one single white hair marred the dark expanse of his long hair. His dark eyes still held the same intensity.

I tried to focus back on my sweet mother. Her loving hold on my hands as she warned me. I had almost forgotten that day. Almost. Her warning still followed me everywhere.

Filing it away in my mind under useless information I held on to, such as how many bones one has in their little finger.

There was a truth to Mother's words. Death had come for me. That much was clear. The proof was on my chest but why would they be hunting me as a child? Who had scared her so much that she believed I was the omen of him? Who tried to take me from her? So many unanswered questions swelled through my mind. I felt as if I were drowning in the depths of them.

The only thing bringing me to the surface time and time again was Maaier. I needed to speak to him. To learn the truth without prying ears. And I knew just the place.

Chapter Eighteen

"Get up," I barked. The pillow I had thrown landed with a soft thud against Maaier's sleeping form.

It was still early in the morning when I finally dragged myself from a fitful sleep. My mind racing with each possibility of what the day and my confrontation could bring.

Maaier stirred in his bed, a fitful sleep evidently taking place. Bending forward, I ripped the bedding from him at the foot of the bed.

His exposed skin now on full display. Eyes clenched shut to avoid the morning sun.

"Vespera, as much as I have craved you coming in here. You could have announced yourself better," He groaned. Throwing his arm down to pull the covers back up.

With a hum of acknowledgment, I walked to the window. The thick curtains blocking out almost all sunlight. I threw them wide. Bright light blazed through the grimy glass.

Maaier hissed behind me. Like a cat startled in an alley.

"Oh shut up. It's not like you are a vampire." I teased. Maaier muttered something under his breath before rolling to face me. His head propped up on his elbow.

"I must say. I rather like you in green."

My brow furrowed as I looked down at my dress. A simple woollen dress suited for going out for a walk in the forest. I filed the colour away in my mind. Not seeing anything but a dark shade of grey.

"But red is my favourite." He shrugged.

"Why? Because it reminds you of blood?" I mocked innocence into my tone. Rolling my lips to hide my smile.

"I am not a vampire." His tone darkened along with his stare.

"Then you must be a creep. Now get out of bed."

"Why?"

"Because you told me that I can't go anywhere alone and I thought that surely my master would escort me on a walk."

Maaier's smug grin covered his face. I made my way to the bed standing just beside it, staring down at him.

"I'm your master?" He drawled, his voice like sin.

"I belong to no one," I said. Recalling my mother's warning. I knelt down onto the bed leaning over him.

Maaier remained as still as stone, watching my every move. His hair tousled from a long night of sleep. My fingers itched to run through it. The urge to climb atop him and pull him close is intoxicating. My hand moved forward. A moment of brief unfamiliar confidence overtaking me. My hand met his cheek. Cupping it slowly before drawing it down the column of his throat. His breath hitching under my touch. He flexed against his will, moving toward my touch. I inched my fingers over the expanse of his chest. His breath stuttered as my hand drifted lower. Fingers gently scratching into him. God I wanted to sink my teeth into him.

As I met his eyes once more I could tell he thought the same thing. Slowly withdrawing, I kept eye contact. The air in my lungs non-existent.

"Quickly now. I hate waiting," I drawled.

Maaier tilted his head examining me. Possibly wondering why I had changed my attitude to him. If only he knew I was onto him. Something strange lurked beneath his surface and finding out what it was was the key to all my questions. And come hell or high water, I was going to find it.

I LEFT WITHOUT ANOTHER WORD. HEADING INTO THE hall now bustling with people. Maids gossiping in hushed whispers.

Mary hissed my name in a soft whisper as I approached her down the stairs.

"Whatever is going on?"

"They found another victim. Another girl was attacked."

"Is she okay?"

Mary's shoulders slumped as she shook her head.

"She was found dead in the streets."

"The poor soul." I deflated, shoulders dropping. Another woman dead. I couldn't help but feel guilty. The pain I felt that night was nothing compared to what she must have felt.

"The police are finally taking it seriously now they have seen the link between both attacks."

"What link?"

"Both of you have an X on your chest." She pointed at the partially exposed scar peeking through the neckline of my dress. "But that's not the strangest part."

I opened my mouth to press for more information. Only for Mary to whisper.

"She looks just like your crazy friend in the flower shop."

My heart sank to the floor. My blood dropped to ice

beneath my skin. My voice trembled. "Mary, clean the spare room beside mine. I want Dorian brought here immediately."

Mary nodded before dashing down the hall.

"Victor!" I called as Maaier stood at the top of the stairs taking in the clamour below.

"What is going on?" He asked over the noise. Eyes raking over the disarray.

"Another woman is dead." I waved him off. Now wasn't the time for my silly little escapades.

I shouted for Victor once more.

I was halfway up the stairs when he called my name from below.

I twisted to face him coming from the back garden.

"Take Arthur and fetch Dorian. She will fight you but I need her sedated. She hates this house but I know for a fact it's the safest place she will be." I didn't care if my words didn't make sense as I said them. I just needed Dorian safe. I needed her with me.

Victor's face paled at the order, his kin grew whiter with each blink of his eyes as he absorbed the situation.

"Please." I pleaded. I wasn't below begging when it came to her.

"Donovan has taken Dorian to London for a few days to see a flower show. I thought you knew," He said gently, not wanting to upset me further.

My shoulders sagged with relief.

"Oh thank the heavens. I want her brought here as soon as she's back home."

"Of course." Victor's smile was strained. As if spending the night in the strange manor with Dorian was enough to bring on a night terror.

Maaier stood behind me. His hand gently landed on my shoulder.

"Come," He said softly. "Let's get some air."

I stifled the thrill that ran through me at his touch. *'A woman just died, Vespera!'* I cursed myself before walking down into the halls. Maaier fastened my coat before turning to Victor.

"We will be back. Don't wait up, doctor." His tone was teasing but firm. I flung my elbow back, the impact of it hitting Maaiers chest causing a slight wince to sound. I looked at Victor from the corner of my eye. His lips curled as he held back a smile.

Maaier gripped that same elbow and thrust me toward the door.

Chapter Nineteen

We walked in silence down the path I had barely dared to travel.

No one wanted to see the place where their mother had died. Why would they? It wasn't like it harboured a happy memory down here.

Maaier eyes me angrily. The rage simmered away under his surface. Why on earth was he mad? He wasn't the one whose best friend was now being hunted because of him. Well at least I didn't think so. But how would I know? It's not like I know the first thing about him. Apart from the fact that he was a lord from somewhere up north and that he favours the colour red.

He was a vampire. There was no other explanation. A vampire that tempted every fibre of my being despite myself. I hadn't the first clue where he was from. But I was certain he wasn't actually a lord. He would have to have been wed by now. Judging by the lack of a ring on his finger. I wondered if there was a lady back up north waiting for him to return home with open arms. A sour taste hit my mouth. I was jealous of a woman I could very well have made up. Silly fool for wanting anything from him. That was me. A pretty fool.

I focused on the sound of the leaves squelching beneath my boots. Picturing Maaier's head beneath my feet with each step. Distracting fool.

"Did you hear what they were discussing?" I broke the silence.

"That another woman is dead or that you are in love with the doctor?" He ground out.

"Oh for heaven's sake. I do not love 'the doctor'." I stopped to face him behind me. Tree branches gripping my puffed sleeves as I swung my arms out with exasperation. "Of course you are too fatheaded to see it." I was sick and tired of everyone weaving their way into my relationships. Platonic or not. It was no one's damned business.

"Fatheaded! You're the one who dragged me out of bed for this utter nonsense!" He matched my stance.

"Why are you so concerned with sleeping Maaier? Out too late slaughtering women I suppose!" I snarled back. I turned away from him once again, this time more hastily. Storming away from the stubborn moron, I hurried to the tiny entrance to the river bank, the trees parting just enough to allow a single person through at a time.

The sound of water running close. I inhaled deep, letting the scent calm my frayed nerves. The scent of moist soil almost called me to my neglected greenhouse. I made a note to check on my plants that evening.

Maaier's foot falls stilled behind me. I stepped forward with a squelch of mud beneath my boots. He remained where he was. Good. Now he will have to admit he knows this place.

I hadn't been here in years. It was my mother's hide away. Where she would often sneak away to come paint or to even sit in silence. My body ached at the memory of her. It wasn't often she would bring me down here with her. But when she did it was always to teach me things. I could never recall what. As if the lessons had faded with age.

Sighing through my nose I made my way to the river. The mossy bank thick, shining from the downpour overnight. The river itself was wild and free. Crashing against the sides as it raced down the current. If one fell in it was certain they would drown. I turned back to Maaier. He remained transfixed on the trees surrounding, his body stiff.

The question felt like lead on my tongue. '*Who are you really?*'

I tilted my head. Admiring the man before me. How could he possibly look the exact same now as he did in those strange memories. Shaking myself I turned back to the water.

I lowered myself to the bank. The soft earth beneath my knees drenching my skirt but I paid it no mind.

This very water took my mother's life. This bank is where she was dragged to. Lifeless and still. Her vibrancy gone. Her colour she bloomed with faded forever to grey.

I swallowed my emotions. Not wanting to cry in front of Maaier. I wouldn't let them fall. He would not see my weakness. Not now, not ever.

My fingers threaded together. Holding on to myself for support. My reflection gazing back through the water. A face so similar to hers stared back. My eyes grew misty. The reflection so much like her I could have sworn that it was her looking back at me through the watery expanse.

"How did you know her?" I called over my shoulder.

Maaier finally left his trance. Moving closer to me until he stood directly behind me.

"I assume you mean your mother," He said evenly. I nodded.

"She was someone I had only ever watched from afar when I visited." He shrugged. My hope deflated.

"How did you know I had known of her?" His voice was not angered. More curious than anything, with the slightest hint of grief.

I stood at this question, facing him once more. My back to the river holding that eerie reflection. A shiver rolled down my spine with a chill.

"You'll think I'm mad," I said small. Wrapping my arms around myself. Maaier moved forward. His hands met my shoulders, slowly moving one to cup my cheek. I allowed him this gentle moment. His eyes searched for mine, pleading for me to continue.

"Little bloom. Everyone's a little mad. But that makes their bleak existence just a little more fun." He smiled as his thumb traced circles on my face. Taking a breath, I told my truth.

"Ever since I was attacked I've been seeing these strange memories of my mother. Things that don't make sense and I can't bring myself to try and see them unprompted. I feel like there is always someone lurking in the halls. Watching my every move. As if haunting me."

"It's not unheard of. Did you read the book I gave you?"

I shook my head, my brow creasing slightly. Why would he ask that of me at a time like this?

"Never mind." He smiled. "There is a dark energy around that manor. It wouldn't surprise me if the darkness somehow latched itself onto you."

"You don't think me mad?" My breath caught, holding until I heard the answer I so desperately craved. Maaier's anger vanished. The rush of the water, the only sound surrounding us as a small smile illuminated his face.

"Vespera, my darling. If I thought you were mad, that would make me a raging lunatic." I smiled despite myself at his words. The swell of being called his darling lightened my heart only slightly but enough to bring me the slightest tendril of hope.

"I just want to know what's going on with me," I said with a sigh.

Maaier dropped his hand to my waist, pulling me close to him. The rush sent my heart galloping. With our bodies almost touching, his hand cradling the small of my back. His dark eyes bored into mine.

"And you will. With time. You have a lot yet to learn."

I couldn't help but frown. The hope slowly faded the longer I remained silent. I was no better off than where I started. Without further word, Maaier led me back to the darkness.

Chapter Twenty

Dorian arrived home three days later. Her battle against moving in now my victory. Her father, Donovan, had moved into the cottage for the time being until he left for London again in two weeks. Victor didn't need much persuading to leave me alone with my thoughts. He was more than willing to get out of the manor for the day. Mary's wide eyed stare followed his every move lately. Always tracking. Always watching. The cold had begun to seep through the halls, each day worse than the last. I woke that morning to an array of noise. The halls clattered with voices and footfalls.

    I rose from the curled up blankets around me. Having slept in the library after a night of studying ghosts and other entities. A groan released from my chest. The vase I had shattered in my frustration lying in pieces on the floor. As if a brutal representation of my mind. Nothing I had researched about ghosts and spirits brought any answers, only more questions. I had bandaged my hand in a shred of cloth torn from my dress last night. The porcelain had sliced a deep wound in my palm. No colour made itself known. I hated to admit a small part of me longed for it to show again. More voices clattered through the hall beyond my sanctuary.

What possibly could have happened now?

The footfalls drew closer. A set I knew better than my own. Light but always quick.

The door flew open with a flurry of motion. Dorian bustled in with purpose as if she owned the room. Her light dress swished as she walked in.

"Why am I never alerted to these attacks by you!" She exclaimed, her arms thrown wide.

"Dorian! You're back!" My heart raced. A smile growing on my face. I stood to face her. My book fell to the floor with a thud.

"Against my will. Father is staying with the cottage. Thought I could use some air today though. I'll be here to stay soon enough. A prisoner to this fucking hell." She scrunched her face as if the thought soured her. I breathed out a laugh. Dorian's hair was only half in a braid. Knotted just as much as I presumed mine was. Minus the leaves and twigs. Dorian smirked as she made her way to the lounge.

"Show me your scars." Her eyes lit up like a child.

"You morbid woman," I chuckled, nodding toward the door "Go close that."

Dorian hurried to the door slamming it shut before scurrying back to me.

I pulled down the neck of my dress. The pale pinched skin of the X on full display.

Dorian's eyes grew wide. Entranced by the mark. Unintelligible words fell from her lips in a hushed whisper. Her fingers rising to the scar tentatively. Neither of us dared to breathe. Dorian's soft fingertips drifted over the cold risen skin.

"Something isn't right, Vessie," She muttered. Her eyes

never leaving the scar. Their colour darkened the longer she stared.

"I know." I admitted.

"You shouldn't be alive. This mark..." She trailed off. I urged her with a squeeze of my hand on her free one.

"The mark reeks of death. Yet you're alive." Silver lined her eyes. "You shouldn't be alive."

"I know," I said once more.

"I watched you die, Vespera. You died. I saw the whole thing. It was fate. But something changed. Someone tore the thread. The dark one will come again." Her voice cracked as she began to sob. Her arms wrapped tightly around me, pulling me to her with a tug. Embracing me in a tight hug.

"Whilst I am most glad you are alive. You shouldn't be."

I remained silent. Burying my head in my best friend's hair. She was right. I should have died that night. She pulled back from me searching my face. Pleading with her eyes.

"You need to find what tainted you, Vespera. Before that darkness swallows you whole." Her eyes caught back on the mark. Clouding over before she stood back. Glancing from the door to where I sat.

I lay back on the couch, considering her cryptic words. It was true. I did need to find who did this but how. I needed to trigger more of those strange visions. But how? This was all a mess. Much like that prized vase grandmother will throw a fit over.

"The book you gave me." Dorian swallowed thickly. Her breath came in shallow.

"Yes?"

"It was blank," She sighed as she sat on my lap, moving so I was more comfortable with her weight. I watched as she pulled the book from her skirt pocket.

She tossed it to me, I opened it cautiously, waiting to see what lay between the pages.

"The energy that book radiates is as dark as your mark but I can't read it. Whatever is in there is yours and yours alone to read."

I cursed lightly before dropping back on the cushions.

"I need to prepare for my return here. God, this place gives me the creeps." She shuddered before rushing to the door.

I DRESSED NOT LONG AFTER SHE HAD LEFT. VICTOR had run off to follow Dorian before I could see him. I was grateful though, I was in the mood for no one after that entire exhausting interaction.

What darkness could possibly have tainted me more than the manor? Did Dorian see the colour I had glimpsed in her in one of her visions? Surely not. She would have noted it. She would have surely shared that. Most definitely with a grin on her beautiful face.

Maaier's voice called from beyond the door before he shoved it open. My heart leapt into my throat. The memory of our small touches came rushing back over my skin.

The smirk on his face confirmed he recalled it too. My cheeks heated as he approached where I sat on the couch, fastening my hair into a knot at the nape of my neck.

"You should come down and eat," He said, stopping behind me. His face was cut off from the reflection of the glass windows before us. I watched as his hand gripped my shoulders. My breathing grew short as his thumb drifted toward my throat.

"Why don't you bring my lunch into here?" I said, trying my hardest not to focus on his touch.

He laughed softly. "It's almost dinner. You slept half the day in here."

I looked at the window before me. Surely he was mistaken. But he wasn't. The sun was already setting in the tree line.

"Oh." The word fell from my lips. Another day wasted in this useless existence and I was no closer to anything.

Maaier lowered his hand giving my shoulders a light squeeze. My eyes drifted closed at the motion. Only to fly open as Maaier's lips brushed my forehead.

"I'll bring your dinner up. You look as if you still need rest, little bloom."

My heart thumped in my chest. Why did he kiss my head again? The interaction was more gentle than the first instance, as if he was truly restraining himself from me.

I turned back toward him, watching as he strode out of the room.

A smile crept across my face. My whole body is growing tingly. I looked down at my hands in my lap. The bandage coming loose. I pulled at the knot. Loosening it, my stomach dropped.

The wound had healed. The thick scabbing wasn't grey. It was red. I blinked again. Raising my hands to my face for closer inspection, admiring the colour, more with surprise than horror.

Maaier returned in the doorway. Frozen as he watched what I could only assume was a mystified expression flicker over my face. The colour now slowly fading back to grey.

He cocked a brow but said nothing, moving past me to sit on the couch.

I remained seated beside him, waiting for him to pass me the stew. He didn't though. Instead demanding to allow him to feed me. I scowled before relenting to the command. I needed to focus on my hands. Why had the colour faded? Why was it only there for a brief moment again? God, I wished I could ask Grandmother about this without being interrogated or locked away.

Maaier watched intently as I wrapped my lips over the spoon. His posture straightened as my eyes met his, briefly before he moved back to my lips.

Each and every time he fed me, his eyes never left my mouth. Heat rose through my body. Who knew being fed by your personal guard could be so exhilarating? Warmth pooled in my belly. His tongue darted out over his lips. And by God, I needed to feel it against mine.

"I must go. Urgent matters to attend to." He choked out before hurrying out of the bedroom. Leaving me alone with half a bowl of stew.

Shrugging a shoulder, I continued my meal. Wondering if I'd got under his skin just as much as he was mine.

Chapter Twenty-One

Night was beginning to fall faster now that winter was here. The grounds surrounding the manor slick with sleet, snow not far away either. Gregory had made sure we all knew it was on its way as he always had. He also shared Grandmother's fear of us going out in horrible weather. Whispers of his favouritism of Magdelena had always been common in the manor. Never anything predatory or untoward but always as if he were an uncle watching his niece.

Something that line of the family tree had never had. Most men of the Florian line had died before the next generation were born.

The ghost of Maaier's touch lingered on my wrist. My gaze fell to my sleeve that covered the flesh he touched. The weight of his eyes on me still ghosting over me. My hands flexed in the bandages that Arthur had wrapped over my hands per Maaier's incessant request. The man was becoming more and more like a thorn in my side with each passing hour. His eyes always followed my every move. At first I was uncomfortable but now, I found myself longing for him to approach me rather than stare at me like I was his most prized possession.

My mind wandered to his dark eyes. A small shred of me wondered what colour they would be. If they would mirror the darkest seas or whether they truly were midnight itself. I hadn't seen a shade or even a hint of red since that ill fated night in the library after Maaier left. A small shred of me longed to see it again. Even if only once.

I hadn't dared to tell anyone, believing that in my dying state I imagined the foreign colour and those that come after it. That I was hallucinating as a result of Arthur's tonics for the pain that he was still feeding me daily. They had stopped working long ago as there was no more pain but I wasn't going to tell him that. It seemed as if the small task gave him purpose in the manor despite his job outside.

The bedroom door creaked as I pushed it open. The stiff neckline of my dress was stifling in the cool air. My fingers moved to pull it away from my neck. I would rather look at that horrible mark now scared into my chest than be choked any longer.

Letting my hair down, I shuffled toward the bed. The silken sheets called to me like an old friend.

A small wrinkle caught my eye amongst the fabric. Only it wasn't a wrinkle. As I approached, I noticed a small shred of parchment laying on the surface. My breathing hitched. My heart pounded as my mind raced with fear. The paper trembled in my grasp.

> *Meet me at the greenhouse.*

Curly delicate handwriting written on a shredded piece of a faded novel. A familiarity with the font took me by surprise. Where had I seen this script before?

Bile rose into my throat.

Who left this? Was it my attacker? Were they back to finish me off?

I should tell Maaier. I *needed* to tell Maaier. Yet I remained still, rooted to the spot. My mind spinning. They were in my room. A wave of dread washed over me. This was it. My last night alive. Again.

The moon shone through the windows, full and bright in the sky through the forest. My throat thickened. A lump lodging itself within.

Clenching my fist around the paper, I walked toward the door. A chill of brisk cold air rolled over the doorway. Only getting thicker the further I ascended into the hallway. My heart picked up once more, pounding against my tight chest. A scuttle sounded down the hall toward Grandmother's room. Stepping as lightly as I could, I made my way down to the kitchen. The moonlight guided me through the halls as I crept past each room. No sound coming from any.

Arthur was supposed to relieve Maaier at night for a few hours so he could rest. I didn't want to be caught by him. Having any of the men hover over me each moment of everyday was bad enough.

I searched the benches. Finding what I needed. My fingers toyed with the knife's handle. It wasn't the biggest but it would have to do. The same scuttle sounded beyond the room. My eyes followed the sound. I gripped the handle tighter, holding it out as the scurry got closer. I braced for impact. The cold air still covering the manor only growing thicker. I waited on baited breath. Hoping that whatever was out there would leave. The scurrying stopped. I stepped forward. The dark hallway illuminated only slightly, the moonlight dimming from clouds. Narrowing my eyes. I watched as the sound began again.

A rat moved its way through the doorway scurrying out a hole in the wall and back out. A horrified scream lodged in my throat. I hated rats. But this time, I had never been more welcoming of the vermin in my life. As I hesitated to go outside I pondered my choices. I could go back to bed and act as if I never found the note or I could go be a fool and investigate who wanted me outside.

This fear ended tonight.

I MOVED AS SILENTLY AS I COULD, MOVING BACK toward the back gardens.

The greenhouse loomed in the yard. Only a slight walk from the house.

Greenery that once bloomed within now withered in the harsh cold. The breeze bit at my exposed face, prickling my nose. My heart galloped in my chest. Blood roared through my ears. Whoever was lurking within would have seen me by now. There was no point at delaying the inevitable. With one last look behind me at the looming dark manor, I entered the greenhouse.

The scent of soil and shrubbery filled my nose. My once most calming scent now sending a shiver of unease through me. The glass house was silent. I strained my ears for a noise. No tell of anyone being here.

My fingers ran over the wooden bench in the centre of the room. The greenhouse was only the size of the library. Grandfather had once been interested in plants but never once continued his endeavour after Mother was born. Or so I was told. I didn't believe it for a second. The tools in here were worn long before I ever stepped foot in here.

The knife glinted in the soft light beside me, shuffling briefly sounded behind me.

I froze. My bandaged hand gripped the blade tighter. I spun to face them.

No one. I was losing my mind.

With a rush of air, a gloved hand gripped my face. Cupping my mouth. I froze. Silently cursing myself for not fighting.

"Aren't you an obedient little thing?" A velvety voice sounded behind me. Despite the circumstance, my body softened. The scent of saffron and cedar filled my nose. The hand slipped from my face allowing air to enter my lungs once more. The scent familiar enough to slow my racing pulse.

"This is rather improper, Maaier," I said. My voice failed as

I turned to face him. His grin widened as he noticed the knife in my hand.

"I am glad you came prepared." He tilted his chin toward the useless weapon.

"Well, when a stranger leaves a note in your bedroom, one would assume it best to bring a form of defence." I smiled as sweetly as I could, knowing full well he could see right through it.

Maaier chuckled. His long gloved fingers moved forward. Brushing mine as he gently pulled the kitchen knife from me. My heart bloomed to life at his touch. A dimple arose in his left cheek as he smirked. He placed the blade on the workbench. Turning his dark gaze back on me. Long hair swept back behind him.

"Why am I here?" I straightened as I spoke. Trying my hardest to shake off how much I admired the way he smiled at me.

"I wanted to see how well you took orders from strangers."

The words rattled through me. As if sensing the change, Maaier reached out. A single hand moving forward toward my throat. His fingers closed over softly. The grip slowly tightening. The warm feeling from earlier spread through me. An almost aching need forming within. Maaier's lips moved closer to mine.

"Such a beautiful little thing." He spoke softly as he admired me once more. Drinking in my every feature. Tilting my head side to side as if imprinting my image to his memory. My eyes never leaving his.

The hand on my throat drifting lower. His fingers leaving a wave of gooseflesh over my skin. Stopping exactly at the centre of the cross. My breathing halted in my throat. Maaier towered over me. His hand dangerously close to my breasts. I had never been touched by another man before. Yet I so desperately longed for this strange man's touch. I barely knew him. How could he possibly have this effect on me?

His hands moved down. Gripping my hips, he pulled me up. Setting me down on the workbench. I sat eye to eye with the strange man. His hands were placed beside me, caging me into him. It was not as if I would run. Not now anyway. I craved the demolition in his eyes.

"You smell like roses," He breathed. Words fell flat on my tongue, left unspoken in the heat of his touch.

My own trembling hands reached out to touch him. Meeting a hard wall of clothed muscle on his chest. He drew in a quick breath, his body growing rigid.

"Be careful, Vespera. You have no idea how hard it is to restrain myself around you." He puffed.

"And what if I do not want you to restrain yourself?" I breathed, looking up at him through my lashes. Maaier chuckled darkly. He shifted closer, his hips moving between my legs. I remained still as stone. His lips mere inches from mine.

"Soon enough, sweet bloom. Soon enough I won't need to restrain myself. You will be mine. Mine to indulge in. Mine to lose myself in, only to find myself once more." His tongue darted out to wet his lips, his hand cupping my face. "Tell me Vespera, has another man tasted these lips?"

I shook my head. Too breathless to formulate a response.

Maaier hummed his approval. A wicked gleam in his gaze.

"Good girl."

I don't know why those words had such an effect on me. I wanted nothing more than for him to lay me back and do as he pleases with me. To use my body as we both so desperately craved. I was close to praying when he drifted back.

Panic rippled through me.

"Did I do something wrong?" I asked softly. I was afraid of

his response. He had probably been with multiple women. Why would he be interested in a pure woman such as myself?

"You could never do anything wrong." He smiled. "Come, let's get you to bed." He offered his hand. I took it with my mind racing.

What on earth had just happened?

Chapter Twenty-Two

Darkness surrounded the halls, the brief candle light flickering with each shaky step I took.

The night had fallen early, a storm on the horizon rolling over like an ominous omen. The last storm that rolled over had almost claimed my life. No one had made themselves known since that man lingered in the forest. No more attempts for my life but all those who knew the manor knew it was better to assume you could be taken at any time.

I took a step forward. The knife in my fist a welcome comfort.

The door to the library creaked as I opened it. A frigid breeze blew from the room. I shuddered quietly. Had I left the window open? Surely not, it was never opened in winter. I stepped into the room further. Walking up to the window, I noticed it was closed, the fastened locks secured tightly in place.

"Curious," I muttered before moving to the shelves. The cold air stilled around me. My spine straightened, the feeling of someone's eyes burning into my exposed shoulders. I turned slowly, willing every ounce of confidence I could. Why did I not ask Maaier to fetch me the book? Why was I so dim when it came to my own safety lately? I didn't even think twice about Uncle Arthur not being outside the room before I left.

I turned to the door. No one lingered. No attacker lurked in the depths of the shadows. I exhaled a heavy breath, fogging the air. I noted how strange the room felt, the frigid temperature. The cold breath still lingering. I turned back to the bookcase. Setting my candle on a small table by the lounge. Running my fingers over the volumes of books, I searched for comfort. Anything to heal the ache inside me. The turmoil of whether I would survive another night.

"Vespera," My name whispered ever so gently in the night. My hand froze. I would know that voice anywhere. No. It can't be.

"My sweet winter child." Mother's voice trembled. As if caught with emotion. I whirled to face the empty room. My heart galloped in my chest.

"Not real." I assured myself. I couldn't hear her. Surely it was repressed mania. Footsteps sounded down the hall. My senses strained to hear who it was.

"I am real." The voice crying inside my head pleaded. Sadness dripped from her tone.

"You can't be real. You died!" I hissed. A deeper fear running through me. The feeling of cold air breezed over my shoulders once more.

The footsteps become louder, drawing closer.

"Vespera?" My name echoed down the hall. My already beating heart sped up.

"In the library, Uncle Arthur," I called back, stealing my voice from nerves.

Arthur appeared in the doorway. Still dressed from his day of work.

"Christ Vespera. It's as cold as all hell in here. What are you doing?" He scolded, striding toward me.

"I was getting a book to read." Hating that he made me feel like a naughty child. His strong hand gripped my wrist pulling me forward.

"You were attacked by walking the halls at night and now you think it's safe to pursue the same halls once more? How daft can you be?" Spittle rained from his mouth as his anger rose with every syllable. His grip tightening on my arm.

"I am not daft!" I grunted whilst trying to wrench my arm free. Arthur's grip tightened before yanking me toward the door.

"You clearly are. Now get to bed before you catch a chill."

"Unhand me!" I seethed. Twisting my wrist every way to shake him off. Arthur's eyes blazed with a sudden fury. He didn't like being ordered around at the best of times. Let alone by his niece.

Just as Arthur opened his mouth to retort, a harsh wind flooded the room. The light from the candle extinguishing with it. Arthur's grip loosened as a certain fear washed over him.

A curse fell from his lips. Terror ran through me. Where did that wind come from if the windows were fastened close? I stepped past Arthur, hurrying back up the stairs to my room.

Only I didn't make it that far. Stopping instead outside Victor's room. Without bothering to knock. I shoved my way in. The room was dark apart from one window allowing a sliver of moonlight. The room was the smallest among the manor residents. Big enough for one average size bed, a wardrobe and a desk. Marble floors and dark walls matching the other rooms. The room once used as a nursery, now only used for guests of lower social class. Arthur's voice grunted before disappearing back down to his wing of the manor. My back still pressed against the wall as I counted the seconds until he was gone.

Victor grunted from the bed. I took a shaky step forward.

Not wanting to wake him. The sound of the door opening going unnoticed by him signalling a deep slumber. He grunted again. My brow furrowed. Was he having a night terror? '*Oh the poor soul!*' I noted to myself softly before stepping forward. My long hair falling in pieces from its loose braid. In the dim light, I noticed a small movement under the blanket. I crept forward. Victor moved under the blanket. I continued forward so I could see his face. His expression purely blissful. Eyes closed but still flickering as if in a dream. Maybe it wasn't a nightmare. What a strange dream he must be having. His mouth opened into a slight o shape, a single word falling from his lips. "Vespera."

"Yes?" I answered softly. Not wanting to startle him.

Victor gasped loudly. Jumping from the bed. Obviously startled. He stood before me. His chest rising and falling. My mouth opened to apologise. Only to close as my eyes took in his form. His hands covered his body as he struggled to regain himself. I looked at his hands, noticing the erection behind them. My cheeks flushed warmly. My whole body heating. That was not what I was expecting by any means.

"Oh my god!" I gasped. The words falling from my lips, embarrassment flooded me. "I am so sorry."

"Don't you know how to knock!" He breathed. My embarrassment had nothing on his. The awkwardness radiating from him. I could only just make out the shape of his body as he stepped back into the shadows. My cheeks still on fire.

"Of course I do! But I was trying to get away from Arthur and I wanted to ask you a question about a person's health after an attack and their mind and I just let myself in and I didnt know what you were doing and I thought it was night terror and I-"

"Vespera breathe!" Victor cut off my flustered rambling.

I finally turned away offering him the privacy to dress himself.

"I really am sorry, Victor. I will leave you be."

"After that Vespera. I don't think I am ever going to be able to sleep in peace again," He muttered. But his tone missed the bite the words intended. The sound of him sitting back on the bed echoed through the room. I turned to face him, rolling my eyes.

"Oh come on, Victor. I may be a virgin but I understand that one needs to pleasure themselves."

Victor cocked a brow at me before looking ahead. I looked up to where his gaze fell. A portrait hung above the desk. My mother's smile beamed down at us. Her body covered in flowers of all kinds. The likeness to myself was uncanny.

"You're a virgin?" Victor asked cautiously. I nodded, not saying anything further.

If Maaier and I's relationship continued to progress as it was, I wouldn't be one for much longer. At least I hoped anyway.

"And if it was that picture you used for inspiration, that was my mother. Adele."

Victor stilled. His expression sobered. "That isn't you?" He said, a slight tremor of disgust in his tone.

"No." I laughed. "That would have been most strange for my uncle to hang a portrait of a woman your boss wants you to court over your bed."

Victor groaned at himself. Scrubbing a hand over his weary face. The poor flustered and confused boy.

"Now that I have seen you most awkwardly in this moment, Victor. One would presume we are now the best of friends. And the best of friends share secrets, and you my friend are in for one hell of a story."

. . .

THE WORDS FELL OUT OF ME. THE NEED TO TELL someone everything overcame my better judgement. I didn't truly know who Victor was but inside I felt as if I could trust him. I knew within myself he was safe. At least I hoped anyway.

Divulging the weight of my family secret was like shedding a mountain of weight off my shoulders. Victor listened intently. Not saying a word or interrupting despite the questions I could see forming behind his eyes. To see if I could determine the truth from the lies.

"So you can't see colour when I touch you?" Victor said. A slight sadness in his tone he tried to keep hidden seeping through.

I shook my head. "No. But to be frank, Victor. I never really wanted to see it. I am fine without it but I would be fine with it. I don't need a soulmate to fix any so-called broken part of me. I need to learn to fix myself before placing the broken pieces in the hands of another. I don't see the colour as a broken or missing piece of me. It just is what it is. It's who I am." I shrugged, the confession feeling lighter off my chest.

Victor nodded, taking my hand in his. I stilled at his touch. Not knowing how to react.

"You said you had questions?"

"I did." I smiled before facing him fully. Bracing for the rejection. "Have you ever heard of people seeing ghosts after they almost die themselves?"

"It has been noted in some diaries but there is no factual information behind it. Are you experiencing this?"

I nodded. His hand squeezed mine. "We will monitor it and if these hallucinations get worse, we can treat them then." I let out a sigh of relief at his words. They weren't ghosts! Rather just a figment of my imagination.

"Thank you for telling me all of this and entrusting me," He said softly.

"Thank you for listening. I will see you at breakfast." I stood, walking toward the door. "I truly am sorry I am not the one for you, Victor."

"I know. Me too." He smiled sadly. My heart cracked in my chest. The tension rolling from my shoulders. I turned to leave before stopping suddenly.

"One last thing," I said.

I walked up to the portrait hanging on the wall. My hands ran along the sides of the huge frame. I pushed it off the hook. The painting fell into my arms.

"Best not let Mother watch you sleep. Or whatever else you plan to do when I am gone." I winked over my shoulder before exiting the room.

I didn't know where this new found confidence came from but I was grateful it was here.

Chapter Twenty-Three

Both books sat open in my lap. I was torn on what to read. My curiosity got the better of me. My fingers grazed the cover of the strange book. What was this book? The Cursed Life of Death. My lip caught between my teeth. Dorian had said it was blank like a fresh journal. But I remember there being text when I found it. Surely there had been. Hesitation lingered.

"What are you so scared of?" I chastised myself before wriggling back on the seat by the window. Wind howled outside, a flurry of decaying leaves swirling down the gravel road. Victor's carriage leading their disruption. He had barely spoken to me all morning much to Maaier's delight. Who proceeded to bound around the manor with a spring in his every step. I couldn't tell whether I liked it or loathed it. Seeing him so joyous as to Victor's displeasure of going to work however did bring a small smile to my face

I spread the pages of the old book, running fingers along the seam where the pages met. The scent of old musk hit my nose like a welcoming comfort. The ink on the page worn out with time.

Faded in spots and creased in others. The font not typed but rather handwritten. An elegant scrawl across the yellowed parchment.

> *"This book reflects a life lost in time. A life once so desired to return to now so despised. The life in question is no other than Death himself. How did the angel of death fall so far from heaven or was he on earth all along? Many people know him as many different names and deities. But most commonly he is referred to as The Reaper. The one who helps souls to their final resting place, wherever they decide that be."*

I drank in the text, indulging in every word. The strange story drew me in, captivating my every attention. Who was Death? Was he the same one who had touched me? Who was the author? Turning the page, I noticed the sketch. A small butterfly in the centre of the page above a roughly drawn garden. Although the line work was simple the piece was unmistakably beautiful. An image worthy of a frame on the wall.

My fingers lingered over the page, hesitant to touch the art. Whoever drew this was gifted. Even mother couldn't capture the grace of the insect as they flew. My fingers pressed against the wings. Their sketching was ever so delicate. Small smoke like tendrils of shadow danced up from the drawing. Drawing my hand to the page. Holding it against it.

A light flashed before my eyes. The image of a young girl painting my sight. Her laughter filled the air as she swirled and spun through the tall grass. Not caring who saw. Her wild dark hair fanning out around her with each twist. A single colour slowly seeping into the memory. Her pale dress an almost light shade of red. Pink if I were correct in my guess, from what others had mentioned. The young girl looked no older than seven. Her youth radiating from her with a toothless grin. The butterfly floated past. Her attention locked onto it as she ran. A voice called for the girl but she paid it no mind. Instead she dashed after the creature. Her breathy laugh filled the spring air. I closed my eyes, filling my nose with the scent of greenery and wildflowers as I inhaled.

When I opened my eyes I was back in my room. The laughter from the small girl still echoing softly in the distance. A small smile pricked my lips. I looked back down at the odd book in my hand. The memory of the girl now etched forever in the pages. But who was she? I looked to the next page only to find it blank. My heart sank. Where had it gone? The book was full before. I flicked through the pages, finding nothing but plain yellow paper. My stomach dropped, the hopeful mood now depleted. I needed this book. Something in my soul telling me the answers were all I needed.

Tilting my head back, I looked up at the sky beyond the window. The windstill danced through the trees like the little girl. If I could close my eyes, I had the tiniest hint of the pink colour to remember but I knew that would fade just like the red had. It was a strange sensation. To witness a colour for the first time but not know what it truly was. To not be able to see how each colour blooms through every day.

Footsteps drew near beyond the closed door. With a hushed curse, I flew from the bench. Pulling the cushions back to reveal my hiding spot. I thrust the book in and sat back on the bench. Just in time to hear a knock on the door. I flicked open to a random page in the book Maaier gave me and waited for the intrusion.

"Morning miss Verspera." Mary smiled, but it didn't quite meet her eyes. Her light was somewhat dimmer than usual.

"Are you alright?" I made to move only to have her stop me with a hand.

"I am fine. Just couldn't sleep."

"Because of the attack in town?"

Mary nodded, keeping her distance. I pulled my legs from the bench and put them before me. Offering her my full attention.

"Your friend warned me it wasn't safe here," She said softly, her eyes not meeting mine. Blasted Dorian, of course she would tell everyone that was the case just so she didn't have to come here.

"Dorian just hates this house. That is all. Trust me. You are safer here than you would out there."

Mary said nothing but nodded.

Her gaze fixed to the floor. As if the imprints of the floorboards were more interesting than me.

"Was that all?" I said softly, flexing my fingers on the spare book. Mary shook her head.

"Sorry, Vespera. I lost myself for a second there. I came to see if you required company for today? It was supposed to rain and I thought the greenhouse may be a good place to stay warm." She brightened slowly. How could I say no to that? She seemed genuinely curious as to the plants. I was always happy to help a fellow gardener. A warm smile spread across my face.

"Of course."

THE GREENHOUSE WAS WARM UPON ARRIVAL. THE rain outside still just a mere threat rather than a downpour.

It looked at least six hours later than it was outside. Mary tried her hardest to contain her excitement as she noticed the small sprouts growing from the pots we had soiled last time. Before that strange man was in the forest. A chill ran through me. He wasn't here. He was long gone. I assured myself over and over again until I had some sort of control on my fear.

"Vespera! Look at the tiny flowers on this bush!"

We took inventory of every new leaf and bloom on each plant, myself noting the size, and Mary noting the colour, to ensure they were growing correctly.

I walked to the patch of bare bench. Unmarked by soil or plant matter. My heart catching alight within me. The memory of Maaier's sinful gaze caused my stomach to clench. God that was heavenly.

Mary asked a question beside me but all I could think of was what Maaier's tongue would feel like on the skin.. My chest became hot and tight. This was wrong. I shouldn't be thinking about my bodyguard in this way. I should be more concerned with where he was and why he was only interested in basic intimate acts on his time, not mine. Why was I so enraptured with him? He was nothing to me. Just a man who devoured my attention like his favourite meal.

God above what was wrong with me. I didn't want colour. I didn't need it. But why did he make a small lost part of me believe he was the one who would give it to me. I needed to be committed to the asylum, I swear there was something fundamentally wrong with me. Facing Mary, I raised my brows with a hum. She just grinned and reached for the watering can.

"I see you two are having fun." Arthur's voice rang through the greenhouse. Mary's shudder was small, barely noticeable, but still a flinch not unnoticed by my eyes. I feigned a smile and stepped toward her.

"We thought we would come out and document some growth."

"Lovely. But Mary, your duties are inside the manor, not along with my niece." His expression was that of a father scolding a child. Mary's mood deflated as her shoulders drooped. A small "Yes, sir," falling from her lips with a sigh.

"Arthur, she is fine in here with me."

"Do not argue Vespera." Anger flashed across his expression before settling back into disappointment.

I opened my mouth to protest only to have Maaier appear in the doorway. Looking as cocky as ever.

"Come now Arthur. Shouldn't you be at work with young Victor? Not in here scolding two women for simply learning." His hands behind his back, he looked as arrogant as ever. Even the fake smile reeked of arrogance.

"Shouldn't you be out here protecting her?" He mocked Maaier's tone.

"I should have been. But Sophia requested an update on her safety. I apologise, Lady Vespera, for my delay."

Narrowing my gaze, I accepted the apology. Confusion furrowing my brow at his use of my title.

"Mary, fetch yourself, Lady Vespera and I a pot of tea and some biscuits. I wish to learn more of..." He waved his hands to the plants lining the benches "whatever all these are."

Mary bowed before scurrying out the door, hiding her face from us all. Arthur grunted but left us be.

My body sparked to life at the thought of being alone in the greenhouse with Maaier once again. I faced the bench once more, trying to repress the memory attached to it as I pulled a large terracotta pot toward me with a rose bush blooming from within.

Maaier stalked closer, like a cat to a mouse. I could see from the corner of my eye the same hunger that roiled through him that night still lurked in his eyes now.

"Pass the trowel please." I managed.

Maaier chuckled but ignored me. Instead coming to a halt behind me. His length pressing into my behind. I grit my teeth, trying a failed attempt at ignoring how heated my body felt against his.

"I think I've come to like this greenhouse," He murmured into my ear. His hands sneaked their way up my waist.

I scoffed, "Maaier, people can see how close you are to me. This is highly inappropriate."

"So? That has never stopped me before." He chuckled to himself. His hands reached higher. Fingers ghosting over my stomach. Thank heavens I wore another high collared dress today.

Butterflies fluttered through my stomach under his gentle touch, longing heated his eyes. My heart raced. What if someone had seen this interaction? I could not tear my gaze from Maaier's. His tongue darted out over his bottom lip. The butterflies turned into a frenzy as I leant closer.

The greenhouse door creaked. I scrambled back from him, trying to regain control over my breathing.

"Ah, there you are Mary!" Maaier clapped, turning his attention to the silver tray in her hands. A master of acting as if he didn't just set my every fibre on fire.

My heart thumped against my chest.

What did he mean by he won't wait long. Was I going to die tonight? Would he finally kill me? That would be a better outcome than him teasing me all the time.

I didn't go to the greenhouse. I wasn't about to risk my life for some strange man. No matter how devilish he looked or how he had managed to worm his way under my skin.

Instead I curled up under my blankets in bed with the oil lamp beside me. The rain, falling on the earth outside, a welcome comfort. The strange book in my lap.

I braced for the same blank pages but instead found more writing. With a sigh of relief, I wriggled back in the sheets. Holding the book up to my nose to read in the dim light.

> *"Death is not something to be feared. But to any mortal being, be it big or small, it is but the fear of the unknown that terrifies them more than the end of life. We watch the families mourn their loved one as they pass over. He holds them close as they depart. Some are harder to watch than others. After all, that is how Death got his role in the first place. Every Reaper has an origin. There is more than one. This origin however depicts what was said to be the last reaper. The Reaper to bind all souls. Only this Reaper was cursed because of his origin. He wouldn't find love until that person accepted him for who he was. For what he now was. A person to see past the darkness and into the heart and soul of a man desperate for life."*

The words were like a dagger to the chest. Slicing into me with each syllable. I related to every word. What came after our bleak existence was not something that weighed lightly on me.

It was always in the forefront of my mind. I would need only the deepest soul connection to feel fulfilled. Someone to accept my curse and not feel like they weren't good enough for me if they could not bring me colour. But that wasn't the truth. The truth was, I was terrified of what a world of colour could be for me. Would the colour be worth it? Worth the adjustment? I hated change at the best of times.

Lately it seemed a shift had taken root in me. I wasn't entirely sure it was dark that I had preferred but more that I had felt comfortable in. Anxiety had begun to flourish in me once. Something I had suffered long with. People would always see Dorian as the one who would crumble at the slightest change but it was always me. I just didn't show it outwardly.

Spending each moment inside where it was safe rather than out in the real world. Safe with my ghosts in the walls and an attacker in the halls. I huffed out a laugh to myself at the thought.

I flicked open the next page. The sketch sent a jolt through me. An iris in black ink staring back at me. The bloom was so vivid you could almost pluck it from the page. I touched the picture feeling another faint stab of pain under my fingers before the light took over. Small tendrils of black shadow tying my hand to the book just like last time.

The small girl from before had now grown into a woman, a truly beautiful one at that. Running through the field once more but this time followed by a young boy. His small legs tottering beneath him. The toddler giggled as he called for his mummy. The dark eyes shining in the afternoon sun. The woman called for him but the sound was muffled as if spoken underwater. The young child caught up to her, holding her tight as he squawked in delight. The beautiful woman held him close. An iris poking out from her dark braid.

The boy held her close. Pressing his face against her cheek.

My own smile twitched my face as I withdrew from the memory. Who was this boy? Was his mother a Florian? Was I watching the beginning of the curse or the beginning of the reaper? The woman looked so familiar. I couldn't place where or how I had seen her before. The familiarity gnawed away at me.

The pages faded to blank before me. I fell back against the pillows with a sigh. This was ridiculous. It would take me days to find out what I needed. Why had Death recoiled when he touched me, leaving me with only a memory of red? Footsteps sounded down the hall drawing near.

Panicked, I threw the book under the covers and reached for the flower book Maaier had got me.

The heavy footsteps stopped outside my door. My heart leapt into my throat. The door swung open.

Maaier's heavy breathing filled the room.

"You're late," He huffed before quietly shutting the door behind him.

"Maaier, this is highly inappropriate," I said loud enough for anyone to hear. Just on the off chance I was attacked again. I couldn't be too safe. Despite how unphased I had been lately.

"Brat," He snarled before stalking forward.

I sat up in bed, letting the covers fall slightly. The white of my nightshirt, sheer in the dim light.

"Maaier if you come here to kill me please just get it over and done with. I am tired of waiting for someone to finally take my last breath." I admitted. I was so tired of it all.

"You think I was going to kill you?" He froze only steps from the bed.

"Isn't that why you keep toying with me?" I said, keeping my voice small.

"Vespera." He breathed before walking over to the large

windows. "Why would I kill the one thing bringing me a shred of happiness that I haven't felt in a long time?"

My skin heated as my heart came to life. Was he being serious?

"You've toyed with me over and over again. I honestly can't tell whether I like you or despise you."

"Why not both?" He smirked as he turned to me. I rolled my eyes, falling back into the pillows.

Maaier walked up to the bed once more. Kneeling on the mattress, he lifted the book from my grasp.

He looked at the cover. A mischievous smirk covered his mouth

"Good to see you think of me at night."

He leant over me. The scent of spice and rain clinging to his skin. His damp hair hanging over his forehead.

"You are such a prick," I sighed, looking up to him. His gloved hands settled beside my bed.

"I am a prick. That much is true." He shrugged. "But I am glad that you told the little doctor that he was not the one for you."

Panic rushed through me. "You heard that."

"It is my job to watch after you, little bloom. I hear everything."

"Why you little rat!" My eyes grew wide. Wondering just how much of it he heard. Did he know that I had walked on Victor pleasuring himself too? Of course he did. A man like him would have to know everything.

"Your colour secret is safe with me. When you desire to come out of the darkness, I will help you find the one to bring it to life. Unless you would rather remain in the darkness with me?"

"Oh please shut up," I groaned.

Maaier laughed loudly, the sound like a summer dream.

"It's a fact of life Vespera. You think I am scared of a little curse? We are all cursed. Maybe one day you'll figure out mine."

I furrowed my brow. His lips were mere inches from mine. My tongue darted out to wet my lips. God, I wished he would kiss me. Even just touch me or look at me with that intense dark gaze he wore that flooded sparks of heat through the entirety of my being. Maybe I should have gone to the greenhouse that night.

Maaier's eyes drank in my face. His gaze lingering on my eyes, his pupils blown black.

My body sparked with need.

His gloved hand cupped my cheek. The movement was sweet and gentle, but oddly pleading. One moment it was there. The next it was gone.

He moved back on the bed. Staring at my chest as it rose and fell.

"Get some rest," He muttered before making his way back to the window. I watched as he sat on the window seat. Watching as the clouds rolled by. The rain still pattering on the glass.

Chapter Twenty-Four

The drizzle swirled beyond the library windows, tapping against the glass incessantly. A storm was approaching.

Silence filled the room. Everyone else was entertaining themselves outside of the manor for the day, leaving me and Grandmother alone for the moment.

A smile curled at my lips. The dark rose lay beside me. I had found it beside me when I awoke this morning, the petals brushing my face.

I had a book spread open on my lap. Surely there is no happier place.

I read over the words on the page. Taking in the story the author told of lost love. I couldn't bear to read the medical essays one more time. Even I needed a break from the darkness they described. The afternoon light wouldn't last long. It was that dark that both thrilled and terrified me now. My conflicting emotions mixed with turmoil.

The sound of the door creaking open tore my eyes from my book. My heart leapt to life, expecting to find Maaier coming to see me. Only for it to falter as Victor poked his head through. I tried my hardest to keep my expression positive, not letting my slight smile fall.

"Ahh. I thought you would be in here." He said before walking over to where I lounged on the lounge. My back against the armrest, stretched out over its length. Victor walked toward me. Slowly he lifted my legs and sat on the couch, placing my legs back over his lap. I felt my cheeks heat despite myself. What was he doing? Had I not made myself clear that I had no romantic interest in him?

Victor leant back. His expert fingers began to massage my calf muscles over my dress. Pleasure rippled through me, the action having aided my relaxation. I reclined back against the chair.

"What are you reading?" He asked. Eyeing the book with a curious gaze.

"A romance." My eyes fluttered.

Victor snorted a small laugh. "The great gloomy Vespera. Queen of the Dark and Medical reading a romance novel. Well I never." He shook his head laughing. I laughed with him despite myself, closing the book only to swat his arm with it. Causing us both to laugh harder. My gaze shifted from his smile to his shoulder. Specks of darkness marking the white expanse of fabric.

"Victor. You're bleeding." I shifted to examine the stain further. His stare raked over my face, taking note of my concern.

"It's not mine." He smiled softly, waving me off. Frowning, I laid back, choosing to let it go for now. His hands resumed the massage. I told myself it was a patient's blood. That it was no one in the manors. Although I wasn't quite sure. The wood fire crackled loudly, startling Victor.

The sound brought on a more tense silence.

"The police still have no idea who did it," He spoke gently.

His voice was as soft as the drizzle outside. I nodded once, understanding what he meant. They had given up on the case.

I shifted awkwardly. The high collar of my dress digging into my skin. I preferred to be covered these days, not wanting anyone to see the ugly pinched wound on my chest.

"I haven't given up hope. I will find them myself if I have to." He vowed. His focus on his hands clenched into fists and unclenching slowly as he forced the tension from them. I leant forward, taking one of his in my own, bare skin touching. I stupidly braced for the colour to flood. Yet again. Thank god. I breathed out my relief. I squeezed his hand in mine.

The door flew open the second he squeezed back.

Maaier strolled into the room. An air of arrogance surrounded him. His lethal gaze focused on where Victor's hands met mine. Where my legs were still draped over his. What a sight this would be to walk in on. I was in for it now.

"Sophia has requested your presence in the kitchen," He said evenly.

Victor said nothing. I pulled my knees up, allowing him to move.

He brushed past Maaier before turning to me, offering a sad smile before closing the door after him.

"You could have been kinder to him. We were just talking." I frowned.

Maaier stalked forward. That lethal gaze on mine. "I don't like others touching what is mine," He hummed, looking over me. I swung my legs over the couch, planting them down onto the floor. Looking up at the man bent over me.

"I am not yours, Maaier. I belong to no one."

He sat down beside me slowly, his expression as gentle as a warm embrace as he looked upon me, weighing the depth of my words. I meant what I said. I was no one's to gift or give.

His lips tipped up slightly, approving whatever he saw within my expression.

"They still haven't found who attacked me." I rolled my head to face Maaier now reclining on the sofa, changing the matter of discussion.. His gloved fingers twirling a piece of my hair over his fingers. Lost in his own world.

"They won't find him," He grunted. Eyes still focused on a point at the ceiling.

I turned to face him fully. "Why not?"

"The police don't care what happens in this manor. They think that the bloodline deserves to dwindle away."

I snorted, shaking my head. "That is not the case."

"Isn't it?" He dropped my hair. "Then how come they didn't question you more? They took one statement and haven't been back. Unless another woman turns up dead in the same way. They won't pay you any attention." His voice, not full of malice, but more factual than anyone else has been with me. A quality I was growing to admire.

"So you mean to say I need to figure this out myself?"

"Yes. You will be the end of this."

"Can't I have any help at all?"

"No. They are after you, aren't they?"

"Why won't you help me? Aren't you my bodyguard or personal guard or whatever damned thing they labelled you as?"

"I am not allowed to interfere. I am only allowed to protect you. That is all," He said before leaving. His shoulders slumped as if somehow he was saddened. What did he mean he couldn't help? Wasn't my life more important than his rule? And who gave him that rule anyhow?

Chapter Twenty-Five

I was frustrated beyond belief. Why would this man not help me find who was trying to kill me but was more than willing to help me find love. The stupid fool. Both him and myself. I can't believe I let him touch me at all. If he wasn't so damn attractive I would have smacked that smirk off his face by now.

A loud bang threw my attention from the man beside me to the front door beyond.

"I hate this damned house!" Dorian screeched.

I hurried to her, throwing the library doors open excitedly. Catching sight of her cloak stuck to the door handle. Stifling a laugh, I helped her get free. Her curses made the giggle harder and harder to contain. Her eyes were a storm of emotions but only one rang clear, sobering me instantly. Fear. Pure fear ran rampant through my best friend. Without hesitation, I wove my arms around her. Drawing her close. She froze immediately. Just as she did when anyone touched her. She softened slowly before crumbling into my embrace, dropping the hefty suitcase from her grip

"I want to go home, Vessie, I do not want to stay here," She whispered, her plea piercing my heart.

"I know. You can soon. But I need you here with me for a while. Until all of this is sorted." I pulled her tighter. Feeling the rise and fall of her chest against mine. Her breath came in short as if pained by trying to hold back her emotion.

I pulled away after a long while when she had finally calmed down.

"You'll be in the room beside mine."

"No." Her voice was firmer than I had ever heard it.

I quirked a brow at her protest. Rolling my lips back to keep my words at bay.

"I need to be in your room. It isn't safe to be apart," She said. Her voice was determined. Demanding.

She had seen something. Something shifted in her, that much was obvious. What had she seen?

"Okay. Yeah, of course." I shook my head, hoping to dislodge some of the fear taking root already that she had planted.

Dorian brushed past me, her suitcases back in hand. Leaving me with the remaining few bags to carry up to my room.

"Your bed or should I call for a spare?" She shouted from up the stairs.

"Whatever you please." I called back.

"You cuddle up to me too much. Call for a spare." Her voice drifted as she made her way to my room.

I puffed out a breath of amusement. This was going to be a long few weeks.

AFTER ARTHUR AND MAAIER DRAGGED THE SPARE bed into the room, I sat on my bed and watched as Dorian made herself at home. The room was large enough to fit the two beds but that was about all. We had shifted mine beneath the window as Dorian had announced she hated the night. I had asked her since when, but she just shut down. Instead turning into the suitcases she piled on her bed. I tucked away my interrogation for later.

"You're only here for two months, Dorian. Until your mother goes to France and brings you along with her."

Dorian huffed but remained silent. Clearly unnerved by the thought of being here for two months let alone a day. Her eyes constantly flickering over every inch of the room. Making sure no ghosts or ghouls lined the corners. My own eyes rolled back in my head. I left her in peace.

How could a girl gifted by the paranormal be so afraid of the dark? I had long thought she was just scared of her own shadows but now my curiosity was getting the best of me. Would it be possible for her to see the ghosts too? Would she see my mother? Would she see any of the other Florians passed? Maybe I could test my theory.

I walked past each of the portraits in the halls. Looking at each Florian. Once a dynasty of great thinkers, now tainted with only murder and darkness. If only they could see what had become of their legacy. Grandmother still operated the trade of my grandfather's law firm under a false male name and it was sure to be passed down to me to handle. A gift I was willing to take on if needed from her. Even though I really didn't want to operate a law firm. If only I could survive that long. I had done well to push the attack to the back of my mind and not let it get to me. Only now, I wished I had embraced it ever so slightly, learnt more about the attacker rather than moving on. My body sagged.

There was one room in the house that had always been off limits. A room I had never dared enter. A single space filled with the grief and longing of lives lost too soon. I wandered back down the hall. To the room at the end just past Grandmother's. Her soft snores drifted from the open room. I tiptoed past the door, careful not to wake her. I shut her door softly before facing the lost room.

The paint work had chipped from the wood leaving an abandoned look to the room. The bronze doorknob tarnished with lack of use. So it was true. No one was allowed to touch the room. With a quick glance over my shoulder, I turned the knob. The door creaked like a squealing cat as it pushed open. My body froze. Straining my hearing for Grandmother's footsteps. Only to find her huff in her sleep and nothing more.

I slivered in between the cracks. Leaving the door only slightly open so I could get out when needed.

Light wisped its way through the room. The large back window reaching the ceiling lined with grime and mould. The smell of dust and mildew reeking in the air. Dust covered every surface, lining it like a thick blanket of snow. A room truly untouched in years.

My hands shook as I lifted my skirts. There was a single bed. Still made perfectly from the moment she left. Her night clothes folded neatly on the end of the bed like they always were. Memories of rushing in here in the morning to wake up my parents flooded through me. My eyes prickled with tears. My nose twitched with the onslaught. My heart clenched. God, I missed them. I wanted nothing more than to hold them both.

I walked to Mother's side of the bed. Looking down at her pillow. Golden vines embroidered into the white. Grandmother said the two sisters although only a year apart never dared to sleep in separate beds. They shared the same large bed until they were sixteen. When Magdelena passed, Mother was beside herself. She chose instead to sleep on the couch in the corner of the room. A couch where she still slept when nights were hard. Often curled up with me in her arms, sleepily reading a book on art. Her lips peppering my hair with adoring kisses. The couch still sat bare. Her art books litter the floor beside it. The room as untouched as the day she left the room to reside with my father in a room across the hall.

Thunder cracked outside the window. Causing a creak to run through the room. I shook the thought away. She was gone. She wasn't here.

The air began to turn cold. A frigid sensation swirling over my skin. I exhaled slowly. My breath began to fog out in front of me.

A breeze skittered across the floor. Dust swirling in its wake. I watched in horror as the breeze circled the bed. Leaving a trail of disturbance in its wake. The breeze suddenly stopped. Just at the foot of the bed.

My heart leapt into my throat. Now dry with the pent up scream building there. My tears fell from my eyes. I clenched them closed. Willing all my strength to aid me.

I moved forward slowly. Not wanting to anger anything. I made it to the end of the bed. Nothing. Not a single mark remained. The dust was back to its usual place as if I and the breeze were never here. My brow furrowed. Did I imagine it? Surely I wouldn't have. I lowered myself to the ground. Squatting over the place the breeze stopped. I ran my fingers through the dust. Although soft. It did not move. I tried again. Harder this time only to achieve the same result. As if I were never here.

"What on earth?" I muttered before slapping the ground trying to elicit anything from the cold hard floor. Nothing. Terror ran through me. Was I a ghost too?

I stood slowly. Keeping my gaze on the strange dust. How

curious. How could the dust not be disturbed by me? I was here. The spirits weren't.

A tiny glimpse of shadow caught my eye. I looked at the small mirror on the wall. My heart thudded. The looking glass perched just between a portrait of Magdelena on the left and Mother on the right. I stepped toward it, squinting to look harder. The shadow swayed once more. No bigger than a moth before disappearing. Another step forward. No more movement. I exhaled slowly, letting the scream dissolve in my throat. This was silly. Nothing was here.

I turned back to the bed. Only something seemed different. At the base stood a single set of footprints. Set and facing me. I stepped back. A hand flying to my throat. The footsteps mirrored. I stepped again. The footsteps followed. The sound like a clunk of machinery followed. I opened my mouth to scream. No sound came. The footsteps hurried forward. I blinked once. Bracing for the impact as my back met the wall. Freezing in terror. Nowhere left to go.

My breath fogged around me. I clenched my eyes closed. No more sounds came. I waited on baited breath. Timidly, I tore my eyes open to a blank room. The only sound was my blood rushing in my ears before a screech sounded. A woman with flaming light hair reached for me. Her skin melted off her skull. The stench of decay and burnt flesh burying itself in my nose. The woman's flame covered hands reached for me. I dashed for the door. A scream tearing through my throat.

The door slammed shut. My hands twisted against the knob. It wouldn't budge.

"Please!" I begged over and over again. My fists wrapping against the door. Desperate to get out. The woman twisted like a snake, her limbs moving like a spider. She stalked toward me. A wicked smile covering her burnt face.

"Help me!" I howled. Cowering against the door between

the archway and the wall. Tears falling through my cheeks onto my gown. Pure and utter terror turning my blood cold. A woman's voice called through the room. Gentle but firm. The burnt woman stopped her advance. I couldn't make out what the other woman was saying. The burnt woman hissed before turning to me. The flames receded slightly. The burns on her face slowly healed. Like a spider weaving its web. Milky skin sewing itself back together.

"Death will come for you, child," The now whole woman said as she tilted her head. Her dead eyes never left mine.

"No." I pleaded. My whole body trembled.

"Run, Vespera." The woman beyond called. I didn't wait to register the voice. The door swung open behind me and I took my chance. Sprinting through the opening and tumbling onto the floor. The door slammed shut. Shaking the entire manor. Tendrils of dust fell from the ceiling with the impact.

"What on God's green earth is going on over there!" Grandmother shouted as she drew near. I paid her no mind, rather sobbing into the floor. The entirety of my body still trembled with terror at the image of my aunt sewing herself together. The flames around her head dancing like snakes. I thought she was crushed to death out of the grounds. What was she doing trapped here? I convulsed on the floor with another sob. My body useless as emotions stormed through me.

"Oh my sweet winter child." Grandmother soothed as she dropped down before me. I curled into her embrace. Lifting myself into her arms.

"I'm sorry." I managed through sobs.

"I miss her too dear." She soothed. Her hand ran over my hair.

She didn't know. Grandmother had no clue who or what

lurked beyond the room. I pulled back. Looking into her misty grey eyes.

"I thought it would be too hard on the both of us to clean it out." She admitted softly.

I said nothing, gasping for breath. I looked over her arm covering my neck. My eyes met Maaier who stood just out of everyone's sight on the stairs. Victor's arm stretched out before Dorian as if silently holding both himself and her back.

Chapter Twenty-Six

Grandmother pulled me into her room. Shutting the door behind her. She called for tea from the maids before setting me on the dressing stool. The softness in her eyes was unmistakable. The grief still lingering there after all these years.

"I knew you would go in there sooner or later." She said softly. I avoided her gaze, looking at my hands twisted in my lap. The image of Magdelena's burnt ones twisting my stomach. "I just wish you had asked me to join you."

"I didn't want to bother you." I admitted. It was true in the sense that neither of us wanted to do it alone and had even said that when the time came, we would go in together. But I wasn't going to tell her why I went in alone. Not yet anyway.

"You never bother me." She playfully scolded. Her attempt at cheering me up did not go unnoticed. I couldn't bring myself to smile. I still felt the weight of trying to piece together the story of Magdelena I was told, versus what I just witnessed. Instead wiping away the mess on my face with my sleeve.

She frowned slightly before pulling a chair before me.

"When you are ready, we can clean it out. Together. Make use of the room for a happier purpose."

"And what purpose would that be?" My voice came out small. The words aching with every syllable from my torn throat.

"Arthur is going to offer your hand to Victor."

"No." I stiffened. Meeting her gaze. My face hardened, this can't be happening.

"No?"

I shook my head.

The old woman smiled before bursting into laughter.

"Oh how I wish you could see your face."

My cheeks heated. After all I had experienced today, this was the final straw. My anger rose to the surface.

"I am kidding, Vespera. Anyone with sense can see you do not see him in that way. I mean, you are yet to come to me with boasts of coloured sight aren't you?" Her wrinkled hands reached for mine in my lap. I let her take it. My anger faded with her gentle touch.

I swallowed hard.

"When you are ready, your colour will come. But for now, live your life. You have been given a second chance. Do what you must, but know that life is precious and fleeting. You as a Florian should know that. Don't get to my age and have your greatest achievement be your granddaughter before you. See the world. Eat cake in Paris, drink coffee in Rome. Steal bread and become a convict on that new land for all I care. Just make me proud."

I nodded sadly. Knowing I would never do any of those things. The end of my life was coming. I could feel it. I was waiting for it. The attacker would come back now Dorian was here. Or at least I hoped. If they could finally get rid of my existence, maybe they wouldn't hurt others. Maybe that would be enough for them. The Florian name would die with the woman who upheld it most. The greatest Florian there was.

I digested her words. Holding them close to my heart. She was always one to make light of any situation. Often serious toward others but a joker at heart. A woman I had long wished to resemble. But oftentimes I was told I was just like my father or my wild aunt. I shuddered at her memory. I could never look at fire the same.

Mary brought in the tray of tea, lingering by the door before offering a worried smile. I tried my best to convey that all was well but my smile fell flat. Grandmother noted the exchange but said nothing. Blowing air across the rim of her tea cup. Roses swirling through the elegant vining pattern on the porcelain. Her favourite china to date.

"If I die without seeing colour-"

"None of that." Grandmother cut me off with a stern look. "I will not bury another Florian child." Her brows rose with her forceful gaze. I kept my voice small. Agreeing with her. Did she know the reason Magdelena's body was never recovered was because she was burnt alive? Or was that just another illusion in my mind? I was starting to go absolutely mental. What was going on with me? Why was she able to lock me in the room and why did I freeze so completely like that?

Grandmother put down her tea, sighing loudly. Tearing me from my thoughts.

"I do think it is time to clean out the room though. But only when you are ready." Her grey brow rose as she waited for my response. As if warning me to not go in there alone again.

The grief in my chest expanded. It was the final step in saying goodbye to the legacy of my mother.

I could only nod. Soon it would be time but not now. Too many questions remained unanswered.

JASMINE STYLES

I RETURNED TO MY ROOM TO CHANGE FOR DINNER. Dorian's scent perfuming the air with hints of daisies and orange. The eerie feeling of being watched crept over my skin. I rolled my shoulders. Hoping to relieve some of the tension. The light of the bathroom was dim when I entered. The cool air tender against my face.

The water was cold as I splashed it over my face. Cleaning the feeling of ash from my appearance. My hands scrubbed at my skin. Pushing into my eyes. Images of the burning woman danced before me. Hot bile rose in my throat as I shook the image from my mind. Turning my focus onto my reflection in the mirror.

Despite feeling like a walking corpse, I looked better than ever. My usually sunken eyes were now vibrant and alive. My skin was still pale but my cheeks were no longer as hollow as they had once been.

My fingers shook slightly as I lifted them to my collar. Unbuttoning them one by one. The dark dress slipped open. I pushed it down over my shoulders. Tugging at the tight sleeves that stuck to my flesh. My chest was now on full display in the mirror. The grey scar stared back at me.

My fingers, still half covered by the sleeves, ghosted over before making contact. A flash of light hit my eyes but this time no vision came. Only the haunted ghostly words of my mother. "He is coming for her."

"No he isn't. You need to stop this Adele. You sound mad," Father responded. I turned to the empty room. Searching for the source of the voices.

"I'm not mad! Death may come for us all but he always favours a Florian."

"You talk about him as if he is real."

"He is! The man of night is Death himself. He can kill with a single touch. And he will come for her next."

The voices faded from the hall. I stepped out of the bathing room. Starting as I noticed myself, no older than eight years old, sitting with her back against the door. A rose clenched in her small fingertips. Tears rolled down her face as she sobbed into her knees. My feet carried me slowly to her. I knelt before myself. Willing her to look at me. My pasts' own sobs broke my heart.

They used to argue all the time and it was almost always over me. Endless fights echoing through the hall like ghosts. I watched as I lifted my head. Resting it against the door. My present self's eyes stinging. I couldn't recall this memory. The same thing happened multiple nights and the memories all blended into one. My hands trembled slightly as I reached for myself. My hand grazing my younger self's cheek, expecting to fall through once again only to make gente contact with her. The skin was warm on contact. Younger me sighed as I ran my thumbs over her cheeks. Clearing the tears.

"You're safe." I whispered. My voice drifted through the air like smoke. Younger me stilled.

"Death comes for you but you don't let him take you."

A smile brightened her face in my hands. A simple gesture. Words intended to calm not only her, but me too.

I watched in sadness as my younger self faded beneath me like mist. Growing fainter by the second. I wanted nothing more than to hold myself and tell her we made it through. That we survived that dreadful night. But it would be no use. I'm still as terrified of death now as I was as a child. As much as I had previously thought it was easier to die. To rid the world of my wasteful existence, lately that perception has changed. Something made me want to stay. But still wasn't overly sure what. Was it love? Was I finally craving the one thing I feared? The one thing that chilled me to my core. Or was it both? I would never know.

Footsteps echoed down the hall, drawing closer. Light but scurrying. Dorian was never one to take things slow. She loved the rush and wildness of life. Whereas I prefer to observe, to watch as things unfold and not be swept away into the swirl of chaos that is human life.

I walked back to my bed. Sitting down in the centre and turning to face the window just as Dorian pranced in.

"Vespera." She almost sung my name with excitement. This was new. Since when was she happy to be here?

"Yes?" I faced her with a confused expression. My brows rose with surprise.

"Your roses are looking marvellous this year."

I opened my mouth to question her but closed it. It was no use trying to question Dorian when she was in this state. Her eyes wide and pupils blown. She was in the midst of an episode. That much was certain.

"Victor showed me them. Your greenhouse seems to be put to good use." She smirked. Her slight body twisting as she stalked toward me. More feline than human.

I hunched slightly, bracing myself from whatever she was about to throw my way.

"Don't let the fire consume you, Vespera. The greenhouse may burn hot but you will burn brighter."

Fire. The word rolled around in my mind. The heaviness of it lingering.

"Dorian, listen to me." I said as I stood face to face. Keeping my posture as strong as I could as I held her shoulders. Her wild eyes darted all over the room. "Did you see my aunt?"

"Everywhere." She whispered. Her focus on the ceiling, eyes darting over every cornice.

"What is everywhere?"

"Your family." She tilted her head. Her gaze fell just below where I stood. "They have been watching for you."

An ice chill rolled down my spine.

"Dorian, who is watching for me?"

"The dark one is near." She breathed, her words almost illegible. "Coming... Unfinished... Angel...Martyr..." The words fell from her. Her body trembled as she watched whatever was behind me. The feeling of cold air flicked over my neck. I pulled Dorian close, wrapping my arms around her shoulders, rubbing small circles on the back of her light dress. Much too thin to be walking around outside in. A layer of damp lace caught between my fingers. I pulled her tighter. My chin resting on her shoulder. Her arms that hung limply by her side now slowly reached behind me. Wrapping them around me. Her grip tightening with the embrace. Dorian's breathing became ragged. As if she were running. In a way I supposed she was.

"I will lose you. In every way, I always lose you. I can't lose you. I need you. Please, Vespera. I need you to stay with me." Her voice grew husky. Warmth filled my eyes at the pain in her voice. The desperation in the tone. Longing and pleading for me to hear. My heart creaked inside of me. Collapsing in on itself. Her head burrowing into my neck. "Please don't leave me alone. It doesn't end the way we intend. We won't survive the night. We don't survive."

"Then we go together." I managed. My throat is thick.

"We can't. We can't go. You can't leave me. We won't survive."

I was lost for words. Her cry was near deafening as she

howled out her fear from her vision. The sound enough to rouse all in the manor spirits and all.

"Come back to me, Dori. I'm here." I tried to soothe. Willing my words to calm her. To offer any sort of comfort.

"You're here." She breathed heavily, her chest rising and falling rapidly against my own.

"Wherever you go, Dorian" I cupped her face. Forcing her to look at me through her watery eyes "I follow. I will never leave you."

She softened slightly.

"We are meant to be. The universe put us together for a reason. You are my sister. The other half of my soul, Dorian. I wouldn't give up on you that easily."

Dorian smiled slightly. My thumb brushed away her tears as she huffed in much needed air.

"I'm sorry," She said after a thick swallow. Her hands were still gripping my waist. "I know the visions aren't always right but this one felt too real." She avoided my gaze, dropping her hands by her sides.

"Then we will rewrite our future. One where we run off into fields of wildflowers and lie like old sisters." I smiled through the emotions storming inside me. Dorian managed a laugh. The sound was more strangled than anything. I took it gratefully.

"I think we best prepare for dinner and get you into something dry."

Dorian looked down at her dirt caked hands, a frown lining her forehead.

"I don't remember digging in the dirt," She muttered.

"No matter. Come." I took her dirty hand in mine, guiding her to the bathroom.

Chapter Twenty-Seven

As Dorian bathed, I pulled a dress from my wardrobe. Mary silently pushed into the room.

I held the silken dress out before me. The fabric was so light and gentle, like water in my hands.

"That isn't your usual style." Mary chuckled. Coming up beside me.

"No it isn't." I tilted my head before facing her, holding the garment out. "What colour would you call this?"

Mary looked taken aback by my question but answered anyway "Pink. A soft pink."

"Pink." I repeated. Letting the word roll over my tongue as I looked down at the light grey fabric. "Pink," I said once more. Willing the shade to memory. I placed the dress on Dorian's bed and moved back to the wardrobe.

"What about this?" I asked as I pulled my usual dress I favoured out with the high collar.

"Black," Mary said. Her confusion was still evident but I couldn't bring myself to tell her I couldn't see colour.

"And this?" I pointed to a darker gown that glimmered in the pale afternoon light.

"Blue. Like a very deep royal blue. Almost like an ocean." Mary smiled and stepped forward. Seeming to finally understand why I was asking. I silently thanked the world. "That colour is always very stunning on you."

"Is it now?" My lip quirked. "Then blue it is." I wondered how the colour would look. If it were a pretty colour or if it were downright foul. I trusted Mary however. Letting her guide me through a world I couldn't see. The thought of an ocean, a distant dream. I wondered how it would look. If it were truly as beautiful as Grandmother had said.

Dressed in the deep blue dress, I swirled my hair back and clipped it with an ornate pin. A metal rose glinting back amongst the dark waves.

Arm in arm with Dorian, who had been quiet ever since her bath, we entered the dining room. Each member of the manor sat watching as we approached. I took my seat beside Grandmother and Dorian beside me. The seat in front of me left empty with Victor to the right and Arthur down the end. The only person missing was Maaier. Although I wasn't overly sure I wanted him near right now. Emotions were still running rampant within me from earlier. For all I know I would put my hand in his during dinner. God, I was in over my head. I lifted my wine glass. The deep liquid swirling in the crystal.

The smile on my face lifted as I noticed Victor staring at Dorian. His cheeks flushed as he narrowed his gaze at her. She looked so beautiful in her gown. Her wild hair smoothed to match mine with the same style. She glared at him. Her stare was almost venomous. But Victor said nothing, instead choosing to sigh and begin a conversation with Arthur.

"That is a lovely shade." Grandmother piped up, her hand ran along the sleeve of my dress.

"Mary said blue suits me," I said with a smile.

Grandmother leant back as if slapped. Recoiling in shock

at my words.

"No, no. I can only see grey." I assured her.

Her hand landed on her heaving chest. Willing it to slow.

"Good God, child. You'll give me a heart attack one of these days." She rolled her eyes. Blinking the notion away.

I chucked to myself, sipping on my dark wine.

"It is interesting you asked for a colour though," Dorian whispered. Victor's gaze flicked back to Dorian as she spoke. His face was unreadable.

"I was curious was all." I offered a nonchalant shrug as I placed my linen napkin in my lap.

"You have been rather curious as of late," Grandmother said. Her voice stern but her expression light. Silly old woman. I rolled my eyes. Sighing through my nose.

"Maybe I am. I think I have lived in darkness too long and need to find my light."

"And your killer." Dorian offered over the rim of her glass.

"That too." I tapped my fingers against the glass. "No further word?" I said, changing the subject.

"No." Grandmother exhaled heavily. "But they did find another attack on a blonde woman in the square. She was stabbed in the abdomen. Though they aren't sure if she will survive the night."

"So each victim looks different from the last?"

"It seems that way. The police say the attacker's targets could be random but they always seem to go for a slight woman with either dark or light hair."

Dorian stilled. Her glass teetered on her bottom lip before lowering it back to the table.

"So I can go home?" She said softly.

"No. Donovan has requested you stay with us." Grandmother pressed.

Dorian huffed through her nose. The air caused the candles

in the centre of the table to flicker violently.

"The manor isn't so bad," Grandmother said. Keeping her chin tilted toward Dorian with pride.

"The ghosts are though," Dorian sneered. Her gaze fell on me.

I remained silent and shook my head. Pretending to be more interested in the napkin covering my lap.

The staff came with a plate of food each. Each dinner consisted of three main courses and dessert. The first tonight was a simple soup. Chunks of assorted vegetables floated on the top of the murky liquid. My stomach churned. I hated peas. Yet here they were floating in my dinner. I withheld my scowl. Not wanting to be rude but still moving them away anyway. Disgusting little demons.

Dorian giggled beside me. Noting my disdain for the small bean. Little did she know that we were having lemon tart for dessert. A flavour she hated. I rolled my lips into my mouth to suppress a smile. Lifting the spoon of soup to my mouth, my heart stopped.

"I apologise for my tardiness. I had some matters to attend to." Maaier stood in the doorway. His coat was an almost identical shade to my dress. I froze. Watching as he approached to sit before me.

Dorian's attention fully transfixed on Arthur and Victor's conversion of how medicines seem to be depleting from pharmacies. Grandmother sat whispering in the ear of a server. No doubt demanding a soup for Maaier who looked like he would prefer to be anywhere else but here. His dark gaze flicked over me. Lingering on my partially exposed chest and the scar peaking through. A slight tilt of his lips was the only indication of mood. I stifled a sigh with my wine and turned to Dorian who was still solely focused on Victor. Listening and absorbing like a rag in a puddle.

The servers returned to clear our bowls and place a new plate of more vegetables and duck on the plate. My stomach roiled. I couldn't stand duck either. I shuddered at the thought of it. And here it was on my plate. A gag rose in my throat. At least it was better than peas I supposed.

Maaier shifted in his seat, watching with amusement at my disgust.

Dorian finally twisted beside me. A hiss between her teeth louder than a gunshot. Her hands clenched on the dark wood of the table. Clawing her manicured fingers into the varnish. I whispered her name but her lethal gaze was aimed directly on Maaier. Her eyes were dark and wide like a beast about to hunt their prey.

"You," She hissed, her shoulders rolling back. She stood abruptly as if spotting Maaier for the first time since arriving. Her chair fell back to the floor with a loud thud. I took her hand, trying to pull her back down as a server fixed her chair once more.

"You are the cause of this. The root of our end." Her words like lead fell on the table. No one made a sound apart from Dorian's ragged breathing. Her chest rising and falling. Her nails still cracked and dug into the wood.

Quick as a flash of lightning, she swept up her dinner knife. Holding it before her. "The root of our end." She repeated in a hiss through gritted teeth.

"Dorian." I pleaded. But it was too late. She had leapt onto the table. The candle between Maaier and I knocked over. Hot wax flying through the tense air. Dorian's rage was palpable between the air. The wax stung as it hit my chest. Burning into the flesh of my scar and above. Splattering like blood over my exposed skin. I shriek at the impact. The skin sizzled as it hit. Dorian paid it no mind. Her body collided with Maaier who had risen to catch her. She pulled them both to the ground. Her fists beating into any part of him she could. Bloodlust in her screams and she called for his end. He didn't fight back. Instead letting her punish him for a crime he was yet to commit.

Victor stood first, I followed. Rushing around the table to pull my maddened friend from the strange man who made my heart ache.

Victor's hands wrapped around her waist. Pulling her back with a strong tug. His face twisting with the exertion. Dorian screeched like a banshee as she lost contact. Blood dribbled from Maaier's lips but he remained still, not uttering a single word. His gaze focused only on Dorian. I bent beside him. Kneeling on the ground as I took count of the scratches maring his neck and chest. His shirt now torn open and bloody. The knife was lost in the attack.

I cursed. Looking at the welts on his face.

"Don't touch him, Vespera. His touch kills. He will kill you. He is our end!" Dorian shrieked over and over again. My hands shook slightly as I lifted it to Maaier. The palm of my hand met his cheek softly as I swept the hair from his forehead. A sharp pain flashed in his eyes. What was happening? I looked down at him. Noting the grey skin still showing. Nothing I hadn't witnessed before, but the wound had my blood turning to ice. My heart galloped into my throat. His voice was raw as he said my name. I couldn't focus on anything anyone was saying. Their words but a buzz in my ear.

The wound shone through the bleak expanse of my vision. A red so pure it took my breath away. I gasped in horror.

It was him. It was Maaier I was drawn too. Maaier was the source of my colour. Could it be true? Surely not. Not him. Love was supposed to blind you to all the darkness in the world. It was supposed to bring you light and make you whole. It wasn't supposed to torment you and make you question things. It was meant to help a person become whole no matter how broken they were. Even a person loving themselves could very well do the same. But it was love that evaded me. I was always broken. Maaier couldn't be the one to fix me. He simply couldn't.

My heart threatened to come out of my throat. His voice low as he said my name again. The only voice strong enough to break through. I couldn't let him know. But something in his concerned gaze told me he already knew too. That this wasn't an accident. That fate had finally intervened.

His gloved hand reached up to cup mine. Gently removing it from him. I swallowed my heart before opening my mouth only to close it.

Grandmother's voice shone through my haze of fear. "Get the girls to bed. Victor, attend to Maaier."

Victor hesitated beside Dorian. Not wanting to go near him after her warning.

"I am fine, Sophia." Maaier sat up. Pushing away from me and avoiding my gaze with his back to me. "I will retire for the night." Rejection rolled over me.

Words fell back from my tongue. There was nothing else to say. I needed to find out more. To learn more about him. To find out why I only saw red when I was with him. Maybe he wasn't the one after all.

Dorian fell into bed as we arrived in my room. Neither of us spoke about her outburst.

It was obvious Maaier was the cause of our situation but how? He should have killed us both by now if he was the attacker. Not letting us roam free. As if it were some sick twisted game to him. Maybe that was why he kept us alive.

The sound of Dorian's gentle snores sounded lightly. Moonlight shone through the open blinds.

Striking a match, I lit my oil lantern beside the bed and pulled the one thing to distract me free. The magical book with faded pages.

The words bled onto the empty page like ink to water. Blossoming like a young flower in spring. Slowly unfurling for all to admire.

"Death doesn't know his destiny. Not yet anyway. He only knew his mother and the love they shared. Everyday the same warm bliss emitted from the pair, days of dancing in flowers and fighting with wooden swords. He would watch his mother with fond love. She taught him how to love kindly and to be loved in return. It was a blissful yet captivating upbringing. She had shielded the boy from all the rot in the world. Waiting until he was asleep to invite strange men into the alley beside the house and sell her body as wares. Her beauty always fetched a price. Men would flock to her. Hoping to be chosen as her flavour for the night. Until the moon went behind the clouds that fateful night. Her son, only sixteen in his bed inside the small home. Sleeping away his day of work at a bakery. Dreaming of a young daughter of a lord. Her hair dark as ink. Always dotted in flower petals. The dream of her always the same. The same

words dropped from her mouth. A declaration of love. The sweetest purest kind of love there was. Young love. A love the boy could only hope for. The woman in the dream faded as his mother screamed. The boy shot up and immediately was out the door. Finding his mother's bed cold and empty. He hurried to the door to outside. The scent of metal heavy in the air. His mother was laying in the street outside. The woman who taught him the sweetest gift the world had to offer now taught him the most valuable lesson. Love could kill you just as much as it could heal you. The boy's torn scream ripped through the night air. His soul tearing to shreds. Tears dripped from his face onto the body of his mother, cooling in the night air. Blood streaming from her throat into the cobblestones below. The crimson mixed with the dirt and grime. People watched from their windows but no one approached. They feared for the boy. And what he would do. For the entirety of the town knew the love they had shared. The love in the boy's soul, now consumed by fire. A vengeance that would never be put out. An inferno that burned brighter than the town had ever seen and would burn them all down to the ground. Every last one until his blade was buried in the neck of he who took his mother from him."

My eyes pooled with stinging heat as I read the words. The poor soul. The image of the boy holding his mother so close to his chest. Her arm dangling limply by her side as he cradled her head to his chest. The detail in his face showed the heartbroken and shattered expression on his face. More ink flooded the next page. Urging me to read on.

"The young man now full with vengeance hunted through the night. His soul darkened as he tore through men. Asking anyone for information on the attacker for a slice of fresh bread. He was good with his hands. A skill many men lacked. A gentleness that came in handy as he sliced through the flesh of his suspects. Although, now blood coated his hands rather than the icing of a cake. The man grew each year into a man without love. His young love, lost. Although unknown to him, she waited for him. In a dark room of her family's manor near the woods. She would wait by the window, gazing down to the garden where he would wait for her night after night. As he was as sneaky as his mother. He would prowl like a fox through the roses as she waited. Eager to see him and run into the woods together to share a gentle kiss. Her name is one of darkness. Her name, a caress to his broken soul but he would never return to her. He couldn't bring himself back to her. The only tell of his remaining humanity. But she waited. Praying to every god of his return. But he never did. Night after night she waited. Until she could wait no more. She longed for a life filled with children and love. A love that *she had watched form the shadows that her lover and his mother had shared. The love of a mother loving her child more than anything in the world. A love that would cause her to burn the world for him and he in return.*

The woman watched that final night before finding a new love. A man just like her sweet soul. An artist who would paint her each shade he could find. Her skin littered with his paintings of flowers. Each shade a vibrant masterpiece on her pale flesh. The love within her growing as vibrant as the paint for her artist lover."

The sketch appeared on the next page. A woman drawn so beautifully came to life on the page. Her skin, decorated in all types of blooms. Roses, lavender, iris and peonies dotted her chest. Wildflowers wrapped around her stomach. Her bare body was covered in art. Each bloom detailed with talent. Whoever this woman was, she was blessed with the love of the artist.

I settled back on the bed holding the book close as the words faded. Enough tragedy told for the night. The memory of Dorian's words echoing in my mind. *He will be our end.*

Was Maaier the attacker from the story or was he the boy who lost his mother? Surely he was the attacker. Maaier never radiated the essence of a man to love. Only a man to hold power. Or so I had thought. The concern in his eyes surfaced to my memory. I huffed out a sigh before falling back on the pillows.

The moonlight, my only comfort amongst my twisted thoughts. It was too early to sleep.

Chapter Twenty-Eight

The door creaked as I pushed it open. Maaier sat on a stool just outside the door frame. A book in one hand and an oil lamp in another.

"It is a bit late for a midnight rendezvous, is it not?" He said without taking his eyes from the page before him. I couldn't make out the words garnering his attention.

"I couldn't sleep. I was hoping you would assist me to the greenhouse?"

"At this time? Absolutely not." He cocked his chin, as if this were the final argument.

With a roll of my eyes, I stepped past him, heading down the hall. My name a hissed whisper behind me followed by a curse. Maaier trailed me down the stairs, silently fuming at the interruption of his night.

Stepping into the greenhouse was like a welcome home. The only place I felt peace. The place where I had learned to grow. To love.

"You are the death of me," Maaier grunted as he followed me through. Lighting lanterns with his candle as he went.

"Not yet. But maybe someday." I threw over my shoulder

before ducking through the plant life growing around me. I weaved through the pots and benches until I came to the one Maaier had lifted me on what felt like years ago. A rose bush placed in the centre. My face twisted with confusion. This wasn't here before. The last plant I had left here was a petunia seedling.

How very peculiar. Shaking off the strange altercation, I pushed the bush back to where it was supposed to be. A single petal falling from a bloom. I watched as it floated down ever so softly onto the bench.

"What do you plan to do?" Maaier drawled, coming up beside me to cock his hip against the bench.

"I just needed to find some normalcy."

I worked in silence. Maaier watched as I darted around checking on my greenery, following my every step with his lantern.

"Have they any more evidence as to the attacks?" I asked over my shoulder. Maaier shook his head with a frown. Hope faded within me. We were already losing time. If only I could remember any small detail of who it was that fateful night in the halls lurking with death.

"So tell me. Why greenery?" Maaier broke the beat of silence.

I turned to face him with a slow hum. My bottom lip still caught between my teeth from my concentration on sheering. Maaier breathed out a laugh before continuing.

"Why greenery?" He said again.

"It reminds me of a simpler time," I said with a sigh, memories of my father floating back through my mind. I kept my eyes on the bush as I continued "A time where I wasn't just a cursed woman wandering around waiting for someone to attack her or her friends again. A time where I was just Vespera Florian. A girl who couldn't see in colour but never wanted to. A girl who thought the love of her family was enough."

The confession weighed down my chest as if a pile of stones had lodged themselves in its cavity.

"You never wanted to see in colour?" He said softly.

I shook my head. "I didn't see the need to."

"Colour is but the very beauty of life, Vespera. I thought you would want to experience that."

"Colour is not everything. There is beauty in the darkness and shades of grey. Sometimes the most beautiful things in life come from the darkness. We shouldn't hold faith in beauty and frivolous things. My sight may be one of grey, but that doesnt mean I have not lived the most beautiful existence or longed for anything more. I have learnt to be content with myself and that in itself is a beautiful thing."

Maaier stepped toward me, pulling the sheers from my hands. Slowly, I faced him. My eyes met his as if seeing them up close for the very first time. The dark expanse glistened in the pale light, our breaths mingling as he leaned in closer. My heart fluttered like a bird in my chest.

"You are the most beautiful thing to walk this earth, my bloom. If not just from your being but from your soul." His voice was low, eyes darting down to where my tongue darted out to wet my lips. He was inches away yet I craved him closer.

Maaier's gloved hand reached up ever so slowly. Taking my cheek in his grasp, his thumb smoothed over my skin. Slowly my own hand reached up, sliding over where his pressed into my cheek. I tilted my head into his grasp, holding him close to me.

"You look like you have a million different questions." He smiled.

"You know me too well."

He pulled me slightly closer. "I know you better than

anyone, Vespera. I think it is only fair that you come to know me."

"I think that would be lovely."

"You would love my home back north," He breathed "endless fields of flowers and greenery. Space for you to grow and frolic as you please." His eyes slid shut, his thoughts a million miles away.

"Would I be safe there?"

Maaier smiled once again. "You will always be safe with me. I can assure you of that." He smiled, eyes meeting mine again.

"How can I trust you?" I said as his thumb swiped over my skin once more.

"I believe your soul knows mine, Vespera." His words were barely above a whisper.

My heart thundered in my chest.

Maaier's lips drew closer once more. This time dangerously close to mine.

"Perhaps mine knows yours too."

Within an instant Maaier's lips brushed mine. Slowly at first. Gentle and timid before growing more passionate. His hands cradling my face drifted to my neck, one slowly cupping the small of my back to press me closer to him. He tasted of heaven, of sweetness and warmth. His hands snaked their way over my back, pulling me as if I could somehow be closer to him. Our bodies pressed together. Hands in each other's hair. Learning the feel and sway of the other. The moment was bliss. Pure and utter bliss.

Maaier pulled back slowly, his breath strained. "Keep your eyes closed." He managed through broken breaths. My chest heaved under my cloak.

I did as he asked, listening for what he planned next. All I wanted was his lips on mine once more. My fingers twitched at my sides, desperate for another feel of him against me. A fire inside me undimmed.

A slip of cloth fell over my face. I remained still as Maaier fastened it over my eyes.

"You must keep this on." He ordered softly, I opened my mouth to protest only to have his lips on mine again. A small moan escaped me, my hands digging into his hard shoulders. He pulled back once more. Only to hoist me into his hold with one hand under my knee and the other under my back. The only sound made was his breaths as he extinguished each lantern.

Chapter Twenty-Nine

"Lady Vespera!" Mary's sweet voice called out. My eyes fluttered open. Why couldn't I see? Had the curse morphed into me being fully blind? Trust my wretched luck.

Gentle hands tugged at the silk on my face, pulling it down.

Harsh light pinning through my eyes like needles. I winced at the intrusion. After our brief moment of intimacy, Maaier had led me back to the room with the blindfold still in place. Urging me to keep it on without further explanation.

"Are you alright?" She said softly. I fumbled for a lie. Hoping Maaier wouldn't be disappointed in me. I told her the ribbon helped me sleep a little better when it was completely dark. Mary accepted my lie easily. Believing that I needed darker shade to sleep and not an open curtain with the night shining through.

She bustled around me. Pulling a dress from the closet.

I sat up. My fingers brushing against something soft on my left. A scrap of paper laid bare.

I hope you enjoyed your brush with Death. We will meet

again soon. My throat tightened at the words. A threat. I was going to be attacked again. I crumpled the note in my fist. Looking down at where it was first laid. The words written in the same handwriting as the book of death.

I shifted the blanket. The dark stem of a rose peaked out of the fabric sheets. I pulled it out. Careful of the thorns. The bloom came free. Beautiful in the morning light. The colour blooming against the white sheets. A red so sure I knew I wasn't dreaming. My heart leapt to life.

"Vespera?" Mary's voice grew distant as my heart thundered in my ears.

A grin widened over my face.

Dorian sat against her bedhead. Gazing at her hands still dotted with Maaier's blood. Confusion lining her features.

"Is Grandmother awake?" I beamed despite her tense mood lingering in the air. Mary was startled at my sudden expression.

"She is in the back garden." She cocked a brow but said nothing further.

"Do you really want to know about the curse? Such a dark topic for such a beautiful day." The old woman smiled. I looked at the garden. A thin layer of snow covered the lawn. A frown covered my face. She was losing her mind the older she got.

I sat beside her on the bench, fixing a woollen blanket over her legs.

"You know all about the curse already." She hugged herself tighter. An expression of annoyance lining her face. Dark circles lined her sagging under eyes.

"I know but has there ever been a record of colour slowly fading in rather than all at once?"

"Why do you ask?" She raised a brow. Eyes scanning my face.

"I was just curious as to what it would be like when I find my love." Wasn't exactly a lie. My mind had been wandering more often to that instance.

"No. The colour comes as a wave. Like a wave crashing on a dark shore. At least it did for me. Your mother was the same," She sighed, turning back to the garden. Clearly not believing a word I said.

"I knew my colour was coming the moment I laid eyes on your grandfather."

I smiled, taking her hand in mine as she spoke. The tale, though told a million times over, still warmed my heart each and every time.

Snow fell lightly on the lawn.

"Your great aunt Agatha never found her colour. Never wanted to either. You remind me of her sometimes." She tilted her head at me, plucking a stray thread in the blanket free.

"Really?"

"She was the only one to be born a twin along with my mother in the whole of our bloodline." Grandmother smiled, lost in the memory of her parentage. I focused my gaze back on the lawn covered in a coating of powdery snow.

"How did it all come about?" I asked. Keeping my voice soft. "Mother never told me." I added. She was forewarned of the curse before she conceived but never expanded on how it came about to me.

"Six generations ago, Lizbeth Florian was said to have met a man who fell madly in love with her. He pursued her for months. Showering her in gifts and affection. Only to find out she was courting another man. Lizbeth had kept it hidden. For months she assured him that there was no other man. Until one night she found the man she was truly in love with dead in his bed. His skin was void of colour. She looked around only to find that she could see no colour at all. The man who had fallen madly in love with her appeared from the shadows and told Lizbeth that he had taken her colour and cursed her and each of her female descendants to bear the same effect. So they could see the world as he did. He warned that only when they find their love can they have their sight back.. That he took away her ability to see the beauty of the world just as she had taken it from him."

I listened intently to the tale Grandmother told. Drinking in the information. A million more questions swirled through my mind, weighing heavily on my tongue.

A tremor ran through her. The cool breeze ghosted over her skin. Without a single word she stood, pressed her lips to my forehead and went back inside the manor.

Leaving me with the questions swirling and a million more forming.

I LONGED FOR THE BOOK TO SHOW ME MORE. To teach me about death and what to prepare for. Seeing as both Death and Maaier were showing me red, I needed to determine which one was the correct one and the other half of my dark soul.

I lay on the library floor, staring at the painted ceiling. Boredom seeking out in the early afternoon.

Rolling my head as Dorian and Victor entered, I flashed them my widest smile.

"You truly have gone mad," She sighed before laying beside me. Stretching out so our heads touched, our bodies forming a triangle. A bubble of laughter left me.

"Not as mad as you." Victor teased, laying on my other side. His head touched both of ours.

"You must be pretty mad yourself, daisy boy," Dorian said with an amused snort.

"Yes, well I suppose that it is true," He noted. "But being around you two makes me seem like the most normal lad there ever was."

I laughed deeply. Dorian herself cackled at the statement.

"We are said to be the most mad people in all of England," I said through my giggles.

Dorian barked out a laugh once more. "Remember that time old man Ronald chased us down to the docks because you coughed in his store and they thought you were speaking a curse?" She said with a wheeze. Victor joined the laughter, his laugh like sunshine.

"Oh that man hated me! Completely believed I was the devil at ten years old."

"Were you?" Victor chuckled.

"Oh yes. I was a terror." I turned to him.

Dorian's hands met my head. "Bullshit! You used to make me do the dirty work and you would run.

"I did not!"

"Yes you did. Remember when you said you wanted that candy from Madame Peters but you thought she would eat you so you convinced me to steal it for you? My bottom hurt for a week after that caning!"

"That was one time!" I laughed.

Dorian sat up, looking down at us both as she rattled off names of all those I supposedly forced her to terrorise. Victor was in a fit of laughter by the end of Dorian's tale of how we stole a plant and brought it back to her father's only to find it poisonous so we told the man we found it in the middle of the street when we returned it and told him a stray dog had stolen it too. The old man was so confused as to why two eight year olds were stealing his plant. From a church nonetheless.

Footsteps sounded outside the open doors. I didn't have to look to notice the shuffling foot falls.

"I had to convince that priest for an hour that you weren't possessed by a demon after that incident," Grandmother said as she passed. The three of us fell back laughing. My stomach and cheeks ached with the exertion. I hadn't laughed this hard in a long time. I don't think I had ever laughed like that prior.

"Alright, I guess I was the instigator," I said as Dorian resumed her spot beside me.

A comfortable silence fell between us. The afternoon sun was beginning to creep in, illuminating Victor where he faced the window feet first.

"Tell us about you, Daisy. How much of a terror were you?"

Victor huffed out a laugh.

"I wasn't a terror. I was the one sweeping the pews when you two came in with the pot plant."

I roared with laughter at his words.

"Were you really?" Dorian said, her tone genuinely curious.

"Sure was," He sighed. Not going any further. Dorian didn't push, knowing full well it would spoil the mood.

"If you stepped foot in a church, Dori, I think it would burn down."

Her small hand swatted my side as she reached for me.

"Says you, demon child!"

I grinned whilst the silence settled in, just three friends

enjoying each other's company. Something I had never thought I would be able to see.

"Do you remember when you threw paint on old man Ronald's horse and told him it was magic?"

Chapter Thirty

The portraits shimmered in the dim light. Their paint glistened like stars shining in the glow of the lantern.

Dinner had passed easily enough. This time with no outburst from Dorian and no Maaier in sight. Who now was devouring the book Maaier had given me to search for any information on him. She was scratching notes on parchment as her eyes darted across the page. The library was alive once again.

I had left my book on human anatomy on my couch. Instead, I headed up the stairs to read my strange book in private. As I made my way up the stairs. The door to my mother's room creaked. A gust of cold air filling out.

Against my better judgement, I crept toward it. Needing to know what lies beyond tonight. The sound of my name being called like a gentle kiss. My pulse thundered in my chest.

The anatomy book had said that the burns from a fire could be just as deadly if infected as the fire itself. Something that I was certain elena didn't have to worry about.

The air was dense as I walked into the room. The dust undisturbed by my foot prints padding into the room. The smell of mildew and decay filled my nose. The damp mist swirled around me.

My name still whispered sweetly on the air.

Licking my lips, I said my aunt's name. A woman I had never met before. I just hoped it really wasn't the flaming woman after all.

"Such a strange child." A sweet almost innocent voice cooed from behind me. I stilled. The cold air, immediately, biting into my exposed shoulders. Footsteps creaked as the woman moved around me. Coming up to a stop on my left side. A ghostly hand reaching out. Long delicate fingers running down my arm. The ghostly touch felt so real against my skin almost as if she was not a ghost at all.

"So pale. So pretty," She whispered as she made her way around me. My hair twisting through her near translucent fingers. She admired it, deep eyes transfixed by the locks. Her own twisted back off her face. A long burn covering the majority of the right side. I dared to glance down. Noticing that the burn actually covered most of her body. Tight skin marred with scars and welts. Melted and fused together flesh on full display from her soft nightgown.

"So very Florian." She grinned. Her smile was approving but her eyes shocked me. Flames danced before them.

"I was also a Florian before they got me," She sneered. The flames in her eyes grew brighter.

"You still are." I croaked, my voice hoarse. The smell of smoke thickened the air.

"I was a mark on the family name," She hissed. The flames now snaked from the corners of her eyes to her hair. Dancing like streams of ribbon to the knot twisted at the back.

"You never were." I pressed. The light of the lantern flickered.

"You know nothing. You were but a mere dream when I

was taken." Her anger radiated with her flames. The hair was now falling in hot waves around her. Each strand was alive in its own way.

"Taken in the night. Whisked away by a suitor. Someone who wanted me for once. Not Adele." Her once beautiful face contorted. "So much like her, you are. Poor little Vespera. All alone in this big old dark manor. Scared of her own shadow." She stepped forward. Our chests were almost touching. The stench of burning flesh hit my nose.

"You should have died. He came for you. Just like he did me. I waited so long for you to join me in this hell scape. But you didn't." Her teeth bared as she spoke. I willed myself to stay strong watching as the fiery eyes devoured me whole.

"You couldn't dare to let go of this dark life. A life of grey. How utterly pathetic." She twisted around me once more. Her hands reached for my right arm. Rough as she admired the skin. Smooth and unmarked. Her disgust was evident on her face. Her lip curled.

"He stole me and stole my colour. He stole yours too. But Death seemed to pity you." Her flames died down. Sinking back into her eyes. I dared to breathe. She tracked the movement like a bloodhound.

"He never pitied me. Certain that Adele was his. That she was the one he desired. It should have been her. But instead, it is you." She smiled softly. Turning my hand over in hers. Her fingers tracing the lines of my palm. "Such young beautiful skin. Such an old soul. You are not like the rest of us."

My heart thudded in my ears. What was she on about? Was this woman mad?

"Am I not?" I managed, my voice hoarse from smoke.

"No." She grinned wickedly before spinning behind me. Her hands rested on my shoulders before guiding me to the mirror. "You are more."

I swallowed my fear. Looking at her in the mirror. Her reflection was mesmerising. A memory of who she was before death. Her skin, so alive and plump. Her smile was dazzling. She rested her head on my shoulder.

"I would have liked you, niece. We would have had so many fun adventures." Her face fell slightly. Her bottom lip pouted.

"I like you," I said, trying to keep her mood positive. Having seen what anger and distress made her.

"You do not know me," She said sadly. "Death has only just granted you the ability to see me." Her eyes fell to my hand reaching for hers under her chin.

"What did they do to you?" I dared to ask.

Anger crackled in her eyes before receding. My breath hitched. The flames pulsing alight to fade.

"He thought I was a witch." She sighed. Her fingers moved to my hair as her chin dug into me. I paid it no mind.

"I was taken in a carriage in the dead of night. I don't know how it crashed but I tried to run. Only for them to find me." She rolled her lips together.

"What did they do to you?"

Her lip curled. The fire caught once more.

"They beat me. Abused my body in every way they could. Every one of them before disposing of me like flesh not soul. They burnt me alive. Laughed as I screamed in the flames." Her voice grew deep. I relished in her anger. Feeling it warm the part of my soul that still feels like Death's cold hand. What a horrible death.

"I am sorry that happened."

"I've seen them since. They all met their match. Death may come for Florian's but it is us he protects in the afterlife." I met her eyes. Her smile was mischievous. This seventeen year old woman was still so full of life even now stuck in the manor. It was no wonder she was mad.

"Death lingers here even now," She said softly as her hand drifted to my scar.

I gulped back my fear. What was she going to do? I spun back to face her. Her burnt skin was almost startling.

"Will you kill him for me?" She tilted her head. Resting it against mine.

"Who?"

"The man who took me."

"Who was he?" I urged. Her smile widened into a wicked grin. I didn't hear the footsteps down the hall until it was too late. Victor walked into the room. Watching in silence as I stood rooted to the spot. Magdelena straightened. Giggling as she turned to Victor. My eyes widened. No. No. She couldn't touch him. Victor shuddered. The cold seeped into his skin as she neared.

"No," I said finally. Magdelena turned. Her glare was like poison. She huffed before stalking back to the bed.

"Victor, you need to leave."

"I came to check on you but Dorian said you were playing with things you have no right to." I stifled an eye roll. Of course she knew what I was doing.

"I came to look for my mother's locket." I lied.

"Death has it." Magdelena bubbled. Kicking her legs as she admired Victor. Her playful youth made me hold back a smile. Definitely mad.

"Can I help you search at all?" He offered. His worry sent a dagger through my heart.

I shook my head. "No. It is not in here."

He frowned before offering his hand. I took it gently. Heading toward the door Magdelena giggled once more.

"Your biggest mistake will be choosing him. Death doesn't like a Florian sworn to another."

Her words cemented inside me. I stilled.

The story of Death and the painted woman coming to life in my mind. Grandmother's tale of the curse matching the story almost in my mind.

I dropped Victor's hand. Instead I ran to my room with him calling my name behind me.

Chapter Thirty-One

I flew into the bedroom. My mind was wild with possibilities. I dove for my bed, pulling the book up from its hiding spot. Victor's footsteps hurried through the hall.

"I am fine, Victor." I urged as my fingers met the spine. I plucked it free of the hole it was in and moved forward. Opening the book to the page, the ink swirled like water before settling into the story.

"The young man who hunted in the night like a hound for blood was not one for niceties. Instead choosing to remain celibate instead of finding interest in another woman. He had only ever loved her. Each night his blade met another man's flesh but he always only saw one face. The artist. The man who took his love from him. The loveless one thrived in the dark. He had said it matched his soul. He was tainted. The blood from his victims

mixed with his own each time he fought. It wasn't until his twenty sixth birthday that the man realised he wasn't truly invincible. That he was still in fact a human. He had been walking the halls through the manor. Not wanting another to see him as he snuck into her room once more. He had heard chatter of her growing ill but he needed to see it with his own eyes. Only he didn't find her ill. He found her well. Curled up in the bed with a bouquet of flowers beside her. Dozing softly. He stalked forward. Noting too late that they were not alone. A man darted out of the shadows with a blade. The sharp knife raced toward his love in the bed. Still unaware of what was happening. Despite the darkness in his soul, he knew he had no choice. He could not save his mother but he could save the woman he loved. The man hurried forward. Instead throwing himself in front of the knife as it came down. His throat burned as it made contact, but only for a second as the man met the same fate as his mother."

The sketch came to life on the page. The young man laying over his lost love with blood maring the sheets. The ink continued.

"The morgue is a cold and tired place. No one alive wants to visit and the dead long to leave. But the young man was pitied. A God of Death

watching him from afar. Never interjecting or interfering, only watching just as the boy's mother had requested. He was the one to carry her soul off after all. The man cloaked in black looked over the man's body. Still fresh from death. His skin was lifeless. The god watched as his skin healed when his hand met the man's chest. The warmth slowly came back to him. The god grinned wickedly before leaving in a cloud of smoke.

    The smoke flew all the way to London. To look for an artist with a pretty blonde in his sheets. Paint dotting her skin just as his young love at home washed the stain from hers. The god grabbed him before he could make a sound. Carting him back to the old manor. He discarded the artist's corpse in the maiden's bed. Leaving him there for her to find whilst he lingered in the corner. Waiting for her like a wolf to a lamb. Aching for her scream.

    She entered slowly. Saying his name as she noticed him. Her scream was a delight as she looked upon his contorted face. The woman howled in sorrow. Throwing herself upon the man now in the same position as the loveless man was only hours before. The god peeled himself from his perch. His shadowed hand reached for the woman. His hands covered her eyes. When he removed it, her world was dark. Void of colour. Void of the beauty she found with her artist.

She screamed and screamed for the god to have mercy and to give it back. The god hated her for the pain she had caused his loveless friend. For making him hunt in the night so that she may never feel that same fate of his mother. The god cursed not only her but the babe in her belly and each daughter after. Cursing them to never know colour until they meet their truest love. Until they accept their life and not waste their love on a man who needs it most only to rip it from him. They were cursed to not see beauty, to not see anything worthy of the title until they found what the loveless man once called the most beautiful thing in the world. The god left the woman to find the young man once more now awakening in the morgue. To teach him of his new role. To help guide him back to the light, to find beauty in a soul. To find love once more."

This time the sketch was softer. Less pronounced as if aged over the years. The woman held her partner whilst the cloaked man held out a finger to her. Cursing her. Cursing Lisbeth Florian and each of us after.

My body trembled as I looked at the sketch of my ancestor. So twisted with heartbreak over her artist. A life ahead of her without colour. A lifetime of curses to hand down. Six generations of torture.

"Why are you staring at a blank book?" Victor quirked a brow. Having sat beside me on my bed without my notice. The silver lining my eyes fell as I leant into him.

"It isn't blank to me," I whispered. His warm scent filled my nose.

His hand wrapped back around my waist, holding me tighter to him as I remained like stone. Staring at my ancestor drawn so perfectly on the page. His warmth stuck to my side. Warming my cold heart that was dropping the longer I looked at the twisted image,

"I apologise." Maaier's deep silken voice grumbled from the doorway. I peeled myself from Victor, looking over at him from his shoulder.

"I should probably go check on Dorian," He muttered before getting off the bed. Leaving me feeling cold and alone. Maaier said nothing but looked over the room. His eyes landed on the book on Dorian's bed. A tilt of his lips filling his face.

"Glad to see someone putting it to use," He said. I slowly tucked the book under the blanket on the bed. Hoping to god he didn't see me do it. If he did, he didn't say anything.

He moved closer. I wiped my eyes. Looking up at him, my gaze met his. Dark yet also full of desire. Rain patted on the window outside, a sign of a storm incoming. One almost as deadly as the light in Maaier's eyes.

"What has made you cry?"

I assured him it was nothing but he was not convinced. He laid me down on the bed. His lips but a mere inch from mine. My breath hitched in my lungs. The scent of him encapsulated me. It wasn't enough. I needed him everywhere. I needed to know if he would bring me colour or if I should risk another brush with Death to find out.

"I hate when you lie to me," He growled.

A whispered apology on my lips. Before I could say anything further, or lean in closer. He shifted back.

"Should I scold you for lying?" He breathed, the question more to himself than me but my insides still clenched. Heat rising through me. What was wrong with me? I just learnt of the origin of my curse and here I am almost begging to be held by a mad man who might just kill me. At least if he did, I would meet Death again. I would tell him I was sorry for my ancestors' past behaviour. The sound of a match being struck filled the air. The candle flickering as he held it near letting it burn in silence before meeting my wary gaze.

"Then I should save this slight scolding for another time. When you are feeling better." He smirked before extinguishing the candle. My hope ignited in me instead. The thought of being with him again enough to colour my skin with a slight blush.

"What did you see when you saw me?" I asked without thinking. What was I saying? He considered me for a moment before answering.

"A beautiful woman with her whole life ahead of her." His gloved hand brushed my cheek.

"I meant your sight Maaier. What do you see?"

"I don't know what you mean, Vespera." He furrowed his brow in confusion. His touch turned more gentle than seductive. I lifted my hand to meet him on my cheek. Holding it close to me. I looked into his eyes. Seeing myself reflected back in the dark expanse.

My reflection dishevelled with misty eyes. My skin was void of colour. I wasn't beautiful, I was a mess. Maaier stepped closer, drawing me to him. My head rested just below his chest as I buried myself in him. I breathed in his spiced scent. The heat of him. His hands pressed into my back, holding me closer as I slowed my breathing. Pulling away only slightly so I could see him once more, I asked my most pressing question. The one I knew would change everything.

"Do you see everything in colour?" I whispered. He froze. His thumb stalling close to my lip.

"I always see colour when I see you," He said softly before moving back off me.

My chin dropped to my chest. The tears fell heavier now.

He left without another word. This was wrong. It had to be him. I couldn't be tied to Death. I needed him. Something in Maaier's gaze when he said the tender words told me it was a lie. A slip of emotion pent up to leak out.

I hurried out the door. Only to find him heading out the back toward the woods. My voice dropped as I called his name over and over again. He ignored me each time. Disappearing amongst the trees.

I stopped. My chest heaving. I needed to go after him. To tell him it was fine. This wasn't right. The colour should have come to us both. Not just me. He was lying he had to be.

I needed to figure him out. I needed to tempt him. To get him to touch me. To open my eyes, to admit he loves me. Maybe then I can admit that I was falling in love with him.

Chapter Thirty-Two

With my plan in motion, I had the best sleep I had had in months. Even before I was attacked. The sound of that haunting voice now stored away as comfort. I was going to make him love me. He had no choice. He had disappeared for three days after my question. Although nothing eventful happened within that time, his lack of presence was noted by all.

I planned my future. I would tempt him. Just as he always said I did.

I had dressed with the help of Mary that morning into a square-neckline dress she had assured me was bright red. My breasts pushed up uncomfortably under the corset. Mary had said it was common for women to wear this kind of gown amongst high society. But all I wanted now was to put on my shield of high collared dresses. I had pestered her for the shade as I planned to lure in the strange man who had brought me that hint of colour in the first place. Knowing he would be the one to answer my questions, surely he saw me that night. The real me. The one he was supposed to love.

The silken light grey dress swirled around me as I made my way downstairs. My hair twisted in its usual knot.

I entered the dining hall to find Victor and Maaier in a heated debate. The argument ceased as I stopped. Victor's eyes tracked my body before shifting away from me. The expression he had looked at me with not of attraction but more of a respectful gaze, a brief nod in my direction as he focused on his tea before him. My eyes moved to Maaier who sat rigid as he took me in. His back straight as his fiery stare met mine. The fork in his hand bending as his fist clenched. His jaw set tight.

"Good morning, gentlemen." I bubbled despite my inner turmoil.

Victor offered his good morning whilst Maaier remained silent, chewing on his cheek. The sight was just down right lustful. I picked an apple from the top of the fruit platter. The skin shining in the faint light from the window. I maintained the fiery gaze with Maaier. The tension palpable between us.

My thoughts were a mess. Who was this strange man? And why did he hide himself from me? Unless he was hiding something else. A dark secret perhaps? I wasn't sure what the truth was. My instinct told me he was the one to help me that night but my mind told me it was all a dream. The only way to tell was for him to touch me whilst wearing this odd shade. Maybe then I could tell if it was him. Victor watched as I bit into the apple letting the juice drip down my chin. I left it there. Biting deeper into the fruit, sucking the juice from its sweet flesh.

Maaier's jaw clenched hard enough to crack a tooth. Good.

I bowed slightly before heading back into the halls. Tossing the apple back into his vicinity.

WALKING TO THE BACK GARDEN, I FASTENED THE cloak that Mary had left out for me. Assuring me that the red matched that of my dress. The grey looked all the same to me.

The wind blew softly over the yard. Snow followed in its wake. The soft little flakes danced on the breeze. My boot touched the snow covered ground. Taking a deep breath I willed myself to relax. This was a truly foolish idea. I cursed myself as I stood on the edge of the treeline. Why was I tempting him? Was I that desperate for a man's touch? No. I needed to lure my attacker back. I needed to put an end to this madness. The forest loomed over me. Bare branches and roots calling me forward.

A heated feeling washed over me. I turned my head to find Maaier advancing.

One word charging the air between us.

"Run."

HE DIDN'T HAVE TO TELL ME TWICE. I LEAPT forward. Holding my skirts in my hands. Running as hard as I could through the forest. My heart beat loudly in my ears. The wind whipped at my exposed face. Sharp stings of cold running through me. My breath fogged as it left me. Maaier's footfalls sounded behind me. I darted right. Down to the thick brush of trees.

"When I catch you, little bloom. I will make you regret tempting me in the first place." His voice echoed through the air. I kept pushing forward. Knowing the man was true to his words. The thrill of the unknown excited me.

"I will own you. Every inch of you. Little temptress." His voice was closer.

I darted to the left. My lungs were on fire with exertion. I couldn't go on much longer. My skirts weighed me down. The snow crunched beneath my boots. The sound mingled my hurried pants. Bare tree branches reached for me as I raced away from the man chasing me like his most prized prey. I dared to look back. Maaier stalked forward. Much like a vampire, that lethal gaze trained on me.

Footfalls sounded behind me. Racing toward me. Within seconds a hard body collided with mine. The air in my lungs dissipated as we fell toward the snow covered earth. My chest hit the ground hard, the cloak slipping open. Exposing my chest to the ice. The damp ground stinging on contact. Maaier's weight left me for a moment only to roll me over to face him.

My lungs heaved as I gulped down air. The fear of the unknown sent a thrill through me, my every nerve alive with apprehension. Maaier's dark gaze landed on me beneath him, tracing every inch of my face with wonder. His gloved hands wisped along my sides, gently at first only to grow bold as he neared my face. His thumb traced my lip. Circling my mouth before cupping my neck.

"Clever little bloom," he praised.

The cold ice beneath me seeped through my clothing, drenching my back. But I paid it little mind. My body was on fire. Sparks of heat danced over my skin, warming me from within.

"My sweet girl. You have figured me out haven't you?" I shook my head at his words. I thought I had but I wasn't so sure. I wasn't sure of anything right now. The only thing I was sure of was how much I craved this man's body.

His hand skimmed from my cheek to my shoulder, one hand still holding my throat with a gentle grasp. Expert fingers drifting across my tight corset. A whimper escaped me as his fingers glided over the neckline of the gown. His rough skin against the smooth expanse of my chest. His eyelids fluttered shut as he leant down. His lips met my skin, kissing softly. Savouring the taste of my flesh. Another moan left my lips as Maaier's curled against the top of my breasts. The rise and fall of my chest beating in time with my heart racing through my body.

"God, how long have I waited to taste you, Vespera," He groaned before slightly hardening the kiss. His teeth gently dug into me. His grip grew tight as if losing control over himself.

"Do you crave me as I crave you?" He whispered, his eyes meeting mine as I looked down at him. Heat filled my core. He looked down right sinful.

"Always." I managed through my thick throat.

"Do you want me to touch you, Vespera? To claim you as my own? To hold you, mind, body and soul?"

"Please, Maaier." I begged. I didn't care what I was agreeing to so long as it involved him and claiming me.

"Good." He grinned wickedly before tugging down on my corset. My breasts bounced free of their confinement. Nipples puckering in the cold air. Maaier's mouth met my skin once more before taking one in his mouth. His tongue swirling around the bud before sucking lightly.

My entire upper body arched into the movement. His action ignited my flaming skin further. I cried out with pure ecstasy, the noise strained as his hand flexed on my throat.

"Quiet, little bloom. We don't want anyone else seeing you like this. You were made for me and no one else. Not even God himself can drag me from you."

My heart thundered beneath his lips, now dragging back up to my lips.

"I was at your end and I am your beginning. I am your god and your devil. I am your saviour and your destroyer. I will tear you apart only to put you back together time and time again. I. Am. Yours."

Within an instant Maaier's lips were on mine. The sensation sent a wave of relief through my body as if I knew this was right. My heart burst to life in his embrace. As if it knew this was the man for me.

Maaier's hips rolled forward. His body pressed against mine. His kiss grew deeper as he explored my mouth, his tongue dancing with mine. The sparks fluttered back over my body. Maaier shifted back with his hips, reaching between us. One hand back on my breast. He kneaded the flesh as his tongue assaulted mine. His warm hand pulled at my skirt, baring me to him. His fingers glided down my mound, circling my bundle of nerves before lowering to my seam. Wetness gathered on his fingers as he pulled them through.

He pulled away, searching my gaze for something. Finding nothing but pure and utter bliss on my expression. I ached for his touch. My body was already mourning the loss of his contact. His hand moved to his own pants, loosening the button and sliding them down. His length bobbed as it appeared above my core. Long and thick.

How on earth was that supposed to fit inside me?

"I have waited centuries, my soul. I will wait no longer. Unless you tell me not to, I will make good on my claim on you." His words buried themselves within me but I didn't say a word. I wanted this. Wanted him so desperately the ache in my body only grew with each second.

Maaier's hands gripped my hips as he pushed forward. His length pushed into me. A fire like no other burnt within me. The feeling of him stretching me a delicious sting. His lips moved to my neck as he pulled out only to push back in. Slowly at first, only to quicken with each thrust. The delirium was like no other. The intoxication of feeling him within me brought endless pleasure. The pressure built in my core once more. His lips met mine once more. One hand gripped my hip as the other wove itself into my hair. The head of his cock pressed deep inside me. I was close to release. Maaier's hands explored my body as he continued to thrust. Our moans were swallowed by the other. Desperation rolling from us. My nails dug into Maaier's exposed back. The pain only stirred him on. He thrust harder, yet still gentle enough to not cause me any further pain or discomfort.

"Come with me." Maaier's husky voice ordered as he broke the kiss. He didn't need to tell me again. The orgasm hit like no other. Nothing felt like this. The sound tore from my throat as Maaier thickened inside me with one final thrust. Warm spurts filling me.

I opened my eyes, searching Maaier's gaze. My eyes fell to his lips. The faintest hint of colour lining them. Maaier remained inside me. His heaving breaths matched mine breath for breath. I looked down at his wound. The scar remained. Raised and red.

My heart dropped to my stomach.

I had found him. It was Maaier all along. Not Death.

"I am yours, my soul." He smirked above me.

"How?" I choked out.

"Every reaper needs his Angel of Death. Just so happens you are mine," He said before kissing me one more time.

Chapter Thirty-Three

I pushed Maaier off me. Instead, straddling him with my knees caging him in. Holding his two large hands in one of mine was a feat in itself. Horror ran through me. I could still see the colour.

"No." My words fell like a whimper, lacking the bite I had intended. What did he mean? Was he truly the grim reaper? Was he the one who saved me that night? Was I right all along? The questions swirl through my mind. Nausea rose in my stomach, edging throughout my body.

"Yes, my soul." He almost pleaded, begging me to accept what he was. The warmth of the embrace before slowly ebbed as his words and gaze sunk in

"This can't be happening. You are lying." I slumped my shoulders down, the weight of the confession weighing me down, letting his hands free. I stumbled back, pulling my knees to my chest as I sat on the cold forest floor.

"I can't help what I am, Vespera," He said softly.

"What are you?" I pressed. Why could I only see one colour with him? Why was he here? What did he want with me?

"I am a reaper. The Reaper I should say." Maaier's tone

rang with the slightest hint of cockiness. As if proud of what he really was.

"I can't handle this!" My heart raced within me. Pounding painfully as blood roared within my ears. This was wrong, this was all wrong. Heat prickled behind my eyes.

Slowly, darkness faded in. Overtaking my senses. A tear leaving my right eye. He was Death. I was the grim reaper's lover. No. it can't be. It was all my mania induced brain that was it. I was insane. The word no uttered from my lips before the darkness consumed me whole.

I came too on the floor of the greenhouse. Warm hands wove through my hair as the last tendrils of blackness ebbed from me.

"I didn't mean to scare you back there," Maaier said softly from behind me. "My emotions got the better of me."

I craned my head back to look at him, head resting on his bare chest. He sprawled behind me on the floor, holding me tightly against him.

His expert fingers rotated in circles around my scalp. The silence was almost unbearable. My lower body stung slightly.

"So it was all true? Not a dream?"

Maaier smiled small with a slight nod.

"Yes. You are my intended. The other half of my soul," He whispered, his lips brushed a sweet kiss on top of my head. My eyes fluttered closed despite my anxious heart.

Maaier said nothing more until I turned to look away from him. Gazing out at the grey woods beyond the window.

His strong arms wrapped around me. It was fruitless to shake him off. His chin rested on my shoulder.

"Now that you know who I am Vespera, the choice will remain yours."

I spun to face him. Still held tightly in his arms against him, my eyes met his. Our chests rising in time with our breaths. Synchronicity mirroring the movement.

"You will always have a choice with me." He kept his voice low as brushed my hair back from my face.

"Why do I have a choice?" I said softly. Maaier's usual cocky expression was gone. Replaced by woe. As if saddened and pained by the weight of the confession.

"You have a choice of living a full life on earth or an endless life serving by my side. You can have a life with your family to find another love and create life for yourself or you can spend eternity aiding souls to the afterlife with me. That is your cross to bear. Whatever you pick will be your choice and yours alone."

"I choose-"

"Shhh," He cut me off with a brush of his lips to mine. I knew my choice. I didn't want to be away from him. I needed him now that I knew who he truly was. I needed his help to find the killer. To help me end my curse. To bring me back to life. "I don't want you to choose me just yet. You need to think about this. To consider what you want. You have been given a second chance at life. Whatever you choose I will accept. But think about it."

His voice was solemn as if expecting me to change my mind.

"Now that you know who I am and your choices, my soul. I must go." My arms tightened around him. My emotions at war inside me now rose to a slaughter. I shouldn't want him. After what he did in the forest and confessed, I should run. Run far away and never return, never look back. But something in his gaze told me that he was expecting that. As if so many before had done the exact same thing.

"Will you come back?"

"Always, little bloom. I will be here when I can." My panic lessened at the words he pressed into my forehead. The tightness in my chest shifted. Feeling lighter with every breath. The feeling of abandonment dissipating.

"Will the red stay?" I fumbled, changing the subject before I broke down in tears. Maaier chuckled.

"Yes. You can keep the red. I won't take it again."

"You can take my colour at will?"

Maaier said nothing but placed a gentle sweet kiss on my lips. Pulling back just as quickly, his gaze roaming over me one last time as if committing me to memory.

"Goodbye, my soul. May the moon light your way until I am home again."

His final words rang through the air as he stood, slowly backing away from me. The expression on his face full of grief and sorrow. His body was completely enveloped by shadows until they dissipated. Leaving nothing but his dark scent behind.

A warm tear rolled down my cheek as I exited the greenhouse myself and headed to my rooms. The cold air prickling my skin. Where was he going? Was another one I loved leaving me once more?

Confusion and hurt setting in amongst my brief happiness still lingering. The manor seemingly empty as I drifted down the halls to my room.

I looked up at the portrait of my mother now hanging at the end of my bed. Her beautifully dazzling smile on display. The red roses surrounding her blooming to life. I admired her beauty. Only stopping to notice the tiny mark poking out through the neckline of the white gown. Two faint diagonal lines peeking through. Her right shoulder peaking through the scrap of fabric covering her. A small blemish the shape of a petal painted so small you could barely notice it came into focus. My heart leapt into my stomach. It wasn't my mother. It was me.

A BRIEF GASP FILLED THE AIR.

Dorian stood in the doorway. Her hair combed. Not as manic as she usually looked. A red rose perched in her hand. A small smile lifted my lips despite myself. Dorian smelt the air. Her eyes shined in the moonlight.

"I had the portrait moved for you." She explained keeping her eyes locked on the bloom in her hands.

I thanked her softly. Not wanting to startle her. The tension was crackling.

"I think you ought to read the book he gave you." She nodded toward the book at the foot of her bed. The one of flowers Maaier had given me. "Not the strange blank one."

"I'll get to it," I said, facing the portrait once more. The detail was immaculate. Right down to the birthmark on my shoulder I had not noticed. A small blemish like a rose petal only someone who had seen me intimately would notice.

Dorian eyed me cautiously before moving beside me. Her hand grasped mine. Her head rested on my shoulder.

"When you are ready," She murmured.

I wasn't sure what she was referring to but I knew she knew more than she was letting on.

Chapter Thirty-Four

I woke with a start. The memory of Maaier's confession was like a song on repeat in my mind. He was Death. Dorian was right all along. He killed with a touch but why wouldn't he kill me? Was it because I was sworn to him in some twisted way like a prophecy? This was all too much. I had tossed and turned all night before creeping into bed next to Dorian. Just to feel the warmth of another once more. She was still curled into a ball beside me, as if cradling something to her chest. Her breathing heavy in the cool air. The moon hung low in the sky. The sun slowly rising from its bed. The dark of the night slowly lightening.

Creeping away from Dorian, I padded gently downstairs to the main hall.

The lantern in my hands flickering through the halls. The doors to the piano room were already open. I stilled. Feeling the strange presence of another. The air became frigid. I stepped over the threshold. Not a soul in sight. Not one that I could see anyway. But I couldn't shake the feeling I was being watched. The feeling of their stare burning through my shoulder blades. I stilled my nerves. Convincing myself that all was well and that I was under no threat although I knew I was. Maaier wasn't here to save me now. But I supposed if I were to die, he would be the one to take me back, would he not? Or would he have to take my soul over and find a new love? God this whole matter was confusing.

I made it to the piano alive despite my sense that something terrible was about to happen. My intuition was stronger than ever. Sitting on the bench before the grand old instrument, fingers wary as they reached for an ivory key. The G note sounded like a gunshot. The sound booming through the empty room. A sound of brisk movement sounded beyond the door but receded. I narrowed my gaze. Scanning the expanse of the dimly lit room for any abnormality only to come up short. I was alone again.

I faced the ivory keys again. The early moonlight hidden through the curtains. Although it was now snowing. I wasn't sure the moon light could guide me back to him. Wherever he was now. I stood firm. Telling myself no one was around. I pressed the same key. Only lightly this time. The sound somehow quieted before another flash of white pulsed before my eyes. The pain seared as the light pushed its way in.

"Theodore, you need to find her!" Grandmother's voice urged. Her posture was rigid. The tension roiled off her stooped form, decades of grief weighing her down.

"I have tried Sophia!" Father's voice sounded from down the hall. I sat at the piano. Watching the two as they entered the room. Father lingering in the doorway as Grandmother made her way to the window behind me.

"She wouldn't just leave. She will be back soon." He nearly pleaded, urging the stubborn woman to see sense. Grandmother narrowed her gaze. She was younger here, only a few strands of white marred the dark expanse of her hair.

"You don't understand. You never have and you never will." She seethed. Her fists clenched beside her, utter terror radiating from her. The look in her light eyes was near wild with fear. I lifted my hand to hold hers. Only to find it fruitless, my palm falling straight through her fist.

"It is just an old tale to scare you into behaving." My father scoffed. I hadn't seen this side of him in a long while even before he had left. A man so enraged and narrow minded. He was always so calm and gentle until the day mother passed. Was this the day it all changed?

"It is not. Death favours a Florian! He always has," She snarled as she turned to face him. Her finger pointed at his chest as he approached her. "I have lost almost all I love. Death has taken them. My daughter, my sisters, my mother. Everyone. I will be damned if I let anyone take Vespera from me. Now you will go find her mother. And bring her home. I will keep Vespera safe here."

"I am her father-"

"You are nothing but a stain on the Florian name if you do not find your wife."

If looks could kill, Father would be six feet underground. He huffed before leaving, his footsteps heavy as he stormed to the door. Grandmother stood firm until the door slammed behind him. A single tear rolled down her cheek. Followed by another. They fell until she could bear their weight no longer, instead falling to the ground with them. Her knees landed with a heavy thud as she bowed to the floor. Praying for her daughter not to be taken, begging for her safe return. Pleading for them to take her instead. But she knew in her bones that her daughter was gone. She wailed to the floor. Her fists beating against the marble.

I stood in my ghostly form. Hovering beside her before kneeling. I ached to touch her. To hold her close but she did not move. Her back heaving with her body as her grief poured from her.

I looked up from her back. Noticing another pale hand holding her on the opposite side. Slowly I tracked my arms up the torn and damp white dress. Landing on a scar in the middle of her partially exposed chest. Her eyes met mine.

My mother blinked. As if not sure who she was seeing. A figure appeared behind me. I could feel their presence. Like a god commanding power. The scent of cedar and saffron filled my nose. I didn't have to look at him to know Maaier stood with his arm outstretched. His hand ready to take hers. Mother blinked between us. A single *no* falling from her trembling lips. The depth of her situation sinking in. She pleaded softly for him to let her stay, to allow her this one sympathy.

"It is your time, Adele," Maaier said gently, a tone scarcely heard with his voice.

"No please. Maaier please." She begged, her voice raw. The sound like a knife to the heart. A voice I craved more than anything before. Tears streamed down her cheeks. Grandmother was still sobbing on the floor oblivious to what was happening around her.

"Maaier, please. Don't do this. I wasn't ready." She begged the man before her.

"I know," He responded, his voice void of emotion. Years of death honed into his mannerisms.

"Maaier, please no. I'll do anything, don't take me from her." Her gaze darted to me before flashing back to him. Could she see me? Or could she feel me as I felt her in the present time?

"Sweet girl, I am sorry but I can not change your fate. You chose your colour."

"But it's not my time." Her voice grew small.

"I'm afraid it is."

"I can't go. I won't go without her." She tilted her head sadly. Looking at Maaier with the weight of a thousand deaths on her shoulders. As if her soul was so burdened by death that she could handle no more.

"I will take care of her." Maaier stepped forward beside me. "I promise you that much."

"No. She can't cross without me." Mother pleaded. Her tears ran down her already damp cheeks. Her hair sticking to her forehead in inky strands. Just as it had when they pulled her body from the river.

Without warning Mother stood. Her gaze on Maaier.

"When Vespera is ready. I will cross paths with her then. Not a moment before." Her voice was soft yet firm. Commanding.

"As you wish, Lady Florian. But I shall return." With a final word Maaier dissipated just as he had leaving me in the bathtub, in a mass of heavy dark shadows. Mother held herself tightly. Her arms wrapped around her legs.

The doors flew open once more. Mother untangled herself as I watched myself rush into the room. Grief poured from me. I remembered this all too well. Watching them pull my mother's lifeless body from the river. I had run off in search of Grandmother. Running from Father and into the manor. My young heart was broken and shattered in my chest. It was as if the pain from my mother's scar had embedded itself in my skin. I watched in wait as a younger me burst through the door. Torn apart by loss. Holding onto my skirts as if they were the only thing holding me up, barreling into Grandmother's arms. My mother watched with more tears flooding her cheeks. Her body heaving with her shattered sobs as she watched her daughter and mother mourn her. But little did they know she was still here. She wasn't leaving. She never would. Not until I go with her. But how could I take her with me if I joined Maaier? She would never find peace. She would be stuck here in the halls watching as we all aged and grew and she stayed the same. Not ageing. No longer growing.

She moved forward clutching her hands to her chest, crawling over to where her loves sat huddled together. Her arms reached out to hold them only to have them fall through. She watched in desperation as they cried for her. But she could do nothing.

I FADED BACK TO THE PRESENT. CATCHING MYSELF just as I fell back on the bench. I looked to where the vision occurred. No marks lined the floor. No tears stained into the ground. A reflection that with time, grief fades. It never truly disappears for it will live under the surface even though we have wiped the remains clean.

Lifting my hands to scrub my face, I wiped the wetness from my cheeks.

"I visit this spot most often too, at night." Grandmother's voice broke through the silence.

Her stooped frame leaning against the door.

"She's still here." I admitted.

"I know. I feel her most in here. She used to paint in that corner almost every day." She pointed to the only spare corner of the room. Right as you walk in. The same space mother used to line the floors with sheets and paint to her heart's content.

"She loved it in here," I said as Grandmother approached.

"She loved having you in here with her more." She smiled

lightly before offering me her hand. I couldn't bring myself to smile. Instead nodding and taking her hand as she led me back to her room.

    I lay beside her just as I did when I was a girl. Only now I couldn't get the sound of her wailing screams out of my head.

Chapter Thirty-Five

"The soil is sort of dry." Mary's voice tore back through the swirl of thoughts racing in my mind. Without saying a word, I watered the tomato plant she was looking into. Plucking a ripe tomato off and popping it into her mouth.

The forest loomed outside, covered in a thick blanket of snow. Hiding the remains of Maaier's confession under its weight. Now a moment lost in time. I didn't know when he was coming back, but I yearned for him regardless. I ached to ask him why he didn't take my mother and aunt to the other side. To ask why they were allowed to remain in the manor. The question had eaten at me most of the morning.

Grandmother had forced me to eat breakfast with her before ushering to go outside and garden despite my every protest. Assuring me it would serve me well. The heavenly scent of roses wafted through my nose. The blazing red peeking out from beyond the mass of grey. Everything in this greenhouse reminded me of Maaier now. No matter where I turned, I could not escape him.

"Did you hear of another attack?" Mary lowered her voice, gazing conspiratorially at me.

I shook my head, my heart pounded painfully.

"A brunette this time. They said she was caught in the streets with her throat sliced."

I trembled. My skin prickled with fear. Why were his killings so random?

"Did she make it?" My voice, hoarse.

Mary shook her head. "The police are still interviewing witnesses but they say she was a woman of the night."

My heart thumped in my chest. The murder almost mirrored the killing of the loveless man's mother in my book. Of possibly Maaier's mother.

"Did she have a son?"

"Not that anyone is aware of, but they were new to town." Mary quirked a brow but said nothing.

I put down the trowel I had clenched in my hands and leaned back against the bench.

"It won't stop," I said. This was all because of me. If I had died that night maybe the man would have left us alone. Not chased after women linked to my likeness.

"Mary, can you fetch Victor for me?"

She scattered away quickly, eager to help whatever thought she assumed I had.

VICTOR ARRIVED WITH A SMILE. BUT IT DIDN'T MEET his eyes. He looked exhausted. His right hand bruised on the knuckles. Red dotting the grey flesh.

"You're bleeding." I noted as I hurried toward him.

"It's fine." He shook me off. Rejection waved through me. I shook it off before meeting his gaze.

"How many women does it make now?"

"Eight," He said softly, avoiding my gaze. My jaw fell open, my fists clenching beside me.

"And you didn't think to tell me?"

Victor went on to explain that he didn't want to cause me any more panic because I was already weighed down enough. He had even argued the point with Maaier before I had interrupted that morning.

Victor had been so upset at himself for withholding the truth that he took his frustrations out on a tree in the yard. A lie almost believable. Victor wouldn't hit a tree and the tree wouldn't leave those marks.

I shook my head turning back to the bush, Mary came up beside me. Picking another tomato and popping it into her mouth.

The smile on her face was out of place for the current mood.

I thanked Victor before turning away. He didn't move away, instead, coming up beside me.

"You need to leave, Vespera. Take Dorian and Mary and go."

"I can't just leave Victor."

"Yes, please do it for me. Please." He urged. His hands cupping my shoulders. His expression turned desperate. "Do it for Dorian."

"What has she told you?" I narrowed my gaze.

"Nothing." He shook his head. Light curls bouncing around steely eyes.

"Then I'll be fine!" I said exasperated. "If the man comes back it'll be the end of it all. Don't we all want that?"

"No." Both Mary and Victor responded in unison.

"You think we are just going to let you die?" Mary sighed before sitting on the bench.

I looked down at my boots on the floor. At the dirt caking them like a secret holds a heart.

"I can't leave my grandmother."

"Well. We will take her too."

"You and I both know that she will never leave this damned house." I pressed. Victor's fingers dug into my flesh.

"I am begging you, please Vespera. Leave."

"I am not leaving Victor. My place is here with her."

If I died away from here I would never see my mother again. I had to stay, if only for her. If I left, her soul would be lingering for nothing. And that was a weight I could not bear. I was already drowning on my own.

Victor slumped with defeat. Pulling me into his embrace. "Then I will stay with you."

"What if I want you to be safe?"

He pulled back from me. Searching my face. "Nowhere is safer than you and the lunatic you call a friend." His cheeks colouring slightly.

My lips quirked. The smallest hint of a smile showing through.

MAAIER APPEARED THE NEXT NIGHT. HOVERING below the window outside in the gardens. I looked down at him with a grin before heading out to the greenhouse where I knew he would be waiting.

I had just read the book he first gave. Nearing the end of the book of flowers. Learning nothing I didn't already know.

I leapt into his arms. Feeling his lips crash against mine. My body lit up for him. My hands snaked their way through his untamed hair falling to his shoulders. The dark waves falling over my skin.

"Oh how I have missed you, little bloom," He whispered against my lips. Not breaking the embrace.

"It's only been three days." Three days of agonised hell trying to figure out if I truly wanted to accept his words after our encounter.

"A second away from you is like an eternity I wish not to bare." His hands glided over my body. Committing my form to memory as he led me further amongst the shrubbery. Our tongues greedily explored the other's. His name was a breath of air caught in my chest. The word buried itself in my soul, marking it as his for eternity..

His arms went lower. Pulling me up against the bench. His hands pushed my skirts up. Gentle palms cupping my waist.

"I can't wait any longer." He spoke, his voice raspy and strained. As if holding himself back with a firm restraint.

"Then devour me. Devour my soul," I whispered softly.

Maaier's eyes grew dark as he did as I commanded. Thrusting into me as his teeth met my neck. Nipping and sucking all over the expanse of bare skin. Hungry hands pulling down at the buttons of my nightgown until they popped free. A moan filled the night air as it fell from my lips.

I gasped for air. Feeling him fill me over and over again. The feel of him was the closest to heaven I would ever have the pleasure of experiencing. The snow falling outside but inside the steam swirled, fogging the glass. Maaier's hand gripped my waist. The other bracing on the glass pane of the windowed walls.

"Anyone out there could see how well you take me, bloom." He grunted, thrusting harder into me. I was a wordless mess. The effect only he could have on me. My hands gripped his hair pulling it tighter as his lips found mine again. Our desperate pants filled the air as we both reached the edge of the cliff only to come tumbling down together. The ecstasy lighting a fire within.

Maaier withdrew but still held me in his arms.

"You're making the choice harder than it has to be." I managed.

Maaier chuckled darkly. "I am a man of persuasion."

I beamed up at him. My breath coming in short.

This man was surely going to be the death of me. And I wasn't sure I minded.

I looked into his eyes. Seeing myself reflected in them. A sight I would never be sick of.

My gaze fell on something over his shoulder. A brief flicker of a shade before vanishing. My already pounding heart picked up speed. Did I just see that flower in colour? And why did it look so vibrant? Mary had said roses can come in pink or yellow but I had never seen the colour to know. In the daylight, the flower looked much like the supposedly pink dress I had selected for Dorian. A soft grey. So gentle and pure.

Maaier smirked before kissing me once more. Knowingly distracting me from the colour.

"Not yet, bloom. All with time," He murmured. "All in good time."

Chapter Thirty-Six

The memory of the colour burned into my mind long into the next day.

The shade haunting me every time I looked down at the red scar as I dressed for the day. The shade was only slightly lighter than the rose I had seen last night. Was it pink I had seen?

The sun was now high in the sky as I pulled on my corset ties. Hissing as I pulled them tighter than necessary. Desperate to hide the peppered marks Maaier had left across my skin before he led me back inside for the night.

It took an age to find a dress to cover my skin that wasn't my usual black one now hung out to dry after being washed. Peeling each piece out of the wardrobe with a hissed curse to Maaier and his lineage. I selected a high necked light grey gown and left the room.

A chill rolled through me. The tall oak trees bent in the wind. Another storm drawing near. Grey clouds drawing near in the distance.

My name sounded from down the hall. A screech followed not long after. Lifting my skirts, I rushed toward them.

The library doors were swung wide open as Arthur hurried from the room.

"Vespera." He gasped, breathless from whatever was happening behind him.

"What is happening?" I stepped forward only to be halted by Arthur's risen palm.

"Go back up the stairs," He said softly. I craned my neck to the sound of sobbing in the library.

"Now!" Arthur barked. Walking backwards, my gaze remained on the room. The scent of cedar drew stronger. Warmth covered my back as I met his front.

"Come with me." Maaier ordered softly.

An angry snarl covered my face. "Do not touch me." I barked. I was so sick of men telling me what to do in my own home. Do not go out alone, Vespera. Don't do this, Vespera. Oh no, don't even think of doing that, Vespera. It was enough to drive anyone mad. No wonder Dorian hated authority so passionately.

Maaier gripped my bicep. Hauling me back with him. I tried again and again to pull my arm free. Even going as far as to try and pry his fingers with my free hand.

He led me out to the back garden, still holding me against him. Silent as the wind howled around us. The woman screamed once again. Pain filled howls sending a wave of guilt over me. Why was I not allowed to help her?

I turned my head only to be stopped by Maaier's hand gripping my face with a gloved hand. Squeezing my cheeks hard. His hard dark eyes met mine, a silent warning brewing in their expanse. My heart raced in my chest. But not because he was touching me. I loathed that. What I was more concerned with was the commotion now taking place in the hall.

"Ghosts," Maaier murmured. I blanched at the word. The warmth drained from my skin. I choked out a simple what.

Maaier's gaze softened. "They're escorting one of your grandmother's maids away. She's being tried for the murder of her husband. Says the ghosts told her to do it."

My stomach flipped. My heart plummeted. Please for the love of god don't let it be Rosemary.

"It's not your friend." I relaxed at his soft spoken words, as if he read the expression on my face. The air coming back into my lungs.

Maaier raked his gaze over my form. My long hair hung in tangled waves. His grip dropped before leading me to a chair. I watched in silence as he removed a tie from his hair. "They won't let you back inside until she is gone. The police are on their way."

Maaier stood behind me. Pulling my head back to look up at him. I studied him silently. His hair brushing his shoulders. Dark eyes shining with mischief.

I gulped. Knowing the last time I saw that glint I was burned all over. Maaier's gaze tracked my throat. Watching silently as my lips parted. A million questions ready on my tongue only to fall silent as he lowered himself to my ear.

"Did you read the book in its entirety?" He asked, his voice low. I froze. Trying my hardest to remain neutral.

"What book?"

Maaier grinned before rising above me once more. His hands wove into my hair, tilting so I looked toward the greenhouse.

"The one I gifted you."

I almost sighed with relief.

"Not yet." It's not totally a lie. I had read a page before my mind wandered to the strange book. Maaier hummed before moving his hands through my hair. Fingers moving in time as he braided it back. He twisted the length into a knot. Sliding something in to hold it in place. The smallest hint of rose hit my nose.

The sound of horses drew near. Maaier moved to stand before me. His hard stare looking through the windows at the arrest.

"Don't watch." He ordered as I shifted in my seat. I trained my focus on the forest in front of me. Chewing the inside of my cheek to keep from retorting. The tall bare trees swaying in the gathering wind. The familiar creak of the front doors crashing open sounded. The branches swayed once more as if drawing my attention.

Maaier stood beside me. Still more focused on the woman screeching.

The tiniest shadow flickered through the expanse.

I stood slowly. Training my gaze on the flicker. Now growing larger. As if drawing near. "Maaier," I whispered. Hoping he could hear me over the commotion.

"I told you not to watch." He snarled. I grit my teeth. Never looking away.

The figure lingered just beyond the tree line. My skin blanched cold. A river of ice cold terror ran through. My limbs shook as I stood at full height. My trembling hands reached for Maaier. His name fell from my lips as my heart pounded against my chest. My trembling hands gripped his black cloak. Blood roared in my ears as I shook him.

Maaier turned quickly, his attention snapping to me. Wild eyes searching mine only to find where I was stuck staring into the trees.

The figure stepped into the light. Leaving the cover of the dark forest behind. The man rolled his shoulders back. His head turned as he took in the old manor looming before him.

Maaier stepped forward but I was faster. Tears stung my eyes as I hurried toward the figure. My stomach in my throat.

It had been years since I saw him. Now I would never let my father go again.

"Vespera." My name fell from his lips like a blessing. I rushed toward him, skirts flying around me with the movement. He was older than the last time I had seen him. His thin arms opened wide as I crashed into them. He stumbled backward, steadying us as his arms wrapped around me. The long familiar scent and warmth of his chest caused the tears lining my eyes to fall. I heaved a sob as my hands wound tightly into his crisp shirt. As if he was going to disappear in an instant just like he had all those years ago. His hold crushed me. His lips kissing my hair over and over. The sound of my name falling around me.

The distant sound of the police carriage pulled away but I paid it no mind. The only sound I could hear was the thump of Father's chest. He's here. He's back. He is truly here this time. Not some hopeless childish dream.

I smiled through the tears. Slowly pulling apart I looked into his eyes. He looked down at me, still towering over me. His hands lifted to cup my face. The tears mirroring those on my face covered his.

"You've grown." He breathed a laugh. I grinned at him.

"You look so much like her." The ice cold terror had thawed into a river of warmth. I couldn't speak. Not knowing what to ask first. Where were you? Why come back now? Did you know about my attack? Will you stay here with me this time?

"Vespera." Maaier called behind me, his footsteps sounding toward us. Father stiffened before me, watching over my head as Maaier stopped behind me. His hands falling to my shoulders.

"Hello," He said cautiously.

"Good afternoon, Master Florian."

"Long time no see, yard hand." Father smiled. His concern fading as he assessed the man behind me.

"Father, this is Maaier. My..." I trailed off. What was this man to me now?

"Keeper." Maaier finished.

"Keeper?" Fathers brow quirked.

"I was hired to keep her safe," He said, pride ribboning his tone.

"I see you've done it well." If only he knew.

I looked over at my father. His hair now tinged with white strands at the temples. Wrinkles crinkled his forehead. Wherever he was these last few years, the world was harsh on him.

"Come. Let's go see Sophia." He squeezed my shoulders before turning me to face Maaier. His steel gaze focused on my smile. Shuffling awkwardly, he smiled back. The expression was forced.

He led the way inside and I couldn't be happier despite the ordeal of the morning.

I CALLED FOR GRANDMOTHER BEFORE FINDING HER IN the main hallway.

My grin plastered to my face. I held fathers arm in mine, not wanting to let him go.

Grandmother froze. Her nose tuning up as she recognised the man who entered her home.

"Theodore," She drawled. Distaste evident in her voice.

"Sophia. You look well." Father beamed.

Maaier met Sophia, whispering something in her ear before moving out toward the front door. I frowned slightly before lighting my expression once more. Where was he hurrying off to?

"You're back," Grandmother stated. Her hands clasping in front of her. A sign she was most displeased with the situation.

"Yes. And I intended to stay this time."

"For now." Grandmother retorted but forced a smile. She's turned her attention to me. "Vespera, the library has been cleared for you. The girl caused quite a mess in her fight to flee this morning but it is all cleaned up now."

"What happened?" I dared to ask.

"Young Gracie was taken away. She was suspected of murdering her husband," She said matter of factly, she was never one to lie to me. As brutal as the truth could be, she would always tell me it.

"Gracie couldn't even kill a fly." I was shocked. How could this nineteen year old kill her husband? She was peaceful. Sweet. Not a murderer.

Grandmother hummed her agreement. "Maaier has gone into town to find out more information. I need to know if this was in any way related to your attack."

"Her attack?" Father questioned. That answered one of my questions at least.

"Yes." Grandmother rolled her eyes. "Vespera was almost murdered a few weeks back. We have been keeping her here safe in your absence." Her jaw ticked. I had never seen her this mad. The rage radiating off her was palpable.

"What happened?" He said, his voice low.

"A man tried to drown her," Sophia said. Her tone snide as she looked over Father once more, "And another attacked her in the kitchen, slicing her open like fresh meat. She's lucky to be alive at all."

"We believe it was the same person." I offered, having slipped my arm out of fathers.

Up the hall Dorian fluttered through the people. Weaving through with Victor close behind her. It was the norm lately. I was finding the two were always close together.

"Theodore," Dorian gasped. Drawing up behind Grandmother. Her head tilted, wild curls littered with flowers falling over grandmother's shoulder.

"My my, Dorian. Haven't you aged well." Father beamed.

Victor stood behind her. His nose wrinkled slightly as he took in the scene. Noting the tension in the air.

"Well, well fucking well. Now we know that the killer is back." Arthur's voice echoed from upstairs. He clapped his hands with each step he descended, his grin viciously savage. Father's expression darkened. The two had never gotten along. Dorian stiffened as she stood beside me. Her hand drifted to my back.

"Speak for yourself." Father kept his tone cheerful but his eyes were wild with anger. Arthur huffed before coming up short beside me.

"What makes you say that? Are you blaming me for the deaths of those young women? Wasn't it you that hated any woman that resembled your wife after she passed? A lot of women killed looked like her..." He trailed off with a shrug. I threw him a withering glare to which he paid no mind. A twisted giggle sounded from up the staircase. Of course Magdelena would find this funny. I exhaled a heavy breath.

"Enough! Surely enough time has passed for you two to simply get along." I raised my brows, daring them to fight me on the matter. They both opened their mouths to protest but were silenced by grandmother's hand lifting into the air. Her approving stare on me.

"Vespera is right. This has gone on too long. What matters is that our girl is safe. With Theodore here, we can keep an eye on him to make sure he was not the one stalking in the night."

"Me?" Father blubbered. "It wasn't me!" He turned to face me. I believed him. How could my own father hurt me?

"Why did you leave?" Arthur pressed.

"Enough!" I raised my voice. "We can discuss this at dinner. Dorian, come with me." I extended my hand to which she took gratefully. Smiling as she led me up the stairs to our room. The men left alone as Grandmother pushed past them and down into the kitchens. No doubt barking orders for a dinner that would be tougher than eating leather. Although I think I would have preferred that than the night that was to come.

Chapter Thirty-Seven

"Do you really think he killed all of those women?" Dorain said in hushed tones as she sat on the edge of my bed. I paced before her. Maaier and Victor sitting side by side behind me on Dorian's. Maaier had found out nothing I didn't already know from the police and returned instantly. Not wanting to leave me in my father's presence any longer than he had to.

I shook my head.

"Why is he back now though?" Victor looked at Maaier who sat chewing his cheek.

"His journey ended." Maaier shrugged. Leaning back on his elbows. All I wanted was to climb over and have my way with him. A swat to the behind caught my attention. I sat beside Dorian who threw a disapproving look. She leant back the same way as Maaier. My eyes bulged as I realised what she was laying on.

"Why is this stupid old book in your bed?" She grunted, rubbing her elbow.

"I was making notes last night on a medical study." I lied, pulling it out of her way.

"So that is what you were doing with the strange blank book." Victor cocked a brow. As if it all made sense to him. Dorian paled beside me. Realising what she had said.

"What book?" Maaier sat forward, dark eyes on mine. I shifted under his gaze. He couldn't know about the book. Not yet.

"Nothing, just a sketch book I found." I tucked the book behind my pillow and stood.

"I need you two to watch him," I said to the men. "As much as I love and trust my father, something is amiss here and I will not rest until I find out what it is."

The men nodded before leaving the room. Maaier excused himself with another job. No doubt dissipating out through the woods to the other side or wherever it was he went these days. Victor went to check on Grandmother.

"Have you found much in the book?" Dorian said when we were in the clear.

I spilled all of the information I had about the Florian curse and the loveless man and how he became Death. Dorian listened intently. Not saying a word but drinking in the information. She stood suddenly, grabbing her notes before nestling in beside me.

"I knew something was off about my vision. All this time I thought he had killed you but it turns out he saved you. I don't know how but there was no correlation to how you survived that attack but utter luck." She breathed. Her voice grew shaky as she flicked through her stack of parchment.

"Dorian, I need you to listen to me. Maaier is safe. He will keep me safe." She huffed but I pressed on, "I don't know how either but he saved me."

"Death only kills, Vespera. He will take you away soon enough." She snorted. I bit my tongue at her tone. Holding back my venomous words. It wasn't worth it.

"So you knew?"

"Always," She said as she found the paper she needed.

"There was a note in the book about rosemary. The page was marked. Maaier had listed a date there. I checked the records and it's the date our Rosemary was employed here. But it also had the words 'trust her'."

"That's why you didn't go mad at her?"

Dorian nodded before continuing "She felt safe. I saw no harm in her future. But then on the page about roses, he had marked your name. So I went through old books and found a story of a man whose mother was murdered in the street and he buried her in pink roses. Saving his red roses for the woman he loved."

"The young man in the strange book's mother died. He mourned her for years. Avenging her soul any chance he could."

"The man in this story went on a murderous rampage. Killing anyone who looked like that man. But the man never found love. The story ended with him drowning in his own blood."

"The loveless man did that too. But the book hadn't shown me anything further than him dying."

Dorian ordered me to open it. And sure enough. The ink spread across the paper. Dorian draped an arm over my shoulder. Huddling close to look at the book. But her eyes found nothing. They remained still.

The words bled to life before me.

The loveless man awoke alone. Something he was used to but dreaded everyday. He felt no pain. Despite not moving for days. The god had watched him sleep that night. Making sure the gift was complete. The god knew his worth. Knew that his young love would return to him. The god kept a shred of that young soul. A single fibre that he would offer to Life to weave into the future. Life did not like this at first but after having watched the horror of the man's life. She agreed. She wove the soul through a bloodline. A wealthy bloodline that matched the thread. Each woman was still cursed but the thread would be their only offer of a cure. Unbeknownst to the man, he became the Reaper. A man who would carry souls to the God of Death. Aiding them into whatever belief of an afterlife they had. He would carry them without complaint. Each and everyone a new love lost. They fascinated him. He had asked about his mother's soul to which the god told him nothing. He was not at liberty to ask again. The soul called for him. He listened. The sound like bells on the wind. He smiled as he approached the old manor. A place where he was reborn and for that, he was grateful. He searched for the soul. Only to find her weeping in the place he died. A hand on her belly. It was not her. Not his lost love. He had to remind himself but the image was remarkable. He knelt before her. Holding his hands out for her to take. Her body lay in the bathtub beyond. Blood pooling over the sides. He held her hand to the otherside. Noticing that shimmer of red thread that danced through her eyes. Each time he returned to the manor was the same. The same crimson thread lining their eyes. He couldn't mistake their beauty. He knew within himself they belonged to him. He learnt from the god that these women of this bloodline were his.

It was his choice to select the one most matched to him but he never made a choice. Instead he would wait for a suitor who matched them and gave them their colour when they found their love. For only he could restore it. He watched the bloodline dwindle. Each woman met a grizzly end. As if life were torturing them for a part unknown. The man sought comfort in a woman though, a young woman cursed at the age of twenty three. The same black hair as his first love but not the same woman overall. He thought she loved him. But he did not love her nor did she love him. He adored her for her companionship but he knew his beloved was on its way. It was no surprise just how much it anguished him to watch her soul refuse him. To stay on the earthly realm in the hopes of protecting her child. A woman whose soul matched the loveless man. A soul tainted by darkness."

The sketch appeared on the page. Heat filled my eyes. My mother lay on the page. Smiling as she painted the loveless man. A man whose face I had come to love.

The words faded once more. Dorian remained still waiting

for me to speak first. The smile on her face was pure wonder. "It was Maaier all along." Was all I could manage for Mary bustled into the room to prepare us for dinner.

Chapter Thirty-Eight

We sat at the dinner table. Tension crackling in the air. No one dared to speak through the first course. The second was no better. Dorian tapped her foot beneath the table. A tell of her nerves about to run wild. Maaier was yet to return and Father had taken his place. Arthur glared at the meat, slicing his knife through and chomping loudly on each piece.

Grandmother sat silently, watching the men like a hawk.

I sighed. This was enough.

"So Father. Where have you been?" I said after a sip of wine to aid my confidence. The red liquid sloshing in the glass.

"I left to try and find a cure." He smiled softly.

"For what?" Arthur barked.

"For Vespera."

"And what exactly do you think is wrong with her?"

"You know what I am talking about, Arthur. It has plagued this family for years." Arthur shot him a severe look at his response. His eyes darted to Victor.

"He knows." Dorian rolled her eyes. Draining her wine glass and signalling for more. Victor remained silent. Focusing on his meal instead looking as if he wished he were elsewhere entirely. I couldn't blame him at all. I didn't want to be here either.

"And what did you find?" Grandmother asked.

"Nothing. Nothing like it had been reported. The only thing close was in France but that was not the colour that the curse took."

"What did it take?" I asked. Curious as to whether the god had cursed anyone else.

"Their ability to hear music. Whole family could hear everything but music." He lifted his glass to his lips but didn't drink. I noted the hesitation. His eyes flicked to the glass of every person on the table. I caught the movement, noting not to drink any more. Something was off about him.

The servers took our meal and replaced it with a selection of sweet pastries. My mouth watered at the thought of the lemon tart. Dorian gagged beside me quietly and I couldn't help but giggle. I swiped hers off her plate and replaced it with a cherry tart. She beamed before stuffing the entire thing into her mouth.

The meal continued in silence until everyone went to bed. Everyone apart from Father that is.

"Come with me," He whispered in the hall.

I followed him out into the greenhouse. My heartbeat picked up speed. The memory of Maaier filled my mind. The memory of his flesh on mine in the forest and his leaving after. I would never be able to look at this place the same.

Father opened the door and ushered me inside. He froze at the sight of it. The smile on his face illuminating the dim room.

"You kept it alive." Awe ribboned his tone. I nodded before fussing with some roses.

"The others will be asleep for a short while." He smirked. I caught his tone and froze. "You are very perceptive."

"Thank you." I responded evenly. Not letting my sudden fear crawl over me.

"You know, I really am terribly sorry for how I reacted after your mother died."

I rolled my lips together. Keeping my retort at bay.

"It wasn't my fault she drowned."

"I know."

"I didn't mean-"

"I know!" I barked, desperate for the subject to change.

Bracing my hands on the bench I looked over the leaves of the bush and to the forest beyond. "You don't have it in you. You never have."

He said my name before I turned to face him.

"You are a coward. You deserted me. You left me and your other problems." I let my thoughts spill out. The taste of the words like pepper on my tongue.

He tried to interject but I cut him off "I longed for you to come home. Begged and pleaded for my father to hold me as the loneliness crept in."

"I tried to help you-"

"You didn't. Dad. You didn't. You left me here to rot and get murdered. Did you know they sliced me the same way they did Mother? Right across my chest." I traced the wound over the fabric of my dress. "They knew who I was. It was planned and some part of me wished that you would come save me. That you would finally come back and protect me like a father should. To love me like a father should. I was so ecstatic that you were home early that I forgot how it felt when you abandoned me."

"I didn't mean to. I thought you would be better off without me here." His voice was small, eyes pleading with me.

"You being here with me would be better. Not leaving me as a fucking orphan." I spat, picking up the shears and taking my frustration out on an overgrown strawberry bush. The words falling from me like a storm.

"You left me alone. I hated you for it. Every damned day, I wanted you to come back. Grandmother had told me you never would and you know what, Father. A small disgusting part of me wished you never did. I wish you never did so I don't have to explain how the last few years have been some of the darkest and most horrible of my life where I actually craved a swift death. But I got myself out of them. No one else. Me. I'm the one who has dealt with two attacks and still breathes air. I'm the one fated to love a damned loveless man and I am the one who will kill the bastard who tried to kill me. I didn't need you then, and I don't need you now."

Father sighed before leaning against the bench.

"I wanted to come home. Believe me I did, but all I could think about was helping you. Yes, it twisted me to look at you everytime I saw you because you look so much like your mother but not once did I ever wish to abandon you the way I did." He pleaded. I faced him once more.

I opened my mouth to curse him out more but the scent of the air took the words from my mouth. The scent of burnt shrubbery caught my attention. I turned to the back of the greenhouse, finding it all illuminated with flames. Devouring each of my blooms and bushes. A horrified scream tore through my throat. Father's hands were on me in an instant dragging me to the door as the smoke filled our lungs. Heavy dry coughs heaved from our chests as the flames drew closer.

My hands made the door first only to find it locked from the outside.

I swore loudly. Father turned to the flames. Hurrying forward, he grabbed the first heavy object he could. A brass pot. He dodged the flames by a millimetre before thrusting the pot through the glass window. The cold night air kissed my hot skin. Sweat poured down my back as Father removed his coat. Wrapping it around his arm and clearing the glass from the pane. I climbed through. Helping him out as my feet touched the grass. The snow was cold against my back as I slipped into its surface. Father fell beside me, falling back as the flames devoured the greenhouse. Sorrow bit into my flesh. My one safe place now no more. My plants, all gone. And what truly made it worse was that the attacker was back to finish his cruel game. Not only for me, but my father also.

The greenhouse smouldered well into the morning. The snow seemingly helped to put it out. Maaier had arrived back just in time to pull us away. Cursing the person who set it alight.

Father had moved back into the room Dorain was intended for as Grandmother wouldn't let him back in the room. None of them realising the flames through the night only to be roused by the smell of fire and rot in the morning. My heart was empty. That greenhouse meant more to me than anyone could know. The walls filled with all of my darkest secrets whispered to my plants. All now fluttering as ash on the wind. It was stupid to ask Maaier if they had souls for him to take so I imagined they did. That he took them to the otherside of plant heaven where there was endless sun and water. He had left that morning. Leaving me alone to deal with the mess of yet another incident.

Chapter Thirty-Nine

The days all blended into one. I would wake, eat, read, sleep. There was no variety. After Maaier's latest departure, Grandmother had taken it upon herself to watch over me. A cautious gaze always fixed as if I were to flee at any moment to follow him. Where did she expect me to go? I couldn't go anywhere, I didn't even know where Maaier went. I wasn't even allowed to see Dorian's father in the town. Whose concerned letters were arriving at least three times a day. I responded each time. Letting the messenger escort the reply back instantly.

Letting him know that everything was okay and not being held imprisoned against our will. Each letter brought a smile to my face. He wouldn't venture here. The manor was too dark for his unending light. Like a shadow creeping over the most beautiful garden.

Victor also took his place by my side most days he wasn't working and throughout the majority of his free time. Spending hours researching all he could about sight and not being able to see colour. It was truly admirable that he was trying to help something he had no knowledge on.

But my mind constantly wandered to Maaier. Always wondering where he was or what he was doing. Or whether his heart felt like it was being torn in two without me. Much like mine was. It was as if I was missing a limb.

Father had locked himself in the library most days. Writing out his notes on herbology and his findings, avoiding my wrath. Arthur chose to work to avoid the same.

"Do you think Lord Maaier will return?" Mary had asked quietly when preparing me for bed. Tearing me from my thoughts.

"I hope so." I offered smally. She smiled.

"Things that are lost always have a way of coming back to us." Her voice sang cheerfully. I smiled back. Hoping to God she was right. Rosemary's gentle hands wove through my hair. Untangling the lengths with ease. Her company was a welcome attribute to my days.

"Your grandmother was speaking about holding a party of some sort. To celebrate your upcoming birthday." She bubbled quietly. Almost squeaking with excitement. "She was most excited for you to play the piano for all of her guests. She was planning a dinner in three nights to arrange for it all."

"Is this all wise, my friend?" The incredulousness of the story was incredible. What was the old woman thinking? The attacker was still at large and not yet caught. That and Maaier was not here to protect me any longer.

I wondered if he knew I would be safe. I was curious as to whether he would show up if I was in danger. I liked to believe he would but I wasn't sure in myself. I barely knew him but it felt like somewhere deep inside me knew him better than the back of my own grey hand. Mary lowered herself to me, hands freezing in my hair. Looking around sheepishly before uttering the words that sent a chill straight to my bone.

"She seems to think it will draw out the attacker once and for all."

Mary watched for my reaction in the mirror. My skin paled as a cold breeze crept through the room. Were they serious? They were going to lure the crazy man back here! Like hell they would succeed. Mary apologised softly before braiding my hair. I waved her away. Assuring her she did no wrong.

After my hair was braided and tied back. I sent for Victor. Needing the comfort of a friend more than anything. My skin felt like the ice slowly creeping in. I watched my hands as I flexed them. Remembering how bright the blood coloured that night. My eyes drifted up to the glass reflecting my exhausted self.

Looking into the mirror, I stared at a patch of fog forming by the window. Like smoke rising. Spinning to face it, my heart leapt into my chest. Nothing remained. No smoke. No fog. Exhaling deeply, I turned to the mirror cursing myself.

The image reflected, causing a screech to shred from my throat. Hovering behind me stood my mother. Her ghostly hand resting on my shoulder. Her pale skin unmarked. Her same soft smile. Just as I remembered her.

I leapt up from my seat. Turning to face the empty room. Tears rolling down my face as sobs racked my body. My behind hit the dressing table, the knuckles on my hands grew white with my grip

The door burst open to a bewildered Victor. He hurried to where I was. Pulling me into a tight embrace. My stare still trained on the spot where she stood. Victor's hands rubbed small circles on my back. Grandmother's voice sounded from beside me. Her hand petting my hair. Sweet words whispered to the otherwise silent room. I shifted closer to Victor, clenching my eyes closed. All I could see was mothers hauntingly beautiful smile.

"Arthur. Send for Dorian!" Grandmother ordered. Footsteps sounded down the hall.

I was no doubt losing my mind.

Dorian arrived in a flurry of silk and weeds. Tiny shreds of her small garden tangled in her tattered skirt. I waited for her in the hall. Her boney arms wrapped around my neck. Only pulling back to pull my head back and forth. Searching for anything she could.

"Who?" She uttered. The word falling from her cracked lips.

"Mother." I croaked.

"Shit." Dorian cursed before pulling me to the front garden outside.

The snow fell around us, like a blanket of plush fur on the hard ground beneath.

"This is wrong. You feel wrong." She wrinkled her nose. Disgust evident as she stepped back from me. I stepped toward her, the snow crunching under my feet. Harsh cold nibbling its way into my skin.

"Dori. You're having an episode. I'm the exact same as I was this morning when you cuddled up to me in bed," I said with an exasperated sigh. I could feel their eyes on me from the window, staring down to where Dorian clutched my shoulders with her sharp nails. After seeing my mother and now dealing with another episode from Dorian, I wasn't sure how much more I could take.

"Death knows your name." Her eyes widened. She whispered her words so softly I had to strain to hear them.

"Death knows everyone's name. It's not something to

fear." I assured her. Keeping my voice level despite my terror inside. I hadn't fully told Dorian about Maaier but no doubt she knew.

"No, but you are." She sneered, her eyes glazing over. A vision coming over her.

I leapt forward, catching her before she hit the ground before her.

I pulled her back into the manor. Collapsing back on the wall with her in my arms. Dorian curled into me. Just as she had many times before.

"A broken portrait will signal retribution. I'm so sorry. I'm sorry, Vessie." She shook in my arms yet her voice remained steady.

I hushed her gently. Petting her hair as she regained control. She pulled back suddenly.

"Vespera. When did I get here? How did I get her? Why am I here?" She scurried back in horror. Her eyes widening at the sight behind me.

The doors to the manor swung open.

Dorian's screech rang in my ears. The sound startled me more than the door flying open. Her sharp nails dug into my shoulders. Frantic eyes searching the hallway.

Like the flick of a switch, Dorian's terror cleared. She stood suddenly. Leaving me on the floor to look up at her as her fists opened and closed. Fingers splaying in between each beat. Her focus was solely on the room now radiating ice cold. My skin prickled beneath my sleeves. Dorian stormed into the room, slamming the doors behind her.

Her voice muffled behind the thick wood. I pressed my ear against the door, knowing better than disrupting her during an outburst. The words "leave" "hurt her" and "killed" were the only ones I could make out. But her next ones made my blood run cold.

"The reaper... brings her harm." Who was she talking to? There was surely no one in there with her. Not that I could hear anyway.

I stepped back from the door. My heart sank into my stomach. He wouldn't hurt me. Would he? Surely not. But Dorian was not wrong. Not ever. The frigid air weaving its way into my veins. My head spun and the world became fuzzy. Blood rushed in my ears. The feeling of the floor was frigid as I tumbled forward. Letting the darkness consume me.

Chapter Forty

My name sounded like water.

A soft gentle stream of words stringing together.

My eyes fluttered open. The library was bare. I sat slowly, holding my pounding head. The pain radiating through my body. I hissed through my clenched teeth.

"It's okay. You're safe here." The words echoed around me. Light flooded in through the windows floating in the cold breeze. Flecks of dust dancing in the light.

I stood slowly making my way over to them. The lace soft against my fingers. A pair of delicate hands gripped my shoulders. The scent of indigo and paint brought a pang of tears to my eyes.

"I've got you, my sweet girl." Mother's voice crooned. Her lips pressed against my hair just as they always had, gentle and warm.

A sob broke through my chest. She held me closer, holding my back to her as my knees grew weak. We slid to the floor but she didn't seem to mind. Instead holding me firmly against her. Her breath cold against my neck.

"Shhh." She soothed. "You're okay. Mummy is here."

The words hit like a dagger.

I twisted in her grasp. Burying myself in her neck.

"I love you." I choked out.

"I love you more, darling girl. Long have I waited for you to tell me that again in my arms."

"Am I dead?"

She chuckled, shaking her head. "I thought it was time I let you know you're not alone here."

"You could see me?"

"Always. But I didn't know you could see me," She said softly as she wiped the hair from my forehead. Her face unaged. Glowing in the light. Just as beautiful as she always had been.

"It was a blessing."

"But also a curse," She murmured as she looked over at me. Taking my head in her hands she studied me before cracking a wide smile.

"My daughter, the beauty. Who would have guessed the little old gloom would turn into the most beautiful bloom."

"You know about his name for me?"

She laughed again, the sound like bells in the wind. "I know everything. I knew he was yours before you were even a babe."

I furrowed my brow.

"Your soul recognises him. Your soul is his."

I longed to bury myself in her chest. To remain with her, forever within her heart. But it was a dream one could not achieve. All I craved was her. To know she was still here was a blessing and a curse.

"But Vespera, things are coming. Very bad things. I can sense them. The attacks have been no accident. You have let your guard fall. You may be blind to death but you are not invincible. You must stay strong. Find who has done this to you and our family. Bring them to justice for us."

"If I do, will you finally rest?"

"When the time comes for you to come with me, my sweet babe, we will cross together." Her words were final. There was no point in arguing. No one ever argued with her and came out victorious. I traced the paint still splattered across her arms even in her afterlife. How could a ghost have paint on them after all this time?

"I had just finished painting when I died," She said, seeing the question in my eyes. Her smile sad. I had never seen that final portrait.

I deflated slightly. Hearing her say she was dead was too hard to hear. To know it was true hurt but to hear her spirit admit it was like a nail to the bone.

My eyes slowly fluttered closed as I embraced her warm hold despite the ice she radiated. Her hands drew circles on my back. "I watch over you, my sweet girl, always. I always have."

"I wish I had known that earlier." I confessed. Mother chuckled lightly. The sound illuminated my soul. I pulled from her grasp. Facing her fully, her hands cupped my cheeks.

"Do you like my final painting?" She smiled.

I quirked a brow. "I don't think I have ever seen it."

She grinned before pulling my head to her chest like a child.

"When you see it again you will know."

I embraced her warmth. The feeling of a mother's touch so long craved finally sinking in. tears filled my eyes as she silently wiped them with her thumb. Holding me close in perfect silence. I didn't want to leave. All I wanted was her. To feel her love forever more.

"I don't have much longer, my sweet winter child. But

please know, I love you more than stars and sky combined." I gripped her tighter. Unable to say the words back before the darkness devoured me once more.

My scream shook the air as I awoke. A protest to take me back to her hanging in the halls.

Dorian hovered beside me. Her wild eyes bored into mine. Fear and sorrow reflected within. She didn't need to speak. She knew she was in there. It only hurt that I could only see her in a vision. Why had she not made herself known beforehand instead of scaring me? My mother was always strange, I suppose.

Maybe she didn't want me chasing after her. Little did she know that once this mess was done, I would follow her into every life beyond this one.

I needed to breathe.

The following days were nothing if not stifling. Maaier had grown distant since Father's arrival. I ached for him but I could not bring myself to delve into that desire. I needed to focus on my killer. I chose to believe that he was giving me space for my task. If only to heal the hurt of losing so much so quickly… yet again.

A dinner had been planned for my birthday just shy of a week away. I protested against it. Demanding it was a waste of time. I did not find the need to celebrate turning twenty five.

I was already an old maid in the town's eyes. Or a freak. Always the freak. Surprisingly a lot of people said yes to attending the function despite the weather and murderer lurking the streets.

The maids had grown quiet. Not discussing their fellow maid as the trial approached. They said the evidence was as good as found. I couldn't bring myself to believe it. It was all too strange and didn't match the poor girl's character in any capacity.

My breath fogged the expanse as I leant against the glass of the library. The wind blows lightly through the barren branches. The last of the winter's snow beginning to slow. The soft flurry still fell like ash to the ground. A pang hit my stomach. Ash just like my beloved greenhouse.

Father had assured me he would build another one himself to replace mine but I didn't want it.

I wanted my safe place with all my most beloved memories and secrets. I watched as Dorian and Victor bickered in the yard below. Dorian no doubt scolding him for something.

Victor however was grinning mischievously. Bending down low to scoop snow in his hands when her back was turned. He rolled the snow slowly between his hands before throwing it at her. The snowball hit her square in the right shoulder. She turned quickly. Her eyes narrowed before she made a snowball of her own. I could hear her laughter. A sound rarely heard from Dorian without her being manic. She deserved it. She deserved to be joyous for once. But something in the breeze made her stiffen. Her shoulders became rigid. She ran from Victor. Heading straight toward the path to the river.

With a curse, I sprinted outside to follow her. Leaving my cloak behind. With my skirts in hand, I ordered Victor to stay put. Whatever Dorian was seeing was enough to throw caution to the wind. Was it bad? Was it her future or mine. Or could it even be ours? She had said we wouldn't survive. Has she seen our ends again? Or was she talking metaphorically? Having a seer as your best friend was more work than anyone could imagine. But I wouldn't trade her for anything. I would remain colourless my entire life, for eternity if I had to, just to see her smile.

I called her name. My voice rough with exertion. Curse Mary and these tight corsets.

Dorian materialised through the brush.

"Vessie, come!" She ushered cheerfully.

I huffed out a breath before kneeling beside her at the river.

"They called for us," She whispered. Her focus on the water running below. She lifted her hand. Skirting her fingers along the frozen surface. I frowned.

"Who called?"

"Them." She pointed to the centre of the river. I stood slowly. The ice was thick. But it wasn't overly strong. I stepped forward, testing the weight of my body on the ice before placing both feet on the surface. The ice creaked beneath me. I took a small step and shuffled until I reached where she was pointing. I turned around to find Dorian with a flask in her hand. She threw it to me, barely giving me time to catch it.

"Where did you get that?" I hissed.

"Pour it on the surface!" She said, eyes wide as she watched the surface beneath my feet. I shuffled back. The sound of a knock beneath the ice rippling through the air.

Slowly, I untwisted the top. My heart was pounding as I poured the liquid onto the surface. The ice grew clearer. I looked down. The shadow of a hand floated just under the surface. My heart leapt into my throat.

The ice creaked beneath me. This time louder. The cracks set in like lightning under my feet. Bursting through the surface. My foot slipped. The ice disappeared as I plummeted into the water. Dorian rushed forward. Catching me just in time before I fell in. The ice broke until we hit the edge. Falling into the abyss below. The hard surface gave way to the secrets hidden beneath. Two white lumps crested the hole where I had just stood. My skirts, now heavy and damp.

Their long hair clumped with leaves. Two small girls bobbed through the ice water. Suspended by a log.

"What do we do?" Dorian fretted her lip. I took her hand.

"We find Arthur?" I suggested.

"Why that daft old toad?" She shook her head in disgust.

"He will know what to do. Victor doesn't need more mess to clean up."

Dorian nodded before scurrying off. I trembled in the cold. Waiting for Arthur to return with Dorian. Who were these poor children? Surely they would not have wandered out here alone. Not at this age. Most children that dared were into their early teenage years. The younger generations were mostly scared off by stories of ghosts. As they should be. I could only imagine how many within our walls were yet to make themselves known to me.

The pair panted as they arrived. The sound filling the silent air apart from my heart pounding in my ears.

Arthur braced his hands on his knees. Gasping for air as he took in the scene around him.

"Why were you on the ice?" He swallowed thickly before panting again.

"I don't know." I lied. Although it wasn't truly a lie.

Arthur swore as he looked at the young girls. His face paled at the sight.

"What do we do?" Dorian said as she moved to stand beside me.

"We can't tell the police." He shook his head.

"Why not!" I barked, horrified that he would keep this from the authorities.

"Think about it." He faced us. "Your father returns home and two girls show up in the river by the house. They will suspect him immediately. They will ask how you knew the girls were there. What are you going to do? Tell them you had a hunch? They would crucify you for that."

"Then what do we do?" Dorian pressed.

"You two will go get warmed up. Leave this with me. I will dispose of them closer to town so that it looks like they died there."

"Why not let them float?"

I shot an incredulous look at Dorian.

"What the fuck do you mean?" I swore, gaining a scald from Arthur in return.

"Too many branches." Arthur waved her help away. Dorian looked at the girls again. Her body shook as she released the weight of the sight.

The two young girls looked so similar, both young with swollen faces. The only difference was their hair, one thick and dark, the other thin and light. Dorian looked over the two corpses once more, drawing the same connection as she looked at me. They looked just like us.

"Take her to the manor. I need you to find your father. I need you to find out if he was by the river at all."

I nodded. Wrapping my arm around Dorian's shoulders. Her saddened sniffs hurt my heart.

"It is too much of a coincidence that they died in the same place your mother did."

"And Aunt Magdelena." I added.

Arthur studied me. Wondering how I knew that Magdelena was burnt not too far into the woods from here.

"And her yes," He said sadly. The memory of his sister

playing in his mind. His shoulders slumped. I pulled Dorian away, leading her up the path.

We broke free of the trees. The yard was now bare of people. Apart from the ghosts of the two small girls now making their way up the front stairs. Their hands clasped together as they entered the house of madness.

Chapter Forty-One

I watched the girls in horror. Knowing that once you were in the manor, you could never escape it's hold. My heart leapt into my throat. I hurried toward the manor, leaving Dorian to stare into the forest like a woman made of stone.

My ears strained as I listened for the girls when I stepped into the main hall. Nothing. Not a peep or single sound.

Dorian shuddered as she entered the home after me. Her shoulders rolled back with her head high. An omen if I ever saw one. The number three whispered from her mouth before she stretched her hand back for me to take. Before I could reach for her, my father suddenly appeared in the doorway. His smile faltered as he looked upon our faces.

"Vespera, you look like you've seen a ghost," He said, a foreign concern ribbed his tone. His posture softened, his arms twitched by his side. As if reaching to hold me close but not strong enough to, I bit back a laugh at his words. If only he knew the truth.

"That's how she always looks," Dorian sneered before pushing past him and to the kitchens. No doubt about to bake a tart to take her frustrations out on the dough. I wished I still had a vice. Mine now lingered as ash on the wind.

"Are you alright?" Father stepped before me. Still not touching me. Fearful as if I were to break before him. I nodded once.

"Yes. Just tired is all."

His shoulders slumped. A pent up breath quietly exhaled from his lips.

"Where did you go?" The words burst from me before I could think. Father raked a hand through his dark hair.

"I've been here all along."

"Not now. When you abandoned me."

"I didn't abandon-"

"You did. But I have moved past it." I cut him off with a raised palm. I was becoming more and more like Grandmother by the day. Something I wasn't even slightly upset at.

Father heaved a sigh before pushing the library doors open. I followed him silently, sitting in my usual seat on the couch whilst Father took the armchair. My nails towed with a loose thread in my skirt as I waited for his excuse.

"I was trying to find a cure." He admitted after what felt like a decade of heavy silence. An icy chill ran through the room. My eyes darted over the room. Wondering who was joining us.

"A cure? I need the actual truth, not the lie you spin to anyone who doesn't care to ask," I said. My expression was cool as he looked upon me with utter sadness in his expression. Pure devastation in his eyes.

"I travelled the world for you. To find information on the curse. To find anything," He said. I met his gaze. His soft eyes pleading. He swallowed before continuing. "I went through England and Ireland. I went to Venice, Rome, France and even as far as Egypt. No one had ever heard of such a curse. I know some were born without the coloured sight but you are different."

"The curse can be broken when I find love. You of all people should know this."

"But you shouldn't have to find love to get your colour back. You should be able to live your life and fall in love not for the end of a curse but because it is truly the most beautiful thing in the world."

"Just like your love for my mother?" I said, not wanting to believe his words. Something was off. He shouldn't have to plead for his daughter to forgive him. A frigid breeze hit my shoulder but I didn't dare look behind me. Knowing mother was there before she even made contact.

"I loved you mother with every fibre of my being." He straightened.

"Yet you left the one thing she created with you. The one thing you once called your greatest blessing."

"I left *for* you," He said, still pleading. I stood quickly. Anger ran through me like a raging hot river.

"You left because you couldn't stand the sight of me. Even seeing me now and how much I mirror her is disgusting to you."

"Vespera... I..." He faltered for words. His posture dampened, the light receding from his eyes but I didn't care.

"I needed you and you left me," I said, keeping my voice as neutral as I could whilst in front of him. "Whilst I understand why you ran, forgiveness isn't in my strong suit."

"Trust me. I will earn it back." He reached for my hands. I allowed him one touch. Maybe there was a truth to his words. Maybe he did leave to find a cure but right now was not the time for research notes. I was not in the mood for anything but lounging on the couch and wallowing in my thoughts. Slowly,

I pulled my hands back. Noticing the warm tender smile on Father's lips.

"I will leave you alone. But please, join me for dinner?"

I nodded. Not knowing how else to respond. He slipped out of the room quietly. I slumped back on the sofa. The anger was still hot in my veins. Why am I always the one who is abandoned? Everyone has always left me.

"I thought he would never leave." A deep velvety voice crooned from behind me. The scent of cedar sent a new type of heat through my body.

"I thought you would never come." I grinned up at him. Maaier reflected the grin before leaning against the rows of books lining the walls. A smirk slashing across his handsome face. I sauntered over to him. A wave of confidence coursing through me. He was all I needed to aid my frustrations. To free some of this anger.

Maaier's gaze darkened as I stalked closer. His hands twitching by his sides.

"This is a bad idea, little bloom."

"And all the other times weren't?" I cocked my head. Loosening the ties on my dress. A deep primal sound caught in Maaier's throat.

"Now that you know the truth, it will be harder for me to retain control."

"What if I don't need you to?" I smirked. My grin was almost feral as I reached him. My hands snaked around his throat as I yanked him down to me. Our lips met harshly. Both fighting for dominance. Moans and groans echoed in the air. A rush of air filled the room. The sound of the lock on the library slid into place. I pulled back breathlessly.

"You can do that?"

"Darling, I can do anything. Now, follow my lead," He purred before pulling me back to him. Our bodies met with heat pouring through us. Hands roaming over each other form as our tongues danced with the other. A sigh escaped me only to be swallowed by him. Just as he did my existence. I was his.

I pushed him harder against the books, demanding more. Deepening the kiss. Maaier growled before hoisting me up by the waist. In an instant, my back was slammed against the shelves. Pain radiated from the impact but I paid it no mind.

"Learn to obey your god."

"And who might they be?" I purred.

"Me." He snarled before hiking up my skirts with his free hand.

He was inside me in an instant. His length filled me perfectly. I moaned when he thrust. Keeping my voice as soft as I could.

"No one can hear you." He managed through his lips peppering my neck. His thrust was slow and deliberate, teasing me to no end.

"You wicked man." I cursed.

He chuckled darkly against my skin. Thrusting so hard into me, I swear the universe flashed before my eyes. My body hit the books behind me. A scream caught in my throat.

"Can't have anyone else hearing how you fall apart for me, can we, my soul?"

The pleasure built higher and higher as his cock impaled me over and over. Hitting the right spot. A hand found my chest, the other still holding me in place by the waist. His expert hands kneaded my soft breast. Fingers tugging at the bud. I groaned louder. He bent down slowly. Thrusting deeper as if that were somehow possible. With a flick of his tongue on my nipple I was gone. The stars burst behind my eyes. My voice broke with the scream. Heat roiled through me. Bringing me life before allowing me to return to earth. To the beautiful man still between my legs.

"Fuck, I love you, Vespera. Tell me you are mine."

God be damned, if this was his way of getting me to choose him, he would win a million times over.

"I'm yours." A whisper was all I could manage as pressure began to build in the small of my spine once more.

"You are what?" He whispered into my ear, his hand closed over my throat.

"I. Am. Yours." I said louder.

"Again." He ordered with a thrust. Books fell from the shelves. Landing with a crash on the floor.

"I am yours." Thrust. "I am yours." thrust. Each repetition sent me hurling toward the cosmos once more.

"You are mine. Until the day you give yourself to me and beyond. You, Vespera Florian, are *mine*." He growled before finally releasing with one last thrust. The stars burst from me again. Blinding light over taking my senses as I cried out once more. His name was like a song to the wind.

Maaier softened against me, removing himself from my core. He slumped down, his forehead resting on mine as our breaths mingled. Closing my eyes, I breathed him in. the scent of cedar and saffron like heaven to my senses.

"I love when no one can hear you scream for me."

"How do you do it?" I opened my eyes to find him staring back at me. Dark and deep eyes like a starless sky shining back at me

"Well you don't exactly want anyone spotting you when you're escorting a soul from a body." His lips twitched with a smile. I couldn't help but smile back.

He stepped back slowly, putting himself back into his trousers. My eyes caught on the ground as I fixed my skirt. The feeling of his seed running down my leg was slightly uncomfortable. The books lay scattered on the ground in a mess.

I breathed his name. My eyes growing wide. Amongst the red lay a new shade. A deep colour I was yet to see.

I swept it off the floor. My fingers danced over the leather as I admired the peculiar shade.

"What colour is this?" I bubbled, turning back to Maaier and holding out the book.

"Your favourite colour. Green." He smiled.

"Green," I repeated, the word foreign on my tongue. "My favourite?" I lifted my brow. Looking back at the dark green book in my hand.

"You always wear either green or black. That and you do have an affinity for plants." My heart warmed at his notice. He noticed the shades I wore more than even I had realised.

"You can keep the colour if you wish." He leant forward and kissed my brow. Hands catching in my hair. Rubbing the strands between his thumbs.

"Is that why you kept my eyes covered? So I would not see colour?"

"No. I did it because when I touched you, I lost control. I couldn't let you know the truth until you were ready. Every touch caused my grip to slip more and more." He smiled softly, almost bashful

"What will our next session get me?" I dared to ask. Maaier threw his head back in a deep laugh. The sound like pure paradise.

"The next time will bring you an eternal life of colour if that be what you wish, little bloom."

My heart swelled in my chest. My choice was made. But I couldn't leave yet. Not with everything unsolved.

Hope flooded through me, replacing the anger that once bubbled.

Chapter Forty-Two

I had retired to my bedroom. Deliciously sore but craving more. My eyes looked over my bedroom. Amongst the usual grey, the new colour bloomed. So much within my wardrobe and dressing heralded the colour. Maaier was right. This was my favourite. I admired the painting hanging on the wall. Green stems wrapped over my arms. The leaves vibrant against the pale skin. A smile filled my face. A genuine admiration for the art I hadn't shown in a long time. I longed to know who painted it.

A small sniff filled the space. The sound of muffled sobbing rebounded through the house. How could no one hear this? It was deafening.

I had tried to find the girls for an hour after they had entered the manor but they were yet to be seen.

The sniffling grew louder. Tearing myself from the portrait, I headed toward the noise. Silently praying the girls had made themselves known. Small and soft voices came from the end of the hall.

I cursed under my breath before storming to the door. They wouldn't escape me now. I had to know who attacked us.

My hand reached for the knob. Only to find the room locked. How curious. The room was never locked, not since I had entered there. A cold chill ran through me. They were in there with Magdelena. God only knows what she was filling their heads with.

The girls cried louder, begging almost, for something I couldn't make out. My heart dropped in my chest. The despair in their tiny sobs was like a knife to the chest. Their small wails, like salt in a wound. I needed to get in there. I needed to calm them down, to assure them all was well.

Willing myself, I tried the door once more. Throwing my shoulder against it for good measure. Only before I could make contact the door flung open. I fell unceremoniously inside, landing with a heavy thud on the dusty floor. The air whooshing out of me.

The girls cried louder at the intrusion. Magdelena screeched from the corner of the room, begging for me to help her with her hands over her ears.

With a groan, I pulled myself from the floor. Finding myself eye to eye with a squatting Maaier.

Wonder blazed through his eyes at me and the door again. His hand reached out for mine. I took it gladly. The contact of his skin zipped through me like a bolt of lightning. The door slammed behind me as I made it to my feet.

"How are you in here?" He muttered, looking back at the door once more.

"I heard crying and thought I could help," I said. It was only half true but he had refused to help me in the past. I still wondered if I was truly his soul mate.

"Very well." He swallowed before turning back to the girls. I finally looked over them. A sharp inhale drawn at the sight of them.

The girls were only young. No older than eight. Their

skin, ice white but their colourings took me by shock. The girl on the right with her arms back toward the smaller girl blinked at me. Her inky black hair was wild with sticks and damp leaves. Wide defiant eyes staring back at me. Her friend sniffled. A light haired girl with darker eyes trembling behind her back. I looked over them. Anger churned through me. The two girls were almost identical to myself and Dorian at their age. Their killer weaving them into this sick game we were all pawns in.

I was frozen in place. Horror masking my saddened expression. Magdelena uncurled from the bed, tiptoeing up to me. Maaier knelt once more. His focus purely on the young girls.

Magdelena wove her frigid hand into mine, squeezing me tightly. More physical than she had ever been before, more corporeal of anything.

"They've been in here crying all day," She whispered. The black haired girl bared her teeth at the words.

"Who are you?" She snarled. Such a fighting spirit for someone so young.

"This is Vespera. My soul," Maaier explained gently. Keeping his focus on the girls.

The girl looked over at me. Noting my aunt's hand in mine.

"Is she dead too?" She jutted her chin.

Maaier shook his head.

"Not technically," He said. His tone was the epitome of softness, a side rarely shown.

"Then how can she see us?" The light haired girl squeaked. Seemingly gaining more confidence with the girl protecting her.

"He's been pleading with them for an hour but still hasn't broken through to them once. I would have punched a wall by now if I was him," Magdelena whispered. I had to hold myself back from laughing at her horrified face.

The dark haired girl snapped her teeth. Even Magdelena startled beside me.

"Hey." Maaier snapped his fingers. The girl remained in place. "You do not threaten my wife."

Magdelena turned to me. Her face a mix of horror and confusion.

When the hell did I become his wife? Did him giving me the colour green mean I was his bride? I shook my head once, pleading with my gaze for her to know that was not the case. Not yet anyway. Magdelena softened again, her usual fire prickling behind her eyes.

"I know how you feel," I said, taking a cautious step toward the girl. Magdelena's hand falling from mine.

"You're alive. We aren't," The dark haired girl hissed.

"But I wasn't." My fingers reached for my neckline. Pulling the fabric down to bare my scar. "It hurts. Dying. Doesn't it?" The girl's facade softened.

"He said you weren't dead," The lighter haired girl responded, peeking out from behind her vicious friend.

"I was. But I was brought back." I offered a small smile.

"Can we be brought back?"

I shook my head at the lighter haired girl's question. "I'm sorry."

The girl's face dropped. Tears rolling down her cheeks in fat droplets. I stepped beside Maaier. The girl rushed forward. Without warning, her arms wrapped around my hips, her head buried itself in my belly as she sobbed.

"But I don't want to be dead," She cried.

"It's okay." I soothed as I pet her back. Letting her release all her emotions onto me. The fabric of my dress grew damp beneath her cheeks. The dark haired girl met gaze. Her facade breaking at the instant our eyes met. She rushed forward. Nuzzling into me beside her little friend. Their cold bodies chilled my skin but I paid it no mind. It was my fault they were here after all. Never to see their mothers or family again. Never to run in fields of flowers or dance under the stars. To grow up and find their talent and passion. Their bright futures ripped away simply because they resembled Dorian and I.

My own tears welled in my eyes. I tilted my head back, willing them to remain hidden to fall later when I was alone.

Maaier stood slowly. Silently watching the interaction.

The girls pulled themselves back from me. The lighter haired one took my hand.

"Can you tell me your names?"

"Abigail," The lighter haired girl said with a sniff.

"Florence," The dark haired girl replied softly.

"We don't want to go to the otherside." Florence stared at me as she reached for Abigail's tiny fist hanging limply by her side.

They took hands, staring up at me as if to argue.

I glanced at Maaier. Begging him with a look to help me, but he remained silent. Magdelena moved to the lounge behind him. Watching with her elbows propped up on her knees. The shadow of another figure lingered beside her. I couldn't make out who it was. Their light was not bright enough to see their features.

"Maaier will take you to the next place. A place of dreams." I forced my brightest smile despite the despair in my heart.

"We don't want to go." They pleaded in unison. The sound reminded me of Dorian and I at their age. There was no talking sense into either of us.

"What if I come with you?" I asked. Maaier's face fell.

Magdelena straightened. "Death! Please! Talk sense into the idiot!" She barked, standing from the couch with her arms out beside her.

"Can you?" Abigail brightened. I nodded.

"In three days, I will turn twenty six. I have a few unfinished things I need to sort out but once I'm done we can all go rest. How does that sound?"

I knew I should have pleaded with them to cross now. But it was simply no use. I knew no matter how hard you tried, a stubborn woman wouldn't budge. No matter the age.

Maaier stared at me, absolutely crestfallen by my decision.

Did he not want me that way? Did he not want my eternal soul like he said?

The girls smiled as I let them go.

"Explore the manor but do not break a thing and do not make yourself known." The girls practically bounced at the permission. Their smiles slowly brightened over their faces.

"Stay away from the wild blonde woman."

"And me!" Magdelena called before flopping back on the couch with a sigh, mumbling curses under her breath.

Maaier reached for my hand, pulling me out into the hall.

I stumbled after him, his heavy footsteps leading to his room.

The room was basic. A single bed with a dresser in the corner. The scent of him was heavy in the air.

His words but a whisper as he said my name.

"What did you mean by not technically dead?" I asked, tilting my head at him.

Maaier sank down onto his bed, shaking hands raking through his dark hair.

"Please," I pleaded. Kneeling in front of him, I took his hands in mine. Prying them from his scalp. He drew in a deep breath. I flashed a small smile, assuring that all was okay.

"You are dead, Vespera."

Chapter Forty-Three

I fell back as if slapped. I wasn't dead. I couldn't be. I was alive. I felt every sensation. People could see me. No. No. It couldn't be real. Maaier pulled me back into him. Holding me close on the floor. I gasped into him, heaving for air. Air I thought that I needed. That I did need.

"You died that night," He whispered into my hair. His lips a brushing kiss. Heat rose in my eyes. But I wouldn't cry. Not again.

"I got there just in time to secure a tether to you but your body was already gone."

"What do you mean?"

"I tied your soul to the earth but also myself. A selfish thing to do. I'm sorry." He kissed my forehead over and over again. Forcing his love into every affection.

"How?" I managed. My hands clawed into his shirt. How could I be dead? I can't be! I was here. Everyone could see me and interact.

"I tethered your soul to the earth here. To the outside world, you would be alive here but no one outside of the manor or town would know you if you were to journey past them. They wouldn't see you. You would remain here forever. Never ageing. Never dying." He took in a deep breath before continuing "I tied the other side to myself. Knowing that you were mine, I claimed you. But you are mine. I recognised your soul. A soul that mirrored mine after so long of being on my lonesome."

"If I'm dead, how do I bleed?" I tried my hardest to find cracks in his story but he always had an answer.

"You still look as if you bleed and feel pain as these are earthly notions."

"You said I had a choice." My voice high as I pulled back staring into his desperate face. A face that no doubt mirrored mine. What had he done?

"I lied. Your choice was always me. You always had to come home in the end."

"Then why did you look so sad when I said I can cross over with the girls?"

"That's the only choice you ever really had. It was me or you crossed over to eternal darkness."

"Why don't I get an 'other' side?"

"Me tethering here you took that away."

"Did you know?"

He said nothing.

"Did you know?" I said, my voice growing firm.

Nothing.

"Maaier did you know what would happen to me?" I hissed through my teeth, pulling him from myself.

"Yes." He uttered softly, avoiding my gaze. I shifted back again, making more space between us. This was all too much. My head was swimming with endless thoughts and accusations.

"You had to choose me." He flashed me a hopeless look. "No one else had ever chosen me. But you. I knew you were different." His words shocked me to my core. My soul teared deep inside of me. Despite it all, I did not find any anger in my heart, nor could I. For I knew his story. The horrifyingly tragic tale and his life after. And even after all of that darkness, I still chose him. Just as I would now. It was like the book had shown me. He was always watching as Florians chose other lovers. Never once choosing him. I breathed in deep before taking his head in my hands.

I understood. I understood what it was like to want love but be terrified of the aftermath. Of the colour coming in. It was terrifying in and of itself. All I had longed for was someone to choose me. To not abandon me the way others had. To hold me through each and every painful or joyful thing that happened. Someone to accept me as I was. Was that too much to ask?

The man before me was offering all of that and more. A comfort I had never dared to fully consider for myself was sitting before me. Having made the choice for me but knowing I would find my own way to him in the end after all.

"I would have chosen you, Maaier. I would have chosen you if you were a peasant on the street. I would have chosen you if you were a man of the night. I would have chosen you if you were nothing but a simple human living their life. And I still choose you. Even after this confession. Not because I have no choice but because I love you." Maaier's eyes widened at my heartfelt words.

"I have loved you since that night you saved me. And I will love you for eternity. I will love you through each reckoning and each disaster. I will love you through each soul because that's what you are. My soul. You're my soul, Maaier."

A long tear dropped from Maaier's eye. His smile wobbled as he pulled me close. My forehead met his.

"Until the world requires us no more."

"Until the world requires us no more," I repeated.

Maaier's lips crashed into mine. The hands holding my back now woven through my hair loosening the knot as he held me as close to him as he could. Our lips met with a bruising force. My heart thundered within. My pulse beating madly through me. My hands explored his just as the door lock sounded. I smiled against his mouth before tugging his shirt over his head.

Our lips broke for a single breath only to allow our tongues to dance once more. Maaier's gentle yet demanding hands drifted down to the buttons on the back of my dress. The bodice falling free to land on my hips. His hands drifted to my front, needing my exposed breasts. I moaned at the contact. Currents of sparks blazing under my skin as he kneaded my flesh.

I needed him. I craved him. Just as much if not more as I had the first time. My fingers ran up his bare chest. Squeezing his shoulders as I straddled him. Taking the lead to where I needed him most. He groaned as I rolled my hips over his clothed length now hard and desperate against the fabric confining it. The sensation against my sensitive skin a welcome delight. I stifled a moan, rolling my lips together just as I did my hips. Slowly Maaier lifted us. I gasped at the sudden loss of the ground only to be thrown on the bed behind us. He stood over. Wild lust filled eyes burning down at me. He knelt forward. His hands tugged at the fabric of my dress until it tore free from my body.

"Like the goddess I knew you to be," He muttered with a smirk. I propped myself up on my elbows. Watching as he loosened the tie in his pants. His hard cock sprung free. My mouth watered at the sight. Maaier knelt over me once more. His hand skimmed my skin over my hips up my waist over my chest only to stop atop my scar. The other landed on the jagged scar just near my belly button where the knife had made its final blow.

"You are utter perfection, my soul," He crooned before lowering himself onto me. I welcomed the weight. His flesh warm against mine. His lips peppered mine again before I opened them for him. Allowing him to taste me. His hand slid under my behind before he thrust into me.

Not as rough as he usually did. Slower this time, as if truly savouring the feeling of me around him. The first time our naked flesh had touched. A movement so intimate, so natural, so utterly devastatingly perfect. I knew I made the right choice.

Maaier thrust slowly, his mouth moved to my neck. A sigh of pleasure left my mouth. His hands gripped my waist. The head of his length hitting just the right spot deep inside me, over and over again. A coil tightened near my spine. Pleasure rolling through me. My body, alive once more. His name, a melody on my lips, sung to him with each brush. The coil finally snapped. Warm heat exploded through me with a deep moan. Tiny rivers of lightning forming behind my eyes. Maaier followed not long after. He panted against my bare skin. Dropping his weight on me.

"Gods, little bloom. You have ruined me," He sighed before nuzzling into my chest.

My hands ran through his hair. Holding him close. I didn't need to tell him he ruined me too. He knew. He knew all along I was his and that I would choose him. I knew it within myself that was always my destiny. All roads always lead back to him.

With the reaper, I was home.

Chapter Forty-Four

Dawn came early the next day. I woke to an empty bed. Maaier had chosen to remain in his own bed to not raise more suspicion than necessary about our situation. Dorian had snored most of the night. Sniffing through her dreams as if saddened by something. She was desperate to return home, anyone could see that.

The two small girls had spotted her yesterday. Heeding my warning as she walked past them. They drifted back into the wall. Running up the stairs in the opposite direction. To be frank, I would have too. Dorain had had a vision that morning that had left her almost volatile. Even the staff dared not to go near her. She had stormed through the manor like a typhoon. Victor was the only one game enough to go after her.

I had dressed quickly before escorting Maaier into town. The Cursed Life of Death sitting hidden in my bag. I didn't want to tell Maaier about it. Not yet anyway. I didn't think he would be upset but I wanted to know the last little shred of the story for myself.

The carriage bumped over the damp road. The rain stilled long enough for us to get through.

My breath fogged the window. The cold chill of the air settled into the cabin. I glanced at Maaier across from me. His focus on something on the horizon.

"They are hanging the maid from the manor today," He said so softly I had barely heard it.

I narrowed my gaze. Confused for a second before the realisation dawned on me.

"No," I responded, Maaier shrugged.

"They found enough evidence to charge her with the murder of her husband and his mistress."

"But Gracie couldn't have done that. She wouldn't have." The woman was smaller than me for Christ sake. How could she have slaughtered her own husband?

"I agree," Maaier said, reading my face. I slumped back in the chair.

"I don't believe it," I breathed.

"Me either."

"How did they say she killed him?" Maaier straightened at my words. His dark eyes never left mine.

"They say she stabbed him sixteen times in the chest."

"And the mistress?"

"Slit her throat."

I exhaled, a small laugh of disbelief falling from my mouth.

"Horse shit. Complete and utter horse shit. The woman was scared of her own shadow!"

Maaier frowned but sat back. "I know. I saw her in the prison cell."

"What did she say?" How on earth was he allowed in. And then it dawned on me. He himself was but a shadow.

"She was pleading to any guard that would listen that she didn't do it. That she didn't commit the murder. But the guards weren't kind." He avoided my gaze.

I muttered a curse under my breath. Damned pigs. My hands fisted in my green skirt. My teeth clenched hard together. Almost cracking under the weight of my frustration.

"Do you have to take their souls?"

Maaier frowned. That was all I needed to know. The poor man had a hard enough job. I couldn't imagine taking the souls of the worst humans to the other side. I only hoped there was a special hell for each of them to live out their lives as if they were the victim on a continuous loop.

"I don't take them to a good place. They go to the darkness. They don't get an afterlife. They get nothing but endless nights with no stars to guide them."

"Like me?" I whispered. Not wanting to hear the response as if I hadn't already chosen him.

Maaier nodded once before turning out the window. His face dropped with despair.

We arrived at the main street in silence. Maaier left me to take the soul he needed and me to find the strange bookstore. I needed to know where the book came from.

I wandered the city. Avoiding the people as they passed, staring at me like a ghost. I snorted back a laugh. If only they knew. The townsfolk didn't bother to hide their stares. Each murmuring to the one next to them as I weaved my way through the crowd. Catching snippets of their words "attacked in the kitchen" "that witch Dorian" and "How could she be alive?". Did they truly not notice me the last time I came? Surely the news didn't travel that slowly.

"I heard that the maid who went mad was her personal maid."

"I would go mad if I was her maid too." Two young women giggled as I passed.

I ran my tongue over my lips, willing myself to stay calm.

There was no use defending myself. Instead as I smiled my way past them, I lifted my hand. Knocking the ridiculous bonnet from the woman's head. The ribbon around her throat tightened as it fell in my grip. The woman gasped before toppling backward with the imbalance.

I stifled my grin as I continued on. The people all gathered around her. Pulling her up from the muck but not one dared to say a thing to me. Good. Stupid people.

The street loomed before me. But the bookstore was nowhere in sight. The same bakery lined one side but next to it was a butcher. Not a bookstore.

The bell sounded as I made my way inside. A large stocky man stood behind a counter. His hands crossed over his large belly.

"Can I help you, love?" He said. His thick moustache moved like a worm as he spoke.

"This is going to sound rather strange but was there ever a book store here?"

The man shook his head once at my words. "Not as long as I've been alive. Been working here for almost thirty years, before that it belonged to my father." The man's gruff voice sounded confused but with the slightest hint of concern lingering through.

"My mistake. Thank you for your time." I offered a warm smile before entering the street once more.

I QUESTIONED MY SANITY. THE WHOLE STORE HAD TO be real. Where else would I have gotten the book? I reached into my bag. It was still there. In all its old faded glory. My fingers ran along the spine. My head spun with scenarios. Was this just another trick from Maaier? I lifted my gaze. Looking over the road before looking toward the police station down the road.

My skin chilled beneath my sleeves as gooseflesh rose. The frown on my face only grew. I squinted my eyes. Trying to see more of the person. A tall light haired man stood over a dark haired girl leaning against the wall of a building. Slowly, I walked down the road. Keeping to my side of the street.

This can't be.

Father stood rolling his shoulders back. The girl grinned up at him. Her stare alluring. Father beamed back almost bashfully. People swept by me, no longer acknowledging my existence. As if I were a ghost once more.

I watched as my father took the young woman's hand and led her down the alley. Bile rose in my throat. My stomach clenched at the sight. The woman was no older than me. My poor mother. She had always dreamed that my father would love her long after she was gone and here he was throwing it in her face.

I sucked my teeth. Anger rose through me, warming my cheeks. Just as I went to take a step to cross the road a hand gripped my shoulder.

"There you are!"

I spun to face the voice. Victor smiled warmly before laying both his hands on my shoulders.

"What are you doing in town?"

"I came to pick up some supplies from Donovan for Dorian. She has insisted on making your birthday dessert," He said brightly, I swallowed my rage. Stifling the fire burning. Was my father the attacker all along? I was annoyed at Victor for stopping me. Maybe I should tell him. He leaned forward. His breath skirted my ear.

"It's not worth it," He whispered softly so only I could

hear. I stilled. My eyes widened. I was confused beyond measure. Victor's words made no sense. "Do you trust me?"

I stopped at his question. My eyes found his light eyes. The same bright eyed expression as usual mirrored back.

"With my soul." I admitted, "But Victor, what if he is-"

"I don't think he is." He cut me off.

I shook my head. More to clear it than anything. My head was spinning with questions. I couldn't make ends of anything.

"Just because you don't think he is, doesn't mean he isn't capable of it." I pleaded with him with my eyes. Needing him to understand and not believe the best in people like he always does. The skill was both a blessing and a curse to possess. One I didn't envy.

"He may be capable of it." Victor dropped his hands from my shoulders. His hands now cupping my elbows. The townsfolk stopped to watch the sweet interaction.

"But?" I dared to ask. He looked around before meeting my gaze staring up at him.

"I will tell you more at home," He said softly before turning and walking away from me.

Frustration roiled like a spark. His distraction from my father was not necessary. I stepped onto the road. Hurrying through waves of carriages to the alley way. The stench of urine and human waste rife in the air. I blocked my nose with my sleeve. The damp earth swallowed my footsteps. My skirts clenched in one hand so they didn't drag through this filth. No voices floated from the shadows. Just my own shallow breathing against the cotton on my mouth.

"Vile people." I muttered before facing the end of the alley way. Meeting a tall brick wall.

"Damn Victor!" I cursed under my breath. My one shred of information was now lost.

"Are you looking for the young girl, lassie?" A man's voice drifted from over the wall, his Scottish accent was thick.

"How did you know?" I called back. My heart beat increased. This was a stupid idea to come down here unarmed.

"She made her way through the door but five minutes ago. Headed right down to the docks she did."

I bit my lip. Looking at the wall once more and finding a small door on the right hand side. I knew better than to open it. I had no clue what was on the other side.

"Thank you."

"Don't thank me, love. Thank the man escorting her down there."

"Shit," I cursed. The man laughed loudly, the sound like a hoarse bark.

THE DOOR SWUNG OPEN WITH A STRONG PUSH. I thrust myself against the old wood. Stumbling as I ran through the alley way. I couldn't spot the Scotsman but I called out a thank you to him anyway as I sprinted as fast as I could down the cobblestones. Stairs met the end of the alley and took them two at a time. Not caring if I fell. I needed to find my damned father.

I hurried down the streets. My eyes darted over each face. Boats loomed in the distance and I pushed forward. The sound of my foot falls pounded against the stones. People darted out of may. Staring at me like a mad woman as I ducked under the logs they carried and various other cargo.

There in the distance stood my father. His focus solely on a ship. The young girl waved to him from the bow.

I hissed through my teeth as I pushed forward. The crowd grew around the boat as they said their goodbyes. Tears and various calls shed to the sea as the ship pushed off. The girl practically leant over the rails to say goodbye to her family on the docks. They surrounded my father, who turned from the boat. Noticing me through the mass of people. A snarl large on my face.

Who in the hell was that woman and why was he sending her off?

My name hit my ears like a weight. Father pushed forward through the bodies of emotional people continuing to call their goodbyes to their loved ones.

I shook my head and turned away. I was so lost. Why was he sending her off?

"Vespera!" He barked my name once again.

I faced him as his hand met my shoulder. Fire burning within me.

"Sent her away so you can't kill her too?" I tilted my head. A savage venom tainting my lips.

Father's eyes widened. His expression turned incredulous.

"Vespera, you have it all wrong!"

"Tell me what exactly I have wrong! Were you not in the alley with that girl?"

He stumbled for a response, his words scrambling over each other.

"Funny how she looks just like all the other girls murdered in town." I kept my voice low. The dock now buzzing with people moving around us as the ship set for its course..

"Come on now. If you ain't working, get off the docks!" A gruff man bellowed from behind. I turned my back on my father, feigning sweetness to the man.

"Sorry sir!" I called before pushing back into the crowd

leaving for the streets. The scent of sea water made me nauseous.

Father called my name again but I paid him no mind. No doubt I would see him at home.

Was that what Victor had distracted me from? My father sending a young woman off? But why would he do that?

Chapter Forty-Five

Night had fallen slowly. I had locked myself in my room with an enraged Dorian. A knife sitting beside her as she sat on the bed with her knees curled beneath her chin, braced against the wall. I had asked her what she had seen but she refused to respond. Only training her eyes on the door. Both Victor and my father had yet to arrive home. I had watched the road from the windows all night. The moon hung high in the sky, now, close to midnight. Close to my twenty sixth birthday.

Puffing out a pent up breath, I fell back against my pillow. A small crinkle sounding. Dorian tore her stare over to me for a split second only to focus on the door once more. My hands snaked under my pillows. A note lay concealed under them.

> *Meet me by the river at midnight.*

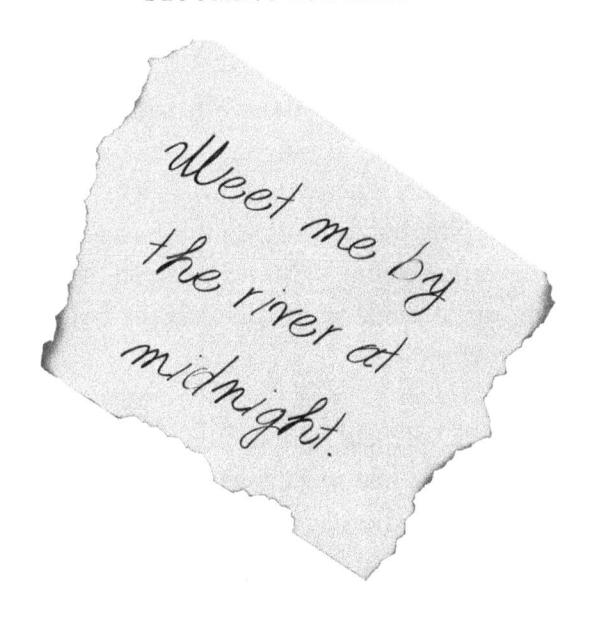

The note read. Maaier's loopy handwriting brought a warmth to my cold, hardened heart. Throwing on my cloak I headed for the door. Turning back to face Dorian before I did. She stared into the wood, as if burning it with her gaze would help.

My feet carried me to her slowly, as they always had when she was like this.

"Whatever you saw, Dori, it isn't real. We will make it through this night one way or another." I assured her. My hands pulled her head to my chest as I kissed the warm silken strands of her wild hair. She remained still. Poised and ready. I let her go. Moving out into the night.

THE SKY ABOVE WAS BRIGHT AND FULL OF LIFE. AS IF the stars were truly leading my way home to him. The breeze rustled the branches of the trees. Leaves starting to form on the claw like growth reaching for those who passed. The moon was high and full in the sky.

The fear of the water was only a light deterrent. The memory of the girls' bodies causing a shiver to roll through me.

"Hello, little bloom." Maaier's velvet voice crooned through the air. A smile widened across my face as I stepped into the clearing.

"Hello, my reaper."

"Your reaper," He said from behind me. His arms wrapped around to pull me close to him. His body warm against my back. "I must say, I rather like that," He purred in my ear.

The ice on the river had yet to form back the hole still remaining. I wondered where Arthur had moved the bodies. Maaier's hands pushed into my belly. Holding me closer as he rested his chin on my shoulder.

"I argued long with myself on whether to give you your gift tonight or not."

I spun to face him. Our bodies flush against each other.

"What gift?"

He smiled at my words. Eagerness flashing in his gaze. Like an excited child.

"I found this many years ago. I thought it was something you would like to keep."

I warmed at his smile. My hands clasped together to contain the warmth to my trembling hands.

"Close your eyes." He ordered. I obeyed. As I always did.

His hands moved behind my neck brushing under my hair until a cold object pressed against my chest just shy above my scar. He fastened the clasp.

"Open."

I did as I was told. Looking down at the pendant hanging from my neck. Tears flooded my eyes. Raw emotion consumed me. I had searched for this long and hard my entire adult life. Coming up fruitless each time. Wondering hopelessly where it ended up. My mother's silver heart shaped locket stared back at me. Blinking in the light of the moon. The tears fell down my cheeks.

"Oh, Maaier." My words fell from me as I collapsed into his waiting embrace.

"I found it just on the bank as her body was pulled out. I had watched her long enough to know it should be yours. But I wanted to be the one to give it to you."

"I looked everywhere for it." I laughed despite myself.

"I know. It was rather funny to watch."

I slapped his arm playfully. His deep laugh filled the night. A sound I wanted to hear over and over again.

"Thank you, Maaier. Truthfully. I love it."

"Long has my soul recognised yours, little bloom. You are mine now and forever. You are the colour to my listless existence." He breathed. The air falling silent around us as the cloud parted away. Leaving a million stars to glitter above us.

"I love you," He confessed softly. The smile on his face was as bright as the stars above.,

"I love you." I repeated. Our lips met under the guidance of the night sky.

Chapter Forty-Six

"Vespera!" My name was called through the manor. Grandmother's shrill voice crying out as I entered the front door.

"I'm here!" I called back.

Dorian's screech filled the night. Maaier darted beside me. Rushing upstairs. I hurried to follow only to make it up three steps. A hooded figure materialised at the end of the hall. Maaier's name but a caught scream in my throat. As the figure moved closer, not a soul was to be seen. The manor was still. As if anticipating his return. Fear ran through me. Maaier had entered my room but not sensed the man lingering down here with me.

"He can't kill you." I assured myself. Willing the words to ring true. Dorian screamed once more and the figure took his chance. He pounced down the hall, sprinting toward me. I screamed. The sound shredded through me. My throat hoarse as I leapt back, my back crashing against the marble stairs. The glint of a knife caught my attention. I scrambled backward up the stairs. The figure taking them slowly. I turned. Bolting toward the room at the end of the hall. Surely Magdelena could help. Voices shouted at each other on the opposite side of the hall. My blood ran as the man drew near. My feet faltered beneath me, caught in my long skirt. Why hadn't I changed for bed when I got home! The man loomed over me, his face hidden in the night. The knife held high above his head. His ragged breath filled the night in a melody with my own.

"Not this time you fucker." I grunted. A wave of volatile confidence overtook me. My leg kicked out. My boot connected with his groin. He toppled over. a grunted curse snarling between his hissed teeth. Dorian howled from the end room. I scrambled toward it only to practically fly down the stairs. I couldn't lure him in there. The man regained himself, stalking toward me.

He raced after me down the staircase, stepping on my skirt as we hurried down the hallway. I fell against the portrait of my aunt Magdelena. The man's smile poked out through the dark fabric concealing him. His hand darted out to grip my throat. He thrust me back against the painting. I clawed at his arm. Knowing you couldn't die was one thing but the human instinct to survive still held me close. He threw me back, the air raced from my lungs. I struggled to draw another gulp of air. The knife raised once more. I reached up despite my fear just as he plunged it down. The sharp edge stabbing into the palm of my hand. I howled with the intrusion. The wound burned as he pushed it through. The blade and my hand making contact with the portrait. He wrenched it out. My blood poured from my torn hand. My eyes flowed with water. Angry and pained tears raining down. I kicked out again. Meeting his knee this time, he doubled over. It was all I needed. I wove my good hand quickly under his hood before clawing into his hair. I smashed my hand into his skull, raising my knee beneath his face. His nose connected with a wet crunch. The impact ricocheted through me. Maaier appeared at the top of the staircase.

"Help Dorian," I demanded.

The man hissed a curse before standing, the sound of his voice familiar. Maaier hesitated before heading toward the room at the end of the hall. Magdelena's hysterical laughter bellowing through the manor.

Letting go of the man I dashed into the library. Leading him right into my little trap.

FEIGNING THE INNOCENT LITTLE WOMAN, I SCURRIED into the room. Allowing the man to come in and lock the door behind him. He breathed heavily under his hood. Panting through his mouth as blood no doubt rained from his shattered face.

"You should be dead," He hissed. The voice was so familiar it was as if I knew it my whole life. The once comforting sound now brought bile to my throat. I nursed my wounded left hand. Blood was still dripping down but I didn't feel dizzy. No. In fact I felt fine. Alive despite the pain. I backed up, my feet clumsily slipping beneath me in my own life fluid.

"Should I?" I managed to croak through gritted teeth. My god, this wound hurt more than being stabbed the first time.

"Insolent brat." The man snapped.

I froze as he lifted his hands. His fingers gripping his hood as he threw it back.

My eyes widened at his face, a small shocked protest falling from my lips. I stepped back in horror, my body collidinging with something hard. Not someone something.

"That's enough, Arthur." They said behind me. Their

chest vibrated with the demand. My father's arm drew me closer to him. Holding me. Protecting me.

Arthur's menacing stare fell on my father. He tilted his head forward. Pure hatred tainting him.

"Let her go, Theodore," He growled.

My father pulled me back behind him. I clutched at his shirt with my blood soaked hands. The white of his shirt forever tainted.

"I knew it was you."

"I was doing the world a favour."

"You destroyed lives. Your own sister's! Your own Mother's life you filled with loss and grief!"

"My mother is a stain just like the rest of them. She deserves the pain she gets." Arthur threw his arms wide. The door knob rattled behind him.

"Vespera." Victor's name echoed through the wood.

"You and that apprentice you stole think you've done the lord's work. Out saving those girls from me," My uncle jeered. His lethal stare on my father. Spittle raining with every word he said.

"We saved them from you." Father stepped toward him, poised for a fight.

"You left the one I was really after." Arthur nodded to me, pointing the knife in our direction.

I stayed behind my father. Frozen as I watched the truth unfold.

"Why kill the others then?"

"I needed to lure you home didn't I?" His grin was wicked as he stepped forward. Father stepped us back. My mouth opened to protest only to close as Father raised his hand back at me. I gritted my teeth but obeyed his silent command.

"Why me?"

"You were the only one to ever suspect me in the first

place. You see, killing off the older ones wasn't hard. My aunt's did love their tea. But you, oh you clever boy, you noticed the little plant I used to kill them, didn't you? You knew it was a nightshade but no one would listen to you. Blaming only age as their downfall." Arthur almost laughed. Glee poured from him as he recounted his kills. Father stood as hard as steel. Listening to the confession. Victor continued to pound on the door.

"You also knew when I took Magdelena that she wouldn't return. Didn't you? You knew that she was next but you let her go. Instead wanting to protect her sister. Your lover." He spat on the floor before continuing. "She wouldn't die though. She was a fiery thing. Absolutely mental. The best friend of the dark haired ones always are. Always are." He spared a brief look at me, stepping forward. Father stepped us back once more.

"She wouldn't drown. No, she was too stubborn so I called in drunken men to do what they pleased. She was scum that needed to be punished. After they had their way with her. I... Well I..." He burst out laughing. Mania bursting from his face. A truly fearless expression. Terror ran through me.

"I burned her alive! Whilst the whole manor searched for her, she was burning far away from here. I couldn't leave her there of course. They would find her charred remains eventually. Instead, I brought her home and buried her in the rose garden."

"You vile piece of shit!" I hissed. Stepping forward with my fists clenched. Father's arm held me back.

"What about my wife?" He said, his voice deadly soft.

"Well her, she was easy. She was always fearful of me. She was obsessed with her happy little family and her colour and her paints. She didn't care for the curse, or the darkness and stain it brought. She wanted to teach her offspring of love and kindness and finding colour." He sneered at his own words as if disgusted by the thought of them. Father lowered his shoulders as Arthur stepped near.

"She drowned easily enough. But she did fight when the blade marked her. If it was any consolation." He shrugged, feigning indifference.

"Why me?" I asked. His hysterical gaze turned back to me.

"Why you? Because the Reaper loves you. I knew he would come for you. The dark one couldn't resist a Florian. My great aunt told me that. She knew all along." He raised his hands to the ceiling as if thanking her.

"She told me to kill you all. 'All the women must die so the Florian name can perish too.' She wanted that. Craved it even. I was but her tool. But you just couldn't give up hope and die, could you? You just had to keep on living. Holding onto your bleak existence. I had no choice but to attack you over and over again but you wouldn't die! I had hoped daddy here would return to you dead to find his legacy lost but that was too much to ask. You're too much like your mother caught up in love and pleasure. A sick little whore!" His words boomed through the space. Victor thrust himself against the door. It shook with the impact.

"It all ends tonight. I lured you both here. Killing each girl I could who resembled you. Even the girl now hanged for murder looked like you."

"You knew her?" Father pressed.

"Knew her? Ha!" He laughed. "I framed her! She saw me kill the girl. I needed her and husband dead. She would have told him otherwise."

"You vile cunt!" I roared.

"Careful now. Watch that tongue of yours." He lowered the knife to point at father.

"Don't." I pleaded, "You can take me."

Father held me back. No this was wrong. He can't take us

both. I won't die. I can't live with him taking Father in a useless attempt at him saving me. But it was too late. Arthur ploughed forward. Knocking father off his balance. The blade entered his chest.

"No!" I roared as they fell in front of me. The library doors blasted open.

Chapter Forty-Seven

Victor pounced on Arthur, landing on his back. Arthur stumbled. Falling straight in Maaier's waiting grasp. His gloved hands held his neck.

I fell to my knees, bending over my father. His blood trickled out around the blade lodged in his chest.

"No." The word fell from my lips. Hot tears filled my eyes. Stupid fool. I cursed myself. His eyes gleamed with emotion. Blood pooling in the corners of his mouth. A torn sob broke through my blubbering lips. This can't be happening.

"You can't leave me." I choked out. My father stared at me. I took my hands in one of his. The blood mingled with the wound still burning. A cold burst of air filled the room. A pale hand took his other.

"Please." I pleaded. I had just gotten him back. The man who raised me. The man who held me when all was fearful in the world. He can't leave me. Not like this. He can't be stuck to the manor like this. This wasn't how it was meant to end.

"My darling Theodore." My mother said softly. Her hand brushed the flop of curls from his forehead. His head lolled as he looked at her. Eyes seemed to widen as if he could see her.

"You've done so well," She said, her eyes watering as she gazed down at her husband on the floor. Arthur's grunts filled the remaining silence. My own shattered sobs filling the other.

"You've come home. I always knew you would come home to me." She lowered her lips to his hand in hers. His eyelids slowly closing. His chest falling softly as his breathing lessened.

"He can't go. It isn't his time." I pleaded. My eyes fell to Maaier in the corner. His saddened gaze told me all I needed to know.

"Please." I pleaded. Calling out to the death god to hear me. To grant me this one wish. To save him just as he did Maaier. Only to receive no response.

"Let him go, Vespera. You can't save him." Mother urged but didn't take her soft eyes from fathers.

I squeaked as I withheld my sob at the sight.

"But I can." Pleaded with her, begging for her to understand.

"Let him come home to me. Let him come home to us." She pleaded. Her fingers grazed his hand, drawing circles as her tears fell on his cheeks. A sad smile on her beautiful face.

I shook my head. This can't be right. It can't be. With one final sob, I let him go. Allowed him that one last breath. His eyes fell to mine before looking up at my mother. Whose lips pressed against his forehead. His eyelids fluttered closed as she brought him home. Back to her loving arms.

The grief and despair heated inside of me. Boiling its way into a rage in my veins. *He* did this. He needs retribution. He tore my family apart. He tore me apart and now, he would tear nothing apart again.

I shook my head. Pulling hand from Father's grip as his breathing stopped.

Maaier had loosened his hold on Arthur. Instead tearing his attention to me. His gaze was concerned as I stood.

"If I accept your offer, Maaier. Do I get to see them again?"

He opened his mouth only to close it. I shot him a withering look. He nodded.

That was all I needed. He stood beside me. Cupping my cheek with his hand as he turned back to Arthur.

"His soul is yours to reap," He whispered in my ear. Pulling his gloves off and taking my hand in his.

Victor grunted as he held back Arthur who was screeching in his arms. Dorian and Grandmother, nowhere to be seen. Good, I didn't need her to witness me killing her son and myself in the process.

"Then I choose you, Maaier. I always choose you," I announced to the room.

A warmth tangled up my skin.

"You need to accept yourself, my soul. You need to accept that you are darkness and you are light. You need to accept that love within yourself."

And I did. I accepted that life could not exist without death. That I would not be here without the death surrounding the manor. That I was both light and darkness. Colour and grey.

The warmth spread through me. Stoking the rage within but heating me to the bone. As if truly bringing me back to life.

My eyes drifted close as I embraced the warmth. Embraced the love the darkness brought.

My eyes fluttered open. The grey of my surroundings flickering like a wave. Colour spread through the ripples. Like a curtain in the breeze. Hues of a world unseen brought to life. The beauty in darkness was now present. The sight was disorienting. The colour shone through the bleak. The wooden floor deepening with the books on the walls beaming to life in all shades. The glow of the lanterns were almost like how I imagined the sun. The night sky beyond the windows now the darkest shade of colour I had ever seen.

Arthur screamed as he realised the change. Knowing he had lost.

"His soul is yours to reap," Maaier purred in my ear again. Pride swelled in my chest. This is what I was created for. This was my journey. This life was my colour.

"Victor. I need you to find Dorian." I kept my order clear. He loosened his grip on a cowering Arthur.

"I need you to keep her away from here. Do you understand?"

"Yes." He nodded. Confused by the outcome of the situation.

"Good." I smiled despite my sadness of never seeing him again. "Take care of her for me."

Victor smiled sadly before leaving the room. Closing the doors after him.

I turned to face Arthur. Letting all my rage seem into my face.

"You brought this on yourself." I hissed, balling my trembling hands into fists. The wound now healed with my sight restored.

"No. You can't do this to me!" He squealed as I drew close. My hands like claws beside me, longing for his soul.

"I can. And I will," I sneered, " You will answer for taking the lives of those girls." As if on cue, the girls entered slowly, hand in hand, staring at Arthur with hostile intent. The maid with a feral gleam in her eyes. And Magdelena. Her fire blazed around her as she looked upon her brother.

They surrounded my mother. Still holding Father in her arms as his soul was yet to come free. She held him close but her eyes remained on me. The ghosts of Florian's past all drifted through circling the man as I neared. I willed him to see them to see the women taken by his hand that hadn't yet crossed. Their souls, not knowing peace until he was six feet under.

I towered over him. Kneeling down as he blubbered with disgusting fear. Taking in the faces of the spirits around him. My hands met his face. I willed his soul to break free. An ancient feeling deep in bones waiting to be awoken. Blood trickled up through his eyes. The man roared with pain. His anguished screams filled the night as the women watched in silence. I willed my hands down. Thrusting them through his ribs to his still beating heart. Warm blood pooled around them before I found what I wanted. A shred of smoke so dark it tainted the air. The stench of decay rife as I tugged it free. Arthur stilled beneath me. The light slowly left his terrified wide eyes.

I held the soul in my bloodied hands. Marvelled at how dark it was. Were all souls like this? I hoped not. This one reeked of death and decay.

A hand touched my back. Maaier pulled me into him. A familiar warmth flooded through me as his lips met my hair.

"Well done, my soul. They can all rest now." I could hear his smile in his voice, pride swelling from him.

The women in the room each looked upon the corpse before fading. A faceless man appeared over him. His hand extended to each of the women. The two young girls smiled as they looked back at me before taking his hands. Fading into the darkness of the room until all that was left were my aunt, mother and father. Whose soul had still not risen.

"You did it," Magdelena said softly, her voice thick with emotion.

I tilted my head smiling at her. Her flames died down to reveal the most beautiful eyes I had ever seen. A shade so vibrant. So blue. A shade I was told I shared but yet to see.

She clung to Mother's shoulders.

"Come." She ordered gently. Mother stayed put. Her focus solely on the wound in Father's chest.

She wouldn't leave without him. Without us. She had said so herself. I lowered myself beside her. Hovering my hands over where she still clutched his. I closed my eyes. Willing the soul to come to me as if I had been doing this my entire life.

His soul was tangled. Knotted around the shadow in his heart. In my mind, I unwound the thread of his soul, like a knot of mattered rope. My hands weaving in and out, pulling it free. A brilliant white light emitted from his body.

The shred of Arthur's soul discarded on the floor. The God of Death returned to take it before lingering to watch the sight unfold.

The light of Father's soul beamed before stilling over his body. He awoke at once. His spirit floating over the corpse. He met my mother's waiting arms with no hesitation. Holding each other close for the first time in years. A love so longing and pure radiating from them.

Never once did their souls part again.

Epilogue
THREE YEARS LATER

The manor loomed in the distance. I had waited for so long for her call. The familiar hum of a melody on repeat within my heart. A place once so dark and gloomy now awash with life. Despite the events of my fateful birthday, the manor remained untouched apart from the sole survivor boarded up within.

The halls were unchanged. The portraits lining the halls now brought new meaning. Beautiful colours amassed on the canvas, proving the beauty of their gaze. I looked past the library, not daring to go near enough to relive that night. Instead, I chose to make my way up the stairs. My door was open at the end of the hall. The room was still open to any. Just as it was when I left. Dorian's bed was still unmade after years of being abandoned. Mine was also still untouched. As if we never left. As if it were all only a single night ago.

THE CALL OF THE SOUL LED ME DOWN THE HALLS. Much warmer now no spirits remained. The room at the end, now clean and bare of belongings. Finally swept away to make way for new life.

The door was already opened as I approached. Grandmother lay on her bed. White hair covering her powder blue pillow. Her breathing was slow and laboured. She had aged gracefully in the time since I saw her last. Memorising the song of her soul. The soul of the woman I owed my life to. I sat on the edge of bed, taking her hand in mine. I willed myself to appear to her. To take off the glamour hiding me from the world. To become corporeal once more. My thumb drew lazy circles in her withered skin.

"Vespera?" She croaked my name. A smile filled my face. Long had I waited to hear her say my name once again.

"Hello Grandmother," I said softly, kissing my lips against her hand.

"You've been gone an awful long time, dear."

I laughed small at her words.

"I have always been around though," I said, my thumb racing her protruding veins. The colour of her skin now pale and lacking life. Dotted with marks of her age.

"Is it my time?" She croaked, sitting up slowly to face me fully..

I nodded, not knowing what else to say. A part of me always believed she knew what we were all destined to be. That she knew and didn't tell us. Not out of spite but out of respect. To give us all the best life she could imagine.

"I knew it would be you." She flashed a smile brighter than I had ever seen

"You carried me through this world. It is only right that I carry you through to the next."

She smiled. Her age showed through with the weariness in

her eyes.

"I am so tired, dear," She admitted softly, her hand clasping mine.

"I know," I whispered. Raising her hand to my lips. Not enough to kill her just yet, but enough to subdue her. It was hard to control my own death touch. Maaier had thought it would match his but mine was less. More of a power than a curse.

"Did you take them over?"

I nodded. Remembering that fateful night. I held my family close as I said goodbye one final time. The Florians were now at peace in their paradise together. My mother had been the last to let go. Holding me tightly against her into a crushing embrace until she faded into the light. I had watched her from the shoreline. The sea air no longer made me sick, now an ever immortal reminder of her final words "You truly have bloomed into the most wonderful woman. I love you more than anything in this world and the next."

Magdelena had twirled into her paradise. Father standing on the edge with his hand outstretched for the love of his life to take. Swallowing them both up with blazing light when she made contact.

Grandmother smiled. I pulled her into a tight embrace. Slowly loosening the tie on my power. She fell quickly, quicker than most. She was truly ready to leave the earthly plain. Ready to meet her daughters again. We fell back, like shooting stars through the night. She watched as lights filled the darkness like stars before landing on the edge of the dark shore in the cave.

A bright light bursting before us. I didn't flinch this time as I usually did. Knowing who was coming through to guide her on. My mother stood with open arms. Magdelena standing beside her. Both wearing matching grins. Their gowns were the same pure white as the light of the other side.

Grandmother softened in my arms, falling back against me.

"Go be with your daughters," I said, holding her up beside me.

"What about you?" She uttered sadly.

"I'll be there soon enough," I lied. I couldn't bring myself to tell her that this was the final goodbye. That I couldn't see what was on the other side where they now resided. The God of Death had assured me of that. He had reappeared after crushing Arthur into darkness to congratulate me on my 'new role' as he called it.

I had him to thank for everything. If he hadn't created the false bookstore to slip me the book I never would have given Maaier my soul. But when I asked him about why it was unfinished, he told me that the story was never finished. His smoke-like persona faded with the confession.

Grandmother smiled up at me, as if she knew I was lying by choosing to believe it anyway. Squeezing me tightly before making her way to Mother's arms.

She practically fell into them. The last glance my mother gave was to me. Smiling as she was enveloped in light.

"It never gets easier." The scent of cedar and saffron drifted over me. Maaier drew behind me. Wrapping his arms over me as I held a single rose in my grip. Just as he always gifted me after guiding a soul over to their rest.

"She is where she really belongs," I said softly. My gaze on the fading light of the other side.

"As are you, my soul," Maaier said. His lips brushing my hair. We watched in silence as the light drew smaller. Drifting away with the edge of the cave. Taking my loved ones with it,

"Until the world requires us no more," He said as the light finally dimmed on the Florian shore one last time.

"Until the world requires us no more."

I wandered toward the place I never thought I would see again. A place so grim and filled with nothing but darkness, even the clouds seemed to hang heavier over it. Florian Manor was still as vast and foreboding as it ever had been. A shiver rolled down my spine. I had never wanted to see this hell again. To see him again.

"Dorian, is that you?" He called from the front steps, a wide grin on his summery face. My heart thundered in my chest. Just as it did every time I so much as thought of him.

"Who else would it be, Daisy Boy?"

To be continued...

Acknowledgments

My biggest acknowledgement is for my beautiful editor and one of my favourite people on the planet. This book would be nothing without you, Callie. My own personal Dorian. Thank you from the bottom of my heart for all of your love and support. For listening to my every worry and helping me with every stress. This book is just as much yours as it is mine and I can't thank you enough for all the love you have given me.

A super massive thank you to another best friend of mine, my beautiful Demi. Thank you so much for all of your help formatting and just in general. You have been a huge help this whole process and I can not thank you enough for all of your love. My sweet racoon queen.

To my girls, Courtney, Shannon, SJ, Mel, Gini, Layla, Jennah, Lauren, Kaitlyn, Maddy, GR Thomas and all of my beautiful friends who have hyped me up and supported me through this entire process. I love you all.

To my Beta readers, thank you all so much for making this story the best it can be. Your feedback really made me believe in myself and I can not thank you enough for that.

I'd also like to thank my best girl Mollie for not only everything she does in my life but also letting me use her house to not only finish Blooming but come up with the idea in her bathroom in the first place. I love you to the pits and back.

To my parents, thank you for everything and always

supporting me through every hair brained idea or issue I throw their way. Love you endlessly.

But last and not least, I would like to thank my beautiful Ben. My soul. My own personal Maaier.

Thank you for holding me through it all. For wiping my tears when I cried that I was not good enough and for celebrating every milestone with me. For being my constant muse. You are my colour. My soul. Until the world requires us no more, mimi.

But also to you, my dearest reader. Thank you for taking a chance on Blooming and a small chaotic author. You have helped me in more ways than you will ever know. Here's to the next one and every book after!

About the Author

Jasmine Styles is an author from Regional Australia who adores all things books. After dreaming of being an author since she was eight years old, Jasmine has pursued every avenue she can to be the best author she can. Her goal in life is always to make her nan proud.

If she isn't curled up reading inside, she's out at any live gig she can.

All of her socials can be found under @authorjasminestyles.